THE
HAUNTED
BOOKSTORE
Gateway to a
Parallel Universe

Wagaya wa Kakuriyo no kashihonya san Novel 3
©Shinobumaru (Story)
This edition originally published in Japan in 2020 by
MICRO MAGAZINE, INC., Tokyo.
English translation rights arranged with
MICRO MAGAZINE, INC., Tokyo.

Seven Seas press and purchase enquiries can be sent to
Marketing Manager Lianne Sentar at press@gomanga.com.
Information regarding the distribution and purchase of
digital editions is available from Digital Manager CK Russell
at digital@gomanga.com.

Follow Seven Seas Entertainment online at
sevenseasentertainment.com.

TRANSLATION: Gwen Baines
COVER DESIGN: Nicky Lim
LOGO DESIGN: George Panella
INTERIOR LAYOUT & DESIGN: Clay Gardner
COPY EDITOR: Jade Gardner
LIGHT NOVEL EDITOR: E.M. Candon
PREPRESS TECHNICIAN: Melanie Ujimori
PRINT MANAGER: Rhiannon Rasmussen-Silverstein
PRODUCTION MANAGER: Lissa Pattillo
EDITOR-IN-CHIEF: Julie Davis
ASSOCIATE PUBLISHER: Adam Arnold
PUBLISHER: Jason DeAngelis

ISBN: 978-1-64827-662-0
Printed in Canada
First Printing: April 2022
10 9 8 7 6 5 4 3 2 1

THE HAUNTED BOOKSTORE

Gateway to a Parallel Universe

VOLUME 3

The Black Cat's Old Friend
and Gemstone Tears

WRITTEN BY

Shinobumaru

TRANSLATED BY

Gwen Baines

Airship

Seven Seas Entertainment

TABLE OF
Contents

PROLOGUE: Peridot Tears—The Black Cat's Dream   7

CHAPTER 1:   In the Garden of the Gods   19

CHAPTER 2:   The Love Lives of the Bookstore   75

CHAPTER 3:   Merry Christmas in the Spirit World   125

SIDE STORY: The Meaning of Happiness
and Where It Can Be Found   159

INTERMISSION: The Man in the Fox Mask Gets Drunk Alone   229

CHAPTER 4:   The Mother and Child from Adachigahara   235

EPILOGUE: On the Day of the Thaw   295

Afterword   303

Peridot Tears—
The Black Cat's Dream

"**D**O YOU KNOW what the most beautiful thing in this world is?"

A world of perpetual night into which not a single ray of sunlight shone; a world where inhuman beings crawled through the darkness, where many eerily glowing eyes eagerly awaited their prey; a world full of blood and flesh and the tang of beasts...

The spirit realm.

The old cat who spoke had spent a daunting amount of time there. His crusty, clouded eyes were trained on the black cat sitting directly in front of him.

The old cat had six tails. The black cat had only two. This was proof that the latter had only just been transformed from a simple beast into something stranger—proof that she was a newcomer.

As she spoke, the old cat looked into the black cat's eyes—one sky-blue and one golden—and saw not a trace of cloud in them; it warmed his heart. Educating the newcomers was the eternal responsibility of elders like him.

"The most beautiful thing in the world are the tears that a person sheds at the point of their death. They're as lovely as gemstones. Don't you want to see them? I'm sure you do. Cats are curious creatures, after all."

Saying this, the old cat told the black cat of all the tears he had seen before.

Tears that reflected the heat of fire were garnet. Crimson tears that captured the flickering of bright red flames, bursting forth as though they would soon burn out completely.

Tears that reflected the moonlight were diamond. Jeweled tears filled with a light cold enough to cut that slipped away and scattered.

Whether the person who shed them was young or old, of high standing or low, their tears flowed like gemstones. They died and faded away, leaving behind only a momentary glimmer. Spirits considered seeing this light their greatest pleasure.

"Young cat, you must devour people. Slurp up their entrails, make them your food. Whoever they might be, do not hesitate. When you have successfully finished your hunt, gemstones of emotion will be waiting for you, more beautiful than anything." When the old cat had finished speaking, he closed his eyes tightly.

Cats have lived alongside humans since ancient times. For this reason, many cats tried to snuggle close to people even after they had been transformed into spirits. But that had caused many tragedies through the years, and so the old cat told the younger: "Humans make delicious prey. You cannot befriend them."

The black cat was only silent for a moment; in the next instant, she stared straight at the old cat and said, "You don't have very good taste, do you?"

The old cat let out a deep sigh. Then he resumed his tale again in a warning tone. "You say that because of your youth. Even you, as you grow older, will come to realize the truth in the natural course of your maturation."

"Speak for yourself. What makes you think you know anything about me?"

Irritated, the black cat looked away. Then she leapt up into the heavens, wreathed in flames. Looking down at the old cat, who in the blink of an eye had become nothing but a speck beneath her, she bounded forward through a sky that was quite different from that of the world of the living.

Fear. Despair. Sorrow. How could tears painted with emotions like those be considered beautiful? To the black cat, who had spent a long time in the human world, it was inconceivable.

But now that she had decayed and come into her spirit form—and had developed a taste for human corpses—she had a hunch that little by little, she herself would be tainted by that same way of thinking.

She would eat humans, laugh at the misfortunes of others, and think only of herself. That was what spirits did.

I've lived longer than other cats. Despite that, will I still end up as he says?

The thought terrified the black cat through and through. Thinking of humans as nothing but prey, her mouth watering as she sprang at them.

How repulsive. Surely I'm not a real monster? ...Either way, that's a long way off. My heart is still with humans.

And so the black cat dreamed. She dreamed of tears that the old cat would never be able to see. Tears that were full of warm emotions.

"I wish... I wish I could see them, someday."

But the black cat's wish was not easily fulfilled. A length of time passed, one that would have felt like an eternity to a human. Only then, after the cat had grown a third tail, and after her heart had been dyed exactly the color of a spirit's, did an opportunity to see those tears arise.

It was summer in the spirit realm, and the cicadas cried insistently.

This was before the black cat had been given the name Nyaa. On that day, shooting stars rained down wildly in the deep green summer night sky of that other world.

It was then that, in the forest, she came across the swarm of glowing butterflies that lived only amongst the spirits: glimmerflies.

That day was somehow special. Special? No, perhaps it would be better to say it was *bizarre.*

Those shooting stars sent out their dazzlingly beautiful light, painting the night sky a shade of green particular to summer. Although it wasn't the right time of year for a meteor shower, star after star fell to earth, ending their fleeting lives.

It made the inhabitants of the spirit realm restless. A shooting star was proof that a human life had burned itself out.

In the human world, shooting stars were a romantic symbol, but in the spirit realm, they were, in all sincerity, a symbol of death.

A person in the human world had died. A whole lot of people!

Although it was nothing to do with the spirits, they didn't have a good feeling about it. The black cat, too, resented it. She couldn't settle down, so she wandered about outdoors, going nowhere in particular.

She finally arrived at a forest a long way from the towns of the spirit realm, thickly overgrown with trees. There, she found innumerable glimmerflies fluttering about.

"Waaah, waaah..."

In the midst of the butterflies was a little girl. She seemed to be about three years old. Her brownish hair was tied up in two buns, and she was wearing a dress patterned with tiny flowers. For some reason, she only had one shoe on. She was furthermore soaked to the skin, and her bare arms and legs were all scratched up. She hugged herself with her little arms, crying big fat tears.

Oh! It's a human!

The moment she saw the little girl, the black cat let out a silent shout of joy.

Glimmerflies... These beautiful but ephemeral butterflies were known to be drawn to humans. If one went to a place where they gathered, there was a high chance one would find a human there.

But humans were rarely seen in the spirit realm. It wasn't uncommon for them to stumble their way here, like this little girl likely had, but many denizens of this world liked to eat those interlopers. Normally, unless the human was very lucky or very strong, someone would chance upon them straightaway and devour them.

I'm the first one here! I'm in luck today.

Narrowing her eyes with pleasure, the black cat walked toward the girl, muffling the sound of her footsteps.

A little girl in a gloomy forest, illuminated by butterflies. The blood dripping from her arms and legs was terribly vivid.

When the black cat suddenly began to purr, her nose twitched. As it did, she smelled the mellow scent of blood, and her face instinctively relaxed. Then she swept her eyes over her surroundings. Establishing that there was no one moving in the vicinity, she chuckled to herself and deliberately let out a coaxing, "Mroooow."

As she did so, she saw the little girl's body stiffen with surprise. Unperturbed, the black cat drew nearer with a dispassionate expression on her face. Her head was full of thoughts about how to make a meal of the little girl.

Fresh innards, fresh blood. I'm not interested in that. After I've killed her, I'll leave her for a few days until her meat is nicely cured. Then I'll munch on her, starting with her head. Ooh, my mouth is watering!

By this point, the black cat was already fully steeped in the spirits' way of life. Humans were a delicacy. She couldn't go her whole spirit life without ever tasting one again; their delicious flesh was the greatest of pleasures. Their screams made her heart thrum, and chasing them as they clumsily ran from her was even more entertaining. Eating a human in the world of the living risked attracting the attention of exorcists if she wasn't careful. But when a human fell into the spirit realm, no one could blame her for gobbling them up. They were the most prized of prey.

Licking her lips, the black cat slowly advanced on the little girl. She could tell at a glance that her opponent was weak and wouldn't be able to put up a fight. The girl wouldn't stand a chance against the black cat's sharp claws and murderous fangs.

So, the black cat let down her guard. She sauntered up to the girl as casually as if she were about to pluck fruit from a tree. She had never imagined that the moment she neared, the little girl would cling to her.

"Gah!"

As the black cat's neck was encircled by the small arms, her mind went blank. This was a counterattack she hadn't foreseen. Ashamed of how careless she'd been, she instantly bared her fangs.

The girl didn't seem to react to the threat. Impatient, the black cat turned her face toward the child's head.

I don't know what she's trying to do, but I've got to kill her before she kills me. I'll bite her little head in half, she thought.

But in the next moment...

"Waaahh..."

At the same time as the black cat heard that frail voice, a warm droplet dripped onto her fur.

It was a tear. A droplet that had overflowed from those big

round eyes. It was transparent—but it captured the scene all around, and it held within it countless different colors.

The night sky, tinged a green that shifted from moment to moment. The shooting stars that fell without pause. The black cat, looking up with a discouraged expression. Those tears, which fell like rain, reflected everything and sent their fresh, twinkling light out into their surroundings.

These must be what the old cat spoke of… "Tears like gemstones."

The cat let out a shocked exhalation as the old memory resurfaced. Her heartbeat picked up and her whiskers stirred involuntarily as her tail stood straight up in the air.

How lovely they are.

In an instant, the black cat's heart was captured by those fleeting tears that lasted only a moment before disappearing. The beauty of those tears far surpassed any expectation she had built from the old cat's tales. As they burst on the surface of her coat and disappeared as if they had never been, they seemed like the most precious thing in the world.

The black cat was fascinated by that endless rain of jewels.

When she remembered the tiny dream she had harbored back then, she immediately sprang into action.

"Don't cry." The cat gave the child's cheek a lick.

"Eek!" Taken by surprise, the little girl let out a hysterical cry.

I should talk her down. "It's all right. There's nothing to be frightened of."

The voice that suddenly emanated from the black cat's mouth was gentle, like a mother's.

How long has it been since I last spoke like that? The cat's chest felt pleasantly warm. *It's just like I'm back in the world of the living, when I used to snuggle up to people...*

As the cat was secretly surprising herself, the little girl blinked her tear-drenched eyes incessantly, as if she had forgotten that, up until now, she had been crying. Then she stared at the black cat...

"Nyaa-chan!" She laughed airily, like a flower blooming.

Tears still escaped from her crinkled eyes. Those tears reflected even more than the ones before them as they slipped down her face and disappeared.

They had all the brilliance of jewels. Just like emeralds made of summer days heated until they dissolved...

Poetically, they were tears of peridot.

Yes... Just as I thought, these are more beautiful, the black cat thought as she gazed steadily at the tears that had begun to rain down upon her again, completely forgetting that, until a short while ago, she had intended to eat the girl.

"Huh...?"

When she opened her eyes, the black cat was in the bookstore in the spirit realm.

She heard the bubbling sound of water boiling. A little ways away sat an oil stove with a kettle on top of it. Unlike an electric stove, it gave off enough heat to make her skin tingle. It warmed her body thoroughly, and as her consciousness wandered back and forth over the boundary between dream and reality, it almost dragged her back into her dream.

"Nyaa-san?" said a familiar voice beside her.

Someone was stroking the black cat's back with a gentle hand. As she slowly raised her head, her gaze alighted on a lone young woman. The cat blinked rapidly. Unable to respond to the girl, she stared at her with round eyes.

The girl chuckled in amusement. "Morning! What's up? Are you still half-asleep?"

She tickled the cat's chin with practiced fingers.

As she softly stroked her, the cat half-closed her eyes with pleasure. "Not really. I was just thinking about how big you've grown, that's all."

"What are you on about?"

"I had a dream about the first time I met you, Kaori."

The girl, Kaori, blinked her large chestnut eyes and smiled, a bit vague, a bit melancholy. "You were the first to find me when I fell into the spirit realm, weren't you, Nyaa-san?"

"You remember that?"

"Well, not really. After all, I was only about three, right?"

Keeping her expression calm, Kaori shifted her gaze. The cat was drawn to look at the same spot. What she was looking at was the courtyard, blanketed in snow. White snowflakes were beginning a fluttering dance. Oh, right, it was winter now. Amused to have forgotten that obvious fact, the black cat smiled broadly.

"But I do remember that the first spirit I met was really warm and soft," said Kaori.

The black cat took a long time to answer. "Huh."

"You found me, Nyaa-san," said Kaori, "and then Shinonome-san took me in. That's how I started out in the spirit realm. I had nowhere in the world of the living to return to, so I'm grateful to you both for giving me somewhere to belong."

Nowhere to return to, huh...?

Kaori had no blood relatives. There was no one waiting for her back in the human world. That was why she lived in the spirit realm.

At least, that was what Kaori thought.

The black cat thumped her three tails on the floor and rolled over onto her back. "Hey, Kaori, you can pet me if you want."

"Whoa, that's unusual! I'll take you up on that, then."

Chuckling, Kaori stroked the black cat's belly. Giving herself over to the pleasant sensation, the cat glanced casually out of the window. It seemed as if the cold outside had deepened considerably. The window was clouded with condensation.

"Ah, I'm so happy..."

Being able to spend a peaceful moment in a room made pleasantly hot by a heater even in this pitiless season, and with someone around whom she could just relax? To the black cat, that was what happiness meant.

Turning only her head, she asked, "Hey, Kaori. Are you happy right now?"

"That again?" Kaori chuckled, amused. That question was practically the cat's catchphrase.

The cat would check whether Kaori was happy at random, whenever it occurred to her. She repeated the same question over and over. She did so again now. The heater kept her heart comfortably warm; since the beginning of winter, she had asked this question frequently.

Grinning, Kaori said, "Of course."

"Hmmm..." said the cat. That was all right, then. "If you're happy, Kaori, then I'm happy."

Through half-closed eyes, the black cat gazed at her old friend, who had given her the new name of "Nyaa."

"Hey, rub my underside a bit more," she coaxed.

"Sure thing!" Kaori responded to her best friend's demand in the way only she could.

CHAPTER 1

In the Garden of the Gods

"WHEW!" I exhaled through pursed lips. In an instant, I was covered in white.

Throwing myself down in a star shape on top of a pile of new-fallen snow was my favorite thing to do in winter. Maybe it was childish, but when I saw brand-new snow that no one had yet made footprints in, I just had to lie down in it. If I could lie down on top of a snowdrift that had just piled up, even better!

Once I'd summoned my courage and thrown myself down on the snow, I stretched out my arms and legs and closed my eyes. Then I heard a certain sound.

Rustle, rustle, rustle.

It was the whisper of snow falling and piling up. Even here on top of the snow, where silence and stillness seemed to reign, the air was full of different sounds. I loved listening to them.

"Oi, Kaori, you're gonna catch a cold."

A rough voice interrupted my moment of supreme bliss. Opening my eyes slightly, I saw someone looking down at me.

The first thing I caught sight of was his hair, white as the fresh snow. His eyes were pale, almost translucent, and his well-proportioned face was as pleasant as a prince's.

His name was Shirai Suimei. A young man who had once worked as an exorcist in the human world, he was now employed at an apothecary in the spirit realm. The red scarf he was wearing had been hand-knitted by Noname, who ran the apothecary; she had also specially picked out his black duffle coat.

According to Noname, the sight of a teenage boy in a duffle coat was more precious than any national treasure.

Really? That's the first I've heard of it.

She said she had deliberately chosen one with sleeves that were slightly too long. Since he was slender, the oversized duffle coat made him look slightly childish.

"That's perfect!" Noname had passionately declared.

I got to my feet slowly and shook off the snow that had stuck to me here and there. "I'm wearing a hat and gloves, so I'm nice and warm. I'll be fine!"

"That's not the point. Where do you think you are?"

"I'm in trouble..."

Being laid into so ruthlessly by a younger man made me giggle.

I looked over at the person standing behind Suimei and bowed my head slightly. "It's okay. The ground might be freezing, but we won't get cold. We can even wear unbelievably light clothing. Isn't that right, Ape-huci-kamuy?"

Her face...Ape-huci-kamuy's face, which was deeply scored with wrinkles, creased into a smile.

Her features were more sculpted than those of a Japanese person. Her thick eyebrows made her look strong-willed, and a broad hachimaki headband was wound about her wavy black hair. Above her mouth, which was lined with age, she had a tattoo like a man's mustache, and her body was wrapped in layer upon layer of fine kosonte robes. A makiri knife was tucked into her belt, and in her hand, she held a cane. That golden cane reflected the soft light, bathing its surroundings in a peaceful glow.

Ape-huci-kamuy is one of the deities—kamuy—worshipped by the Ainu people. She represents fire and lives in an apeoi, or sunken hearth. She appears in the form of an old woman, and the kosonte robes in which she is clad are the red of brightly burning flames. For the Ainu, who live in an extremely cold region, the kamuy of fire is the most venerated yet also the most familiar of beings.

Ainu, kamuy... Yes, Suimei and I had come to Hokkaido.

"Do you think we'll be able to set off soon?" I asked.

When I called out to her, Ape-huci-kamuy nodded silently. As she did, a man—who was slightly on the short side—appeared from a traditional Ainu bark-and-thatch house, called a chise.

Unlike Ape-huci-kamuy, the man was dressed in attush robes made of bark fibers. Over those, he wore a haori coat decorated with feathers, and on his head was a hat made of animal skin. His neatly styled beard gave his masculine features a look as keen as a well-honed blade. His elegant body was captivatingly firm, and it gave him the aura of a powerful man.

"Sorry for the delay. Come on, let's head off. We have to follow Kim-un-kamuy."

Adjusting his tekunpe hand warmers, he took hold of me and Suimei by the shoulders and began to walk quickly.

"H-hey, wait!" Perhaps because he didn't know what was happening, Suimei was pretty flustered.

I spoke to Suimei to reassure him. "It's okay, it's okay! Just keep up with him for now!"

"Tell me what's going on, idiot! You might think it's 'okay,' but it isn't!"

Ugh, getting a bit extreme there, aren't you? Then again, when I thought about it, Suimei had done plenty of extreme things. Casting souls into hell by force, walking high in the sky without a safety rope... He really was incredible...

Quickening my steps to match the man's stride, I smiled uneasily as I explained. "In the spirit realm, the great majority of spirits hibernate during the winter, so shopkeepers have a lot of free time. That means they can do things they wouldn't normally. So, for example...collecting debts from customers who've been in arrears for ages, and stuff like that."

"I've heard about that. This is another job, right? But how did things reach this point?"

"What do you mean, 'this point'?"

"I'm asking you why the guy we've come to collect debts from has run away!"

"Oof. Look..."

As I faltered, the man suddenly broke into a run. Swept along, I started running too. Of course, this also made Suimei's face stiffen in bewilderment, but he frantically moved his legs to keep up.

"You see, Kim-un-kamuy, the one who's run away, right, he's—aaggghh!"

"Whoa—ngh!"

Perhaps annoyed by our slow pace, the man picked us up, one under each arm, interrupting my explanation. Carrying us like that, he rapidly picked up speed.

"A-and—ngh!" I gasped. *Uh-oh, I'm gonna bite my tongue!*

The scenery flashed past us in the blink of an eye. Because of how fast we were going, I closed my mouth and looked straight ahead.

The snowfield stretched out as far as the eye could see, but we were gradually approaching a ridge. Bent slightly forward, the man violently stamped his animal-hide shoe against the ground.

Boom!

With a sound like an explosion, powdery snow whirled up into the air. My field of vision went white; I couldn't see anything.

Air cold enough to freeze my lungs flowed into my body. I held my breath. At the same time, I felt the sensation of my body rising upward, and I landed on something soft. Next thing I knew, the man carrying us had disappeared. Clutching at the fluffy thing underneath my feet, I stared out into the swirling whiteness.

At last, the whirling snow around me died down, and all at once the view opened up.

"Wow...!"

Stretching out before me was a magnificent landscape. The earth was painted white until it reached a great peak. It was part of the Daisetsuzan Range, a series of mountains of varying sizes which extended around the Ohachidaira caldera. On the bare surface of the mountain, I could see something moving.

Hokkaido sika deer!

The graceful sika had gathered in a herd and were clinging to a slope so steep that a human would slip and fall right down it. I also thought I could see white smoke rising from the round crater in the earth.

Volcanic gas? Or could it be a hot spring welling up?

As I stood there, fascinated by this scenery that was unique to Hokkaido, someone put a hand on my shoulder.

It was Suimei, his face ashen. Teeth chattering, he said, "Explain to me what the heck is going on!"

His voice brimmed with anger, and his face was drawn. Laughing lightly, I picked up the explanation that I'd left off.

"Um, like I was saying. There's this god called Kim-un-kamuy, and he's always falling behind on his payments. This time, he hasn't paid up in over a year, and his late fee is getting pretty high."

"I've never heard anything about him."

"Yeah, I didn't mention it. I also didn't tell you that collecting debts in a situation like this is a real pain."

When I bluntly declared this, the blood vessels in Suimei's temples bulged.

As I forced a smile—as if to say "oops!"—I looked around restlessly. I cast a glance behind us to check whether Ape-huci-kamuy was still there.

"Please help us out, Ape-huci-kamuy and Kapatcir-kamuy!"

Then, raising my right hand with a cheer, I shouted, "Good luck to us on our mission to collect Kim-un-kamuy's debt! Yeaaah!"

In time with my voice, Ape-huci-kamuy graciously raised her hand a little. I happily looked back at Suimei.

As I did, he gripped both my shoulders. "I keep telling you! Explain things beforehand! If I know what's waiting for me, I'll be in a completely different frame of mind, at the very least!" He shook me with a frantic look on his face. "Even if someone who looks human suddenly turns into a huge eagle! Even if they're big enough for a human to ride on their back easily! Then I wouldn't end up almost paralyzed with fright!"

"Ah ha ha ha! You were paralyzed with fright?"

"I only said I *nearly* was! It's not funny..."

The Hokkaido winter sky rang with my laughter and Suimei's angry voice.

Kapatcir-kamuy, who had launched himself into the air with a shrill cry, circled slowly and then, with a great flap of his wings, rose higher into the sky.

But why did Suimei and I have to go all the way to Hokkaido to collect a debt?

In order to explain that, I'll have to go back a little in time.

At the beginning of winter, Shinonome-san launched his first book, *Selected Memoirs from the Spirit Realm.*

Along with information about spirits who lived in the spirit realm, it also contained stories that they had told him. Shinonome-san had put over a decade of work into this volume, which was intended to show readers the authentic ways, life, and culture of spirits.

We'd held a massive party to celebrate its publication, and when this most topical book came out, the entrance to the bookstore had been thronged with spirits. Almost all of our rental books were now loaned out, and our sale stock was also pleasingly low.

However...

"In terms of money..."

"Yeah."

Shinonome-san lay wearily in a corner of the living room. Seeing him hug the flimsy zabuton to his body like a pillow was heartrending, to say the least.

Tossing a winter tangerine into my mouth, I stole a sidelong glance at Shinonome-san. I had never imagined he would fall into such a bad slump.

"We need money to print the books too," I said. "As a rental bookstore, we can't very well loan them out at the actual selling price, and even in normal times it takes forever to recoup our expenses. If the books get damaged, we can't loan them out, and repairing them costs money. Sometimes customers lose our books too. Funds are low, so it's not even as if we can print a huge quantity of additional copies. That means we'll have to raise the price of the individual books."

"Oof. Let's analyze the situation calmly…"

"If you're aiming to make a profit in the first place, you'll have to change distribution channels."

"Stoooooop!" Shinonome-san flailed his arms and legs about like a spoiled kid.

Laughing, I peeled another winter tangerine. "That doesn't matter. Thanks to your book, Shinonome-san, we've gained new customers. You've made spirits who've never even touched a book before see how interesting they can be."

"Buuut…"

"At the very least, you should be happy that we're selling more than before."

Because of that, we could eat better rice than we used to (even if we still couldn't afford special A-grade rice). I was thankful for that. Improving one's daily nutrition leads to peace of mind.

"Well, that'll change before long," I said. "After all, everyone's hibernating now, right? Why don't you prepare for the busy spring by continuing to work on your next book while the time is ripe?"

Shinonome-san's face split into a smile so broad it looked strained. Then he rolled over in the direction of the wall, hugged the zabuton to him again, and didn't move.

Huh?!

Eyeing him closely, I sidled up to him. I narrowed my eyes and peered at Shinonome-san's face. I heard him breathing deeply and evenly, as if to say "I'm asleep!"

Gotcha. So you don't want to write today? Quickly raising both my hands in front of my face, I yelled, "Shape…up!"

I swooped down on Shinonome-san's torso with terrific force.

"Ack—ah ha ha hee hee hee! Stop! What're you doing?!"

"Even if you're not in the mood, keep working away at that manuscript! Don't cause problems for Tamaki-san!"

Incidentally, Tamaki-san was a slightly shady spirit who worked as a "story-seller." He had arranged a lot of things for us when *Selected Memoirs from the Spirit Realm* was being published. He took on the job of editing too, so he would be the one most affected if Shinonome-san's manuscript was late.

"I'm eagerly awaiting those beautiful tales of tales..." Tamaki-san had said. *"But put yourself in the shoes of the one who's doing the waiting. Don't you just want to punch that carefree face of his over and over?"*

I shivered. *I'm the one who'll be on the receiving end of Tamaki-san's angry complaints when he comes to collect the manuscript and finds that it's nowhere near finished. I wish you'd at least keep to your deadline!*

"Writers are delicate creatures!" my adoptive father wailed. "Uh... If their hearts aren't absolutely overflowing, they can't write a single word!"

"I don't care about nonsense like that! Surely you won't know whether you can write unless you sit down at your desk! You can talk like that *after* you've actually made it to the starting line!"

"Don't wanna. My room's cold."

"You're such a child!"

My frustration with my father, who'd just looked away in a huff, grew stronger. Shinonome-san could be really moody when it came to writing, and he was always like this when he didn't feel like doing it.

"Ugh, I quit. I don't even care if Tamaki-san gets mad at me again."

"Sure."

I watched my father in exasperation as, not even pretending to be asleep anymore, he started blowing smoke through his pipe.

Oh well.

Exhausted, I smiled wearily. A few days before this, there had been an incident with Yao Bikuni. Shinonome-san had been pretty badly hurt.

In the effort to force him to cancel the publication of his book, she had partially destroyed the hanging scroll that was his true form. As he was a Tsukumogami, the damage to the hanging scroll had dealt him considerable injury as well.

In the end, we had been able to publish his book safely, but he had only just recovered from the most debilitating effects of his injuries. Even now, he wasn't completely well.

Incidentally, we were having the hanging scroll mended at an appropriate place; they would finish the work when it got warmer, so we were anxiously waiting the spring.

He's just published a book. Surely he can rest for a bit? I'll just have to let Tamaki-san's nagging go in one ear and out the other. ... Or am I being too soft on him? But, well, I'm the only one who's allowed to spoil Shinonome-san, aren't I?

"That reminds me," I said as I remembered something. "What d'you want to do about collecting debts this year?"

"Oh!" Apparently, he'd wholly forgotten. He scratched his head, his gaze roaming through the air. "I've always been the one to do it before, but... Naturally, I can't make it this year. I'm not back to my old self yet."

"You might be okay with the spirits who live nearby, but you'll struggle with ones who are far away."

Most spirits set up their dens in the hinterlands. Shinonome-san's wounds hadn't totally healed yet; there was no way he could go. On top of that, the larger the late fees got, the more difficult it was to collect them. I'd gone along with him in the past, but he often ended up having to chase spirits who got away from me. That was why collecting late fees was Shinonome-san's job. However...

"You could wait until spring?" I suggested.

"That's a pain in its own way."

"I suppose so."

In short, the season itself was the reason we went to the trouble of collecting debts despite the cold. For one, we weren't busy at the shop, and for another, many spirits were confined to their homes for the winter. In other words, it was easy to establish where they'd be. In spring, it was much harder to track down errant spirits.

"I spent all our ready cash creating that book..." I said. "We can't afford for you not to go."

"True. If we carry on like this, we might not even make it past New Year's."

Exchanging a glance with Shinonome-san, I heaved a sigh. If I were able to collect the late fees, they would add up to a not inconsiderable amount of money. Those fees are a valuable source of income for us during the winter off-season. Without them, we wouldn't even be able to buy any new books.

While I was racking my brains over what we should do, I sensed someone in the shop. I turned toward the door that connected the shop and the living room. When I opened it, I saw a familiar face.

"Hey..."

"Welcome!"

It was Suimei. There was quite a blizzard blowing up outside, and here and there, white snowflakes had stuck to him. His eyes were drooping and his head swaying as if he was awfully sleepy.

"You okay?"

"Mm."

Suimei took off his shoes and tottered into the living room. Looking as drowsy as could be, he stood right in the center of the room, dazed.

"Hey, what about your coat?! You need to take it off."

"Mmph."

I tried to speak to him, but he barely responded. His eyes were half-closed.

"Jeez."

Sighing, I went and stood right in front of Suimei. I had no other choice but to strip his coat off myself.

Why was Suimei so sleepy? The reason was his previous job.

As I've mentioned before, until a little while ago, Suimei made a living as an exorcist. To him, the spirit realm was a land full of enemies. Subconsciously, he was always on guard, so he couldn't always sleep soundly. But he seemed to be able to actually rest at our house—probably because I, a fellow human, was there. Because of this, he'd started coming to our place whenever he felt truly exhausted.

"Are you hungry? Want something to eat before you go to sleep?"

Next, I took off his scarf. It must have been freezing outside; his skin was as cold as ice.

"It's cold out there! You need a futon?"

I warmed his frozen cheeks with my hands.

Suimei shook his head. "Jus' a blanket."

Then he leaned against me. Suddenly bearing his weight, I almost fell over.

As I hurried to support him, he murmured in a small voice, "Don' like the cold. You're warm, Kaori. All cozy."

Talking like a kid, he nuzzled his head against me. It really tickled, and I tried to stop him, but then—still leaning against me—he began to snore gently.

"Ooof." Conscious that my cheeks were a wee bit warm, I wrapped my arms around Suimei's waist. With a "heave-ho!" to psyche myself up, I half-led, half-dragged him over to the stove. With slight difficulty, I laid him down and slipped a zabuton, folded in half, under his head.

I'll have to go and get a blanket...

With that thought in mind, as I was slowly trying to stand up, I happened to meet Shinonome-san's gaze. For some reason, his eyes were as round as saucers.

"What's with that weird look?" I asked.

As I instinctively tilted my head, all the color immediately drained from Shinonome-san's face. "F-f-for crying out loud!"

"Shhh. Suimei's sleeping."

"S-sorry...wait, no no no, what's with how you two were acting just now?!" Shinonome-san sprang vigorously up from the ground and crawled toward me on his hands and knees. "H-hang on. Don't move, Kaori. Sit there. I want to talk to you."

"Huh? But the blanket—"

"Surely that can wait until afterward?!"

"O-oh?"

Overwhelmed by Shinonome-san's energy, I knelt where I was, baffled.

Extremely flustered, yet choosing his words with care, Shinonome-san said, "I don't want to believe it. K-Kaori... You and that boy..."

Eep.

Shinonome-san broke off, swallowed, and then said, "Are you two dating?"

"Huh...?"

Dating. I didn't understand what he meant right away; for a moment, I froze up.

As I faltered, Shinonome-san watched me with a terrifyingly upset expression. He hadn't had a drink yet, but he had gone as red in the face as he did when he partook too much.

Just as I was absentmindedly thinking how exhausting it must be to go from pale to red like that, I suddenly understood the meaning of his words.

"Whaa?! Wh-wh-what d'you mean, dating?!"

"Owww!"

Instinctively, I'd slapped him hard across the face. A satisfying sound rang out, and Shinonome-san groaned in pain.

"Argh, sorry. You were saying weird things, Shinonome-san!" I hastily patted his cheek.

Clutching the cheek I'd struck with his hand, my father gave me a somewhat thin smile. "Yes, indeed. There's no way you're dating. Well...I did wonder if something had happened while I was being hounded about my manuscript."

I laughed at his behavior. "Yeah, you're right. There's no way we'd be dating! Nothing's really happ..."

At that moment, an autumnal scene flashed through my mind. The dark purple sky. The tranquil surface of a lake, reflecting the stars. The words Suimei had spoken to me on that bridge adorned with beautiful butterflies...

"When I'm with you, my chest feels weird. Is this...love too?"

The instant I remembered that, I flushed as though someone had lit a fire in my cheeks. Our house was old and drafty; there was no way I could be too hot. Yet sweat began to bead on my brow, and I hung my head, wishing I could run away.

"Ack."

There was a strange sound like a frog being squashed. Looking up fearfully, wondering what it was, I was greeted by a terrible sight that made my blood run cold.

"I'll kill him." It was Shinonome-san, his blue-gray eyes burning gold with fury. He usually wore a lazy expression that didn't betray the slightest bit of enthusiasm, but *now*—

The veins at his temples bulged, and the horns sprouting from his forehead crackled with lightning. His unkempt hair stood on end. He looked just as fearsome as an oni.

"Huh...ack! Shinonome-san?! Wait, hang on!"

In a panic, I clung to him and frantically trying to smooth his hair back down. "Don't get the wrong idea, okay? Nothing happened. Nothing! Suimei is a good friend, and he'll carry on being my friend!"

If I don't do something, Suimei will be killed! I screamed internally, heartbroken at the thought.

Then I realized that, in my arms, Shinonome-san had grown quiet.

"Shinonome...san?" Peering cautiously at his face, I saw that he was wearing a worn-out expression.

"I don't really mind if you have a boyfriend... No, I don't mind. It's completely natural for humans to fall in love. Yeah...yeah." In the next moment, his expression turned sour. "Love isn't something a Tsukumogami like me can really understand. But humans fall in love, pair off, have children, bring them up. Such is life. Hah, children...? How are they created again?"

Shinonome-san's eyes rolled back. He must have fainted.

"Come on, wake up!"

I shook him, and he suddenly regained consciousness, only to crumple to the floor where he was and murmur in a hoarse voice, "I liked it when you were little... You used to say you'd be my bride. You were so charming back then..."

This is hopeless...

With a sigh, I left Shinonome-san as he was and headed for the second floor. I took a blanket out of the closet and came back downstairs.

Shinonome-san was still grumbling away. He had looked after me ever since I was little, so even though we weren't related by blood, there were complicated feelings involved.

I wonder what would happen to Shinonome-san if I were to get married...

Up until a few days ago, practically the only thing that came out of his mouth had been, "Hurry up and find a husband." Yet this was how he reacted when I wasn't even dating someone? It did make me worry about the future.

Sighing who knew how many times, I laid the blanket over Suimei. As I did so, I met the gaze of his light brown eyes, and my heart leapt.

"Oh! Suimei, you're awake? Sorry, we were being noisy."

Lying there, Suimei didn't respond to my words, just regarded me vaguely with half-open eyes. Thinking he probably hadn't quite woken up yet, I went to open my mouth again.

That's when it happened.

"Kaori..." Smiling carelessly, he fixed his pale eyes on me. Then, with the innocent grin of a child, he happily said, "I'm so warm... Thank you."

Then, straightaway, he closed his eyes. I began to hear the strong, even sound of his breathing. Just as I'd thought, he had been half-asleep already.

He's just too cute! At that moment, I clutched at my heart in pain. How sneaky of him—he never usually wore such an expression! How could he look so like an angel? How could he be so destructive? Where had the sulky brat gone? Why couldn't this smile be his standard setting?!

As I fought against my urge to stroke his snow-white hair as much as I wanted to, I felt an extremely sharp gaze on my back. That snapped me back to myself. I looked up hastily to see my father scowling at me with bloodshot eyes. I started, feeling cold sweat trickle down my spine. Although I had nothing to feel guilty about, I was terribly ill at ease.

In the next moment, Shinonome-san flopped down spread-eagled on the floor. Then, in a voice that was tinged with despair, he wailed, "Augh, whatever! I don't care anymore!"

"What's with you now?!"

It seemed his "bad" switch had been flipped. Just like a baby throwing a tantrum, he started whining that he wasn't going to do *anything* this winter.

"But what about your manuscript?! And collecting the late fees?" I pressed him.

Shinonome-san covered his face with both hands. "As for the

manuscript... I'll prostrate myself in front of Tamaki or something. Whatever. Leave me alone!"

"And the late fees?!"

"As for them... Couldn't you go and collect them with that e-exorcist?"

"With Suimei...?"

"I don't care about you two going off together! Chasing after fleeing spirits is an exorcist's forte. Yes, yes, that's right. He's much better suited to it than I am!" Then a strange, suppressed heat entered his voice as he said, "Don't tell me...you'd be *embarrassed* if it was just the two of you? You're not dating, so it shouldn't be a problem."

I could see his eyes through the gaps between his fingers. They were emitting a golden light.

Ugh, this really is hopeless! I heaved a deep sigh. "Come on," I said weakly. "I already told you we're not dating. I get it. Suimei and I will go together."

I stole a glance at Suimei's sleeping figure.

"Ergh..."

Just for a moment, I hated this boy who was sleeping so soundly.

That was how I ended up collecting debts with Suimei.

A few days had passed since then. I'd decided that we should go to Hokkaido at once.

"Why do I have to…?"

"Because 90 percent of this is your fault anyway, Suimei!"

"Huh?"

I gave Suimei a sharp look as he tilted his head in confusion, and I hefted the rucksack onto my back.

Incidentally, while Nyaa-san usually accompanied me, she was sleeping at home. "I never leave the house in winter"—that was her policy. The cat was curled up under the kotatsu. "I could hardly call myself a cat if I didn't," she had told me.

As for Suimei's companion, Kuro the Inugami…

"Please don't leave meeeeee…"

The moment I spoke to him, he began to weep bitterly. It seemed this Inugami couldn't cope with the cold at all; he'd grown utterly pathetic as soon as he realized we were going to freezing Hokkaido.

"I'm terrible at running in the snow. Honestly, I feel like I wouldn't be helpful to you at all! But but but…*please* take me with you…"

Kuro's body was much longer than a normal dog's, and his four legs were very short, so if he tried to run in the snow he'd probably end up getting buried. Moreover, the snow would get caught in his fur, and the weight of it would make it harder and harder for him to move at all.

I figured we could ask him to look after the house for us, but he flatly refused to let Suimei go by himself. As a result, Kuro ended up coming along with us inside Suimei's rucksack.

Before we left, Kuro stuck his face out of the top flap of the rucksack and said cheerfully, "Hee hee hee. Now I'm the ultimate weapon! Call me when I'm needed!"

But now in the present, he was sound asleep inside the rucksack, snoring away loudly.

"Aren't dogs supposed to happily run about outside?"

"Don't treat Kuro like a normal dog. Whatever it looks like, he's delicate." Even Suimei, his loyal companion, seemed to have his doubts. His expression was somewhat disappointed.

After some journeying from one point to the next, we arrived in Hokkaido. We got a ride from an oxcart spirit called Oboroguruma and reached our destination around noon. Once we'd seen the Oboroguruma off back to the gates of hell, I found myself at a loss. Everything around us was hazy and white. I couldn't see anything.

The Oboroguruma had carried us to the dead center of a snowfield. The wind howled, and powdery snow blew ceaselessly against us. There wasn't a building in sight. We didn't even have anywhere to take shelter from the snow.

Abandoned in the middle of the snowstorm, we were frozen through in the blink of an eye.

"It's so c-c-cold! We might end up going missing!"

"Stop it, that doesn't sound like a joke!"

We could barely see a meter in front of us, and even the figure of Suimei right next to me was almost obliterated by the blizzard. Frightened, I clutched Suimei's arm.

"A kamuy I know is supposed to come to meet us. I wasn't expecting a snowstorm this bad! If only I'd bundled up more... No, I should've come in mountaineering gear!"

I was dressed more warmly than usual, but it was so cold that it made little difference.

It was definitely below freezing. Cold enough to freeze a banana. But Noname had said that I'd be fine if I wore clothes of this thickness.

Argh, but it's too late! A pang of regret shot through me.

Listening to me, Suimei scowled. "Kamuy? Is that an Ainu god?"

"Yeah, that's right." I nodded, not thinking anything of it.

He gave me a doubtful look and said suspiciously, "You're just as thoughtless as ever." He was clearly exasperated with me. I guess it seemed weird to him to be acquainted with a deity.

"A customer is a customer, even if they're a god."

"Well, I guess. 'The customer is god.' Is that true…?"

"Yes. It really is. Hey, that was a good pun!"

Impressed by that idea, which I never would have come up with myself, I thumped Suimei with a hand that was numb with cold.

Looking annoyed, Suimei batted away my hand.

Whooosh.

Just then, a particularly chill wind blew past us, and I trembled violently. "Wheeew, it's cold…"

I clung instinctively to Suimei's arm. But the cold wind whipping around us was relentless, and I couldn't warm myself up at all.

"At this rate, we might freeze to death…" I was serious. Thinking Suimei would agree with me, I looked up at his face and noticed that his cheeks and his ears were bright red. "Eek, you're all red with cold! Are you okay?"

"Yeah... I'm fine."

I tilted my head to look at Suimei, who for some reason wouldn't meet my gaze. *Whatever he says, he is cold. I hope she'll come and meet us soon...*

Just as I was thinking this, the cold suddenly eased.

"Irankarapte! Hello!"

I looked up in surprise to see an old woman wrapped in layer upon layer of red robes.

"Ape-huci-kamuy!"

She was the kamuy of fire. Heat as powerful as that of the sun radiated off the old woman, who was clad in robes as vivid as flames. Strangely enough, just standing at Ape-huci-kamuy's side, I felt my frozen body begin to thaw out from its extremities, and I breathed a sigh of relief.

At length, Ape-huci-kamuy nodded deeply and turned on her heel. As she began to walk away, the chill immediately worsened. It seemed that this warm feeling lost its effect when one was separated from her. I exchanged looks with Suimei, and we began to hurry after her.

As we did, Suimei asked me, "Where are we headed?"

"Kamuy Mintar, the Garden of the Gods. There's someone there I want to see."

We had probably been walking for about five minutes when the world that had been dyed white by the snowstorm suddenly opened up.

"Wow...!"

A sight I had never seen before stretched out before us. The snowy scene extended in all directions but for where it was interrupted by a circular field of flowers. Above it was an expanse of blue, as if a hole had opened up in the center of the cloudy sky.

The flower field was dotted with stones, though other than that there were no tall trees or plants besides the smooth carpet of flowers. They were all alpine blossoms. Avens, with yellow stamens clustered in the center of sweet white petals. Tiny, bright purple primulas. Clusters of pink, spindle-shaped mountain heather.

The cold had abated; it wasn't exactly warm, but a fresh breeze blew across the flower field. The white world of before was suddenly transformed, and my heart danced at the brilliance of the puddles reflecting blue sky, and at the vivid colors of the flowers that put me in mind of early summer.

"What's going on?" While I was spellbound, Suimei surveyed our surroundings in bewilderment.

I did understand how he was feeling. Looking into the distance, I could see that a blizzard still blew beyond the perimeter of the field. It was no ordinary sight. One could only assume that the place where we were standing was special—that it had been created with special powers.

This is Kamuy Mintar, the Garden of the Gods.

Relieved that we had finally arrived, I saw that our guide Ape-huci-kamuy had come to a halt. Following suit, I stopped still. Then I noticed houses just beyond Ape-huci-kamuy.

They were chise, traditional Ainu homes. The simple wooden houses stood in a line, their ridged roofs resting on pillars sunk directly into the ground. I also saw storehouses with raised floors and wooden cage-like structures. There seemed to be a kotan settlement here.

There were a lot of people near the houses, and they, like Ape-huci-kamuy, were dressed in traditional Ainu garb. Male and female, young and old, they all wore cheerful smiles.

When I asked Ape-huci-kamuy, "Where is Kim-un-kamuy?" she gave me a smiling nod and started to walk again. It seemed like she had a plan.

Then I remembered what Shinonome-san had said before we left.

"Ape-huci-kamuy, the kamuy of fire, is the friendliest of the Ainu kamuy. She is the constant link between humans and gods. If you're in trouble, turn to her. It's all right, Kaori, you'll do fine."

"'You'll do fine,' huh?"

Although he'd foisted this bothersome task on me, Shinonome-san had told me a lot of things about kamuy before we left. I'd been nervous about meeting the gods of the Ainu, whose culture is completely different from that of the Japanese, but thanks to Shinonome-san, my anxiety had lessened somewhat.

Be that as it may, he's still overprotective. I let out a laugh that was half-exasperated, half-happy.

Ape-huci-kamuy stopped in front of one of the chise. Out of all the chise, this was the finest. It seemed that the person we were looking for was here.

Signaling to Suimei with a glance, I moved to stand in front of the entrance to the chise. Then, remembering the Ainu etiquette for visiting, I cleared my throat loudly.

A hairy creature suddenly appeared from inside the house. "Ack!"

Thinking for a moment that it was an animal, I tensed up. The creature was perfectly human-shaped, but it was covered in so much hair that it was easy to mistake it for a beast.

"Ahup wa shini yan. Come on in and rest," he said with a broad smile that showed his canine fangs. He was a fairly well-built man. His wavy black hair fell to his shoulders, and most of his face was covered by a coarse beard. The hair on his body looked too thick to belong to a human; black hair so dense that it looked like fur protruded from the collar and sleeves of his attush, which was embroidered with a complex Ainu pattern. He also wore hand warmers and leggings, but they were so buried by his hair as to be almost invisible. However, he was bald from forehead to crown. The thick hair covering the rest of his body made that fact all the more noticeable.

"Kim-un-kamuy...I presume?" I asked the man, who was just about to go back inside the chise.

Scratching his head with his finger, he replied only, "That's right." He glanced at me with hazel eyes, and his voice lowered even further. "And what can I do for you today, my honored guests?"

Feeling the dangerous light of his eyes on me, I gulped and took a piece of paper out of my bag. "My name is Kaori. I am the daughter of Shinonome, who runs the bookstore in the spirit realm. I am here today to collect unreturned books and late fees."

Kim-un-kamuy's thick eyebrows knitted together.

Then, once again, I recalled the words Shinonome-san had spoken to me before we left.

"Kim-un-kamuy might be a god, but he's also a massive fibber. Be careful."

I wonder what lies he'll tell. I won't put up with it if he tries to send us away with deceitful words. Resolving myself to resist all trickery, no matter what, I gritted my teeth and waited for Kim-un-kamuy's answer.

"Is that s-s-so? But I thought I'd returned them?!"

He's sweating like a waterfall!

His hazel eyes refused to meet mine, and his squeaky voice was obviously shaking as he murmured to himself. "Too obvious!"

"Huh? Did you say something?"

"N-no?!" He hastily shook his head in denial.

I was shaken. I'd thought he would try more sophisticated psychological warfare; instead, he was far too transparent. I could only sigh. As I regained my composure, I gazed intently at him. "There is a precise record of loans in our ledger. Please return your items."

Kim-un-kamuy was the size of a bear and wearing a true scowl, yet at the same time he was mumbling, "Um... Well, you see..."

"My word, how can you stand around talking without even inviting our guests inside? What are you doing?!"

Then someone else appeared from inside the chise. He stood

next to Kim-un-kamuy, smirking smugly. "What's up, Kim-un-kamuy? Need some help?"

When he noticed us, he introduced himself as Kapatcir-kamuy. He was an eagle kamuy; the Ainu view the eagle, like the owl, as a god among birds.

I turned to him and bowed my head, and formally announced that I was from the bookstore.

"Oho? The bookstore? So there's a young woman running it this year..." He gazed at me with great interest, then turned to Kim-un-kamuy with a look that was somewhat sympathetic. "You look pale, Kim-un-kamuy. Did someone refuse to eat your left-over rice again? That is, did they reject your marriage proposal?"

"Eh?! N-no."

"Or did somebody laugh at you? Not much you can do about that. You're Ron-koro-oyasi, the bald-headed monster, after all. That's why you can't get yourself a wife."

Kim-un-kamuy said nothing.

Kapatcir-kamuy kept making comments that we didn't really understand. I silently exchanged glances with Suimei. The conversation was full of Ainu words and metaphors relating to unfamiliar customs, so I didn't understand everything he was saying, but there was clearly a tension in the air.

Why is he doing this...? I watched them nervously.

Kapatcir-kamuy smoothed his hand over Kim-un-kamuy's bald head, which made Kim-un-kamuy flush as red as a boiled lobster.

"If you'd just shut up and listen!"

"Ha ha ha. It's true, isn't it? Everyone knows you'll be single forever."

A vein bulged on Kim-un-kamuy's brow, and his arms and legs—which were thick to begin with—began to swell before our eyes.

This is bad!

He was clearly furious. I instinctively shrank back. As I did, Suimei stepped forward to protect me. But even so, the wrath emanating from Kim-un-kamuy was so terrifying that I clung to Suimei's back.

Kim-un-kamuy wouldn't suppress his rage. Kapatcir-kamuy slung an arm around his shoulders and whispered in his ear, "Is that why you borrowed that book from the bookstore? I know. I know what you did with the book. Don't you think you'd better give it back quickly? You can't keep it with you forever..."

In that moment, there was the *boom* of an explosion, so loud it shook the earth, and the fallen snow whirled up into the air. Instantly, I closed my eyes against the suddenly white world. I had a bad feeling about this, but I didn't open my eyes straightaway; I squeezed them tightly shut and waited.

At long last, the swirling snow settled down, and I could see what was going on.

"Gah?!"

Kim-un-kamuy, who should have been standing in front of us, had disappeared. I hastily looked around until I spied the tiny speck of a retreating figure far in the distance.

"He got away! How on earth did he run so quickly?!"

As I stood there amazed, the situation shifted again. Until now, the sky above the settlement had been clear. But that break in the clouds was suddenly filled as a blizzard whipped up. In the blink of an eye, the entire flower field disappeared under the snow.

"Ooh, Kim-un-kamuy, you scoundrel! He's controlling the weather." Kapatcir-kamuy roared with laughter as he looked up at the sky.

Tearfully, I rushed over to him. "Wh-what are you going to do about it?! He's getting away!"

"While that guy was hiding himself in the snow, I cunningly took the book out of the chise. Ah ha ha ha! Not half-bad, huh?"

"It's no laughing matter! Why did you agitate him like that?!"

Stroking his beard, Kapatcir-kamuy broke into a wide grin. "Sorry, I just hate that bearish black hair of his."

"What?"

"Kim-un-kamuy isn't a bear, but he looks like one, so I don't care for him. That's all!"

"Whaaaa...?!"

Apparently, it was nothing but a personal grudge. In the back of my mind, I recalled what Shinonome-san had said.

"Kim-un-kamuy and Kapatcir-kamuy are on bad terms. Don't let them get near each other."

I deflated. *Argh, it's a bit late to be remembering that now!*

Just then, Kapatcir-kamuy thumped his chest.

"No problem. Shall I give you a hand? Let's get ready—what's wrong?" He pointed at his own golden eyes and smiled. "Prey can't escape an eagle's eyes. I'll spot that hairy guy straightaway."

Riding on the eagle's back, we soared above the clouds. The Hokkaido sky seemed to go on forever. It was a limpid, pure blue. The ocean of clouds that stretched out beneath us looked lovely and soft, as if it would make for a wonderfully comfortable bed.

But in reality, it wouldn't be soft at all.

"Eep—eeeeeeeek! Oh no, I'm gonna fall, I'm gonna fall, I'm gonna fall!"

"Don't talk, Kaori. You'll bite your tongue!"

"Hey, hang on! That's easy for you to say—ack!" *I bit my tongue!*

Several hours had passed since we climbed onto Kapatcir-kamuy's back and soared up into the sky. In that time, I had let out many a pitiful shriek.

Every time Kapatcir-kamuy spotted Kim-un-kamuy below us, he swooped down on the other god, just as you'd expect from a bird of prey. And every time he did, to stop myself from being thrown off, I would cling desperately to whatever I could reach, whether it be Kapatcir-kamuy's wing or Suimei's waist...

At some point, my woolly hat had flown off without my noticing. Even though I was practically fainting, as though I were riding a roller coaster without a seat belt, I did my best to brave the situation. But whereas I was in this terrible state, Ape-huci-kamuy just sat there, her face as undisturbed as if she were having tea by the fireside.

The gods really are amazing, aren't they?!

While I was honestly impressed with her, I looked at Suimei's face with tears in my eyes. I'd just remembered that he wasn't good with heights.

Silence.

Although his face was pale, he didn't let out a single shriek.

Perhaps because I'd explained the situation in detail, he'd prepared himself. He gazed at the ground visible through the gaps in the clouds with an entirely serious expression.

"Ah ha ha ha ha ha! Look! There's that hairy scoundrel!"

Just as he had boasted, Kapatcir-kamuy was able to find Kim-un-kamuy extremely easily. But Kim-un-kamuy was unusually agile; he would nimbly dodge Kapatcir-kamuy's sharp talons, cross a river in a single bound, and pass over a mountain in another.

To put it simply, Kim-un-kamuy—whose name meant "person of the mountains" in Ainu—was a mountaineer. He was also known as Kim-un-kux ("god in the mountains") and Kim-okay-kux ("god who resides in the mountains"). Among the Ainu, it was said that one must never lodge in the hinterlands of the Ishikari River, for that is where he lives.

He was strong enough to kill a bear with only his hands, but there was another side to him. If a person was struggling in the mountains with heavy baggage, they had only to shout, "Aneshiratsuki utara ikasuu wa" ("Help me, guardian deities") and he would make their baggage lighter.

He was also said to despise blood, but there were legends that told of him eating humans. Also, when facing him, there was something it was never safe to mention: his baldness. Kim-un-kamuy was terribly sensitive about the fact that he was bald, and if you carelessly touched on the subject, he would incite a natural disaster that would bring all the great trees by the roadside crashing down.

"It's no use running away! The light bouncing off your bald head makes it obvious where you are. Ah ha ha ha ha ha!"

However, because Kapatcir-kamuy—who hated bears—kept making fun of his bald head and chasing after him, Kim-un-kamuy got completely worked up and kept on running away.

Hmm, I wonder whether we'll even be able to collect those late fees...

Despite my worry, there was nothing I could do, so I stayed quiet and watched attentively.

Clearly exhausted from evading Kapatcir-kamuy's claw attacks time after time, Kim-un-kamuy dove into a herd of nearby Hokkaido sika, straddled one of the bucks, and kicked it into a gallop.

"All right, we're on a roll. I was right to rely on Yuk-kor-kamuy, the god who governs the deer." Kapatcir-kamuy chuckled to himself as he watched Kim-un-kamuy moving along with the sika.

The Ainu, who found their gods in the prey, tools, and nature that surrounded them, didn't consider deer—arguably their main food source—to be kamuy. Rather, the god who governed the deer was the one who had set them free on Earth in response to the prayers of the Ainu. Was Kapatcir-kamuy implying that he'd convinced that god to station a large number of Hokkaido sika here ahead of time?

As I was wondering this, Kapatcir-kamuy addressed Suimei. "Boy! Can you drive the deer on?"

"Yes," Suimei answered without a moment's delay.

Kapatcir-kamuy let out a cheer of satisfaction.

"Kaori, hold on to my clothes or something," said Suimei. "Can't let you fall."

Suimei moved up the great eagle's body and straddled his neck. When I'd done as he told me to, Suimei took Kuro out of the bag he was carrying.

"Zzz...zzz..."

Kuro was still asleep. Murmuring an incantation of some kind to the comfortably sleeping Inugami, Suimei charged the paper talisman that he'd taken out along with Kuro.

At that moment, Kuro's red spots began to emit a dazzling light.

"Kuro! Wake up!" And, holding the Inugami high aloft, Suimei flung him into the air.

"Huh?"

Just then, Kuro finally woke up. However, he didn't seem to be fully awake yet. For a few moments, he spaced out, but as soon as he realized his predicament, he let out a shriek.

"Eeeeeeeeeep! Wh-what's going on?! It's so cold! I'm falling! Eeeeeeeeeeeeek!"

But shrieking did him no good; he was already in midair. At his wits' end, his tail still stuck to his stomach, he plunged downward in the twinkling of an eye.

"S-Suimei! What the heck are you doing? Kuro—Kuro can't—!" Instinctively, I shook him.

Suimei looked indifferent. "He'll be fine."

Just then, a whole load of talismans went flying. Suimei immediately made a series of signs with his hands. The talismans all collected in one place and formed a familiar shape.

A paper plane!

The paper plane slipped swiftly under Kuro's small body and caught him. Kuro immediately got to his feet and wagged his tail with relief.

"Wooow!" I was so impressed that I spontaneously embraced Suimei. "I didn't know you could do that too! Gosh, you really are amazing!"

Overcome with excitement, I hugged Suimei's body tightly.

"Don't cling to me," Suimei muttered. "I'll lose control. I'm serious."

"Huh? What?"

"N-nothing."

Meanwhile, the situation below was rapidly changing. Little by little, the paper plane drew closer to the herd of Hokkaido sika containing the deer that Kim-un-kamuy was straddling. Kuro raised his rump in the air, poised. His red patches began to flicker.

"Let's goooo!"

Kuro twisted his body with all his might and swung his tail, sending out a shock wave of scarlet light. It struck before the sprinting sika and burst with a thunderous roar. The startled deer tried to scatter in all directions, but the shock wave ran ahead of them, gouging into the earth.

As a result, the herd—having lost all means of escape—gradually gathered in the center of the shock wave's impact and began to run in the same direction.

I see! So that's how he controls where the herd goes!

"Ah ha ha ha! Very good, boy, very good!" Seeing this, Kapatcirkamuy laughed in high spirits.

"Damn!"

Right in the middle of the clustered deer was the buck upon which Kim-un-kamuy rode. With the deer packed together like sardines, he couldn't even jump down from its back. He was in a terrible panic.

At length, I realized that the scene had changed. The snow-field had seemed as if it went on forever. But in the center, flowing at a leisurely pace, was a river. White-coated trees dotted pools of various sizes. Birds rested in those trees, entirely carefree. The weather had greatly improved since noon, and the evening sun shone through the breaks in the clouds, making the dimly lit surface of the water sparkle. The snowy earth, tinged red by the setting sun... It was enchantingly beautiful.

"Where are we...?"

"Probably Kushiro-shitsugen. It looks as if the eagle intends to chase Kim-un-kamuy into Lake Toro."

Just as Suimei said, I could see something that resembled a lake in the distance. Parts of it were frozen, but I could tell at a glance that in some places, the ice was thin. If the herd of deer rushed onto the lake at one of those spots, the ice would certainly break, and they would fall in.

"Don't tell me he's going to make Kim-un-kamuy sink to the bottom?!"

That was definitely going too far. I turned pale.

At that moment, Kapatcir-kamuy began to descend gently. We were fast approaching the deer herd and the lake.

"Kapatcir-kamuy!" I shouted desperately.

But just at that moment, a flock of red-crowned cranes took flight all at once. My voice was drowned out by the noise of their wings. It didn't reach him at all. In a flash, we closed in on Kim-un-kamuy.

Argh, what should I do?!

At times like these, I was always stricken with hopelessness. I didn't have special powers, like Suimei. I couldn't do anything the way spirits and gods did. I was just a powerless human.

In spite of myself, I was about to cry when someone pulled on my sleeve. It was Ape-huci-kamuy. The old woman looked at me with a peaceful, poised expression, as if she wanted to say something.

"If you're in trouble, turn to Ape-huci-kamuy."

With a start, I remembered Shinonome-san's words.

That's right. I'm a human. There are things only I can do. There is a correct way for humans and gods to exist with each other, a way that has continued unbroken since ancient times. And that... is to offer up our prayers to the gods, entrusting them with our wishes.

"Ape-huci-kamuy, please... Don't let anything bad happen to Kim-un-kamuy. I don't want anyone to get hurt."

I bowed my head in earnest prayer. Apehuci stroked my head gently with a wrinkled hand and gave me a cheerful smile.

At long last, the Hokkaido sika, kicking up a spray of snow as they ran, burst onto the surface of Lake Touro and immediately lost their balance. As I'd expected, the ice was still thin. They stumbled over it in a panic. But in the next moment, I doubted my own eyes.

"Ha!"

Kim-un-kamuy fired himself up. There was the creaking sound of something solid chafing against another surface; at the same time, the whole surface of Lake Touro was blanketed in white. No—it *froze over*!

"Bwa ha ha ha ha ha! Bad luck!"

Kim-un-kamuy had the power to control the weather. Apparently, freezing over the surface of a lake presented no difficulty for him.

With an amused smile, Kim-un-kamuy—still mounted on the deer—began to cross the lake with nimble steps. The surface of the lake was completely frozen, and it did not yield under the deer's weight.

"He got away?" I murmured in blank amazement.

"Not yet!" shouted Kapatcir-kamuy. "Ape-huci-kamuy!"

As if responding to Kapatcir-kamuy's call, a heat began to spread outward from Ape-huci-kamuy. It was as hot as the midsummer sun. She seemed to be trying to melt the ice of Lake Touro. In a flash, cracks appeared in the ice covering the surface of the lake.

At this rate, won't the ice break?!

Suddenly overcome with dread, I turned to Ape-huci-kamuy. But the goddess of fire smiled placidly and gave me a small nod. I decided to trust her and watch how the situation unfolded.

"You're wasting your time!"

Seeing what was happening to the ice, Kim-un-kamuy used his miraculous powers to freeze it over once more. But as soon as Ape-huci-kamuy sent out more heat, fine cracks once again spread through the surface.

When Kim-un-kamuy reached the center of the lake, things took a turn.

"What? Whaaaat?!"

No sooner had he let out a bewildered cry than the ice beneath the hooves of the deer suddenly began to rise. With a horrible creaking sound, a huge rift broke the surface of the ice.

Flustered, Kim-un-kamuy used his powers again. An even more grating sound rang out as the ice rose. The deer that were running with all their might crashed into the ice and, startled, bolted in the wrong direction. The buck carrying Kim-un-kamuy ended up getting its hoof caught in the rift and toppling over.

"Gaaaah!"

Falling off the deer's back, Kim-un-kamuy went sliding across the ice, spinning like a curling stone. Without a moment's delay, Kapatcir-kamuy headed for him and plunged toward him in a straight line.

"Ah ha ha ha! I win, Kim-un-kamuy!"

"Damn! Damn! Damn!"

Kapatcir-kamuy let out a great burst of satisfied laughter, his beak clacking together as he did so.

Pinned down by Kapatcir-kamuy's enormous talons, Kim-un-kamuy pounded his fists against the ice, his face bright red.

When I had seen this, I somehow got down off Kapatcir-kamuy's back...and sank weakly to the ground just where I was. "Is it over?"

The cries of the Hokkaido sika and the cranes echoed around me. As for Kim-un-kamuy, Kapatcir-kamuy had him securely pinned down; it didn't look like I needed to worry about him escaping again.

"I'm exhausted," I murmured unthinkingly.

"I feel the same," said Suimei, who had alighted next to me.

For a moment, I glanced up at the sky. Then I turned my gaze back to the lake. The ice covering the lake's surface sparkled in the light of the setting sun. And then, just as if it were tracing the path someone had taken, the ice rose. I knew the name of this phenomenon.

"Omi-watari..."

This phenomenon could also be seen on Lake Suwa in Nagano Prefecture, among other places. It was caused by the difference in night and daytime temperatures. It seemed Kim-un-kamuy's chill and Apehuci's warmth had incited the effect.

"Ah ha ha ha! Wasn't it a great idea? As you'd expect from me. Wonderful for killing time!" Kapatcir-kamuy's laughter reverberated throughout our surroundings.

I let out a secret sigh at the excessive scale of the works of the gods.

Returning to the largest chise in the Garden of the Gods, we decided that we should at least have a meal. We'd missed out on lunch, and we were so exhausted that we couldn't concentrate on anything. We sat by the sunken hearth and were treated to food cooked by Ape-huci-kamuy. A pot simmered away on the fire. Inside the pot was ohaw soup, made with salmon. A general feature of Ainu cuisine is that the only seasoning used is salt. There was plenty of salmon in the soup, which had been caught in the autumn and smoked over the sunken hearth. The ingredients had a simple taste, but that taste had been beautifully highlighted, making for a flavorful soup.

"Aah... I'm warming up."

"Yeah, me too."

Our stomachs empty, Suimei and I devoured the ohaw in a daze.

My body had been continually exposed to the harsh cold air of the skies, and as it began to warm up, I was finally able to relax. At this rate, I was going to start feeling sleepy. But we still had a job to do. Once I had eaten my fill, I checked which books Kim-un-kamuy had yet to return.

The books he had borrowed were mainly written records of yukar—heroic epics handed down by the Ainu. The Ainu didn't have a written language. They remembered everything and preserved it as oral tradition. But researchers had collected tales that the Ainu had told them for these books.

There are various kinds of Ainu tales, such as uepeker (folktales) and kamuy yukar (myths); among these tales are yukar, the tales of the adventures of superhumans imbued with special powers.

"This is all of them. Well then, I will be taking these back." I put the books away in my bag as Kim-un-kamuy watched me with a melancholy look.

Suimei stroked Kuro, who was curled up asleep on his lap, as he eyed Kim-un-kamuy. "Why did you run away?" he asked. "Did you not want to pay the late fees?"

"You're...just going to go right ahead and ask me something like that?!"

"It's cold, and I was frightened. Surely I get to ask you this much." Knitting his brows together, Suimei cast Kim-un-kamuy a look that said "Come on, I earned this."

However, Kim-un-kamuy only hemmed and hawed and didn't say anything.

Meanwhile, Kapatcir-kamuy had been studying us from his seat beside Kim-un-kamuy; he had also drained his sake cup. Thus he grinned widely and declared, "In that case, I'll tell you."

"Eeeek! Wait, please!"

Thanks to Kapatcir-kamuy's interference, Kim-un-kamuy finally resigned himself to explain the situation.

"Daughter of the bookstore, how much do you know about kamuy?"

I pondered this for a while. Recalling the things Shinonome-san had taught me, I answered, "I know that they're different from the gods I'm acquainted with. Almost all of them are gods of things that surround the Ainu: beasts, vegetation, nature, tools."

For example, bears or eagles or fire, or utensils, or wild plants. In Kamuy-Mosir, the realm of the gods, they took on the form of humans; when they came to the human world, Ainu-Mosir, they put on a costume in order to appear to people. For a bear god, this costume would be the body of a bear; in the case of a fire deity, they would manifest accompanied by heat.

In other words, what the Ainu called "kamuy" were not messengers of any kind but rather the gods themselves. At the same time, the costumes they wore were gifts for humans.

"For example, the bear kamuy brings meat and fur. In return, the Ainu offer words of thanks and items that only humans can make. It is thought that this allows the kamuy to live a good life in the land of the gods. The Ainu believe that they aren't simply hunting them for their own convenience; the relationship is mutually beneficial. The Ainu and the kamuy are on equal footing. That's what my adoptive father told me."

In short, it was give and take. It seemed to me that this was an appropriate mindset for the Ainu, who flourished through trade.

Then Kim-un-kamuy told me, "Yukar are one of those things that only humans can create. When bidding farewell to a kamuy who has handed over their gift and become just a soul, the Ainu recite yukar of great interest. Those stories are truly amazing. Felling great monsters, flying through the sky! Recovering from injuries in an instant! Isn't that thrilling?!"

Kim-un-kamuy spoke with great excitement, but in the next moment he deflated.

"However, these stories almost always stop halfway through. And right before the most exciting part! I'm in limbo. It's awful."

Kapatcir-kamuy gulped down his sake and stifled a laugh. "From the point of view of the Ainu, the idea is to make people want to come back and listen to the next part of the enthralling story. But the next time, the story stops halfway again. There's nothing for it but to laugh."

"Even here in Kamuy Mintar, there are swarms of kamuy distressed by hearing these incomplete stories." Shaking his head from side to side, Kim-un-kamuy stared down at his own hands. "I thought 'Someday, I want to find out how the stories continue.' That's when I met Shinonome."

He said that Shinonome-san had told him we had a book containing a collection of yukar. In the beginning, Kim-un-kamuy—who couldn't read the characters—had studied frenetically, spurred on by his desire to read these tales. Then he borrowed that long-awaited book and dove into reading it.

"It was so fun. I clutched my belly and laughed; I was so thrilled, I couldn't stop turning page after page. I read through those yukar as if I were gobbling them up. When I finished, I started reading again from the beginning. Over and over again... So I wouldn't miss even a single character."

For Kim-un-kamuy, it was an exciting time. Once he'd read the book so many times that he'd memorized its contents, he recited the yukar to other kamuy he knew. Word got around, and visitors began to descend on Kim-un-kamuy's home.

"Recently, I've had fewer opportunities to be sent from the human world to the realm of the gods. At this rate, the kamuy will forget the stories. I want to bequeath the yukar unto them in my own way. Someday...I want to become a marvelous storyteller. But there's no way I can do it like the Ainu. I forget the stories. So I didn't want to give up the book. I'm sorry."

Kim-un-kamuy had genuinely enjoyed the book—genuinely loved the stories. When I learned this, my heart filled with new warmth.

We want to tell the spirits how wonderful books can be.

That was the wish I shared with Shinonome-san. It wouldn't have been an exaggeration to say that was why we ran the bookstore. That wish had certainly reached Kim-un-kamuy, which made me happy indeed.

"In that case, would you like me to sell it to you?" I offered. At the bookstore, we periodically replaced our stock.

Unlike a library, a rental bookshop like ours always has to change the lineup of books it offers, or our customers will get bored with our stock. For example, books that were borrowed particularly rarely might get sold to secondhand bookshops. In other cases, certain books enjoy a boom, and then when reader enthusiasm fades, we end up with excess stock. But we can sell that excess and put the profit toward buying new books.

We also sell off books that we're about to retire from our shelves to spirits who want them. I figured we ought to have enough of the yukar book in stock. Besides, unlike spirits who make their homes outdoors, Kim-un-kamuy would have no problem looking after the book in his chise.

But to my surprise, Kim-un-kamuy turned down my proposal.

"I'm the person I am now because I met Shinonome. If you sell the book to me, that link will be broken, you see? Besides, it's obviously in the bookstore's interest to keep lending out books. The things you bestow upon people have to be returned in an orderly fashion. I want to keep borrowing the book from you."

I was speechless with surprise, but I found myself smiling broadly at his words. *Yes, I'm glad I started working at the bookstore.*

Overcome with deep emotion, I moved over to stand next to Kim-un-kamuy and took his hand. "Thank you very much! What a wonderful thought! Kim-un-kamuy, we will support you. Go forth and become a fantastic storyteller. Please keep visiting the spirit realm bookstore!"

Kim-un-kamuy's big body had rounded as he sat down.

What's going on? Smiling, I peered at his face.

Utterly silent, Kim-un-kamuy was frozen, still staring at me.

"Huh? What's the matter with you?"

I waved my hand in front of his eyes, but he didn't respond. He looked blank, as if he wasn't focusing on anything. Was he unwell?

Kapatcir-kamuy suddenly burst out laughing. "Ah ha ha ha! He's just stringing together fine-sounding talk. Daughter of the bookstore, what he told you is only part of the truth. That guy is a liar."

"A liar?" Cold with dread, I looked hard at Kim-un-kamuy.

"Kim-un-kamuy might be a god, but he tells lies. Be careful."

Remembering Shinonome-san's words, I found myself glaring at Kim-un-kamuy.

"What does he mean by this?" I asked in a low voice.

Kim-un-kamuy, who had gone pale, mumbled something noncommittal.

In high spirits, Kapatcir-kamuy explained the situation. "A storyteller? He only tells the yukar to young women. And as for visitors descending on him... He invites young women to his home on the pretext of telling them yukar, then distributes his leftover rice to any and everybody."

"Distributes rice? Why?"

"According to Ainu custom, eating half a bowl of rice and then handing the rest to a woman means you're asking her to marry you. If the woman accepts, she'll eat the remainder of the rice, and that's that. But who'd marry a guy who uses such underhanded methods? He's bald, and what's more, he's a coward. He's beyond help." Smiling sardonically, he gave me a pitying look. "Daughter of the bookstore, be careful. Kim-un-kamuy is—"

Kim-un-kamuy suddenly started to vigorously bolt down the ohaw he'd barely begun. I gazed at him, startled.

Uh-oh, I have a really *bad feeling about this. I need to get away from him right now.* I tried to scoot slowly backward.

"Where are you going?" Kim-un-kamuy caught my wrist. His hand, which dwarfed my own, held my wrist securely and would not let go. The blood drained swiftly from my face.

"Um, er... Erm..." I panicked.

In that instant, I remembered something.

"Kaori, you mustn't forget this."

It was something Shinonome-san had said. Before we had left, he had told it to me with a terribly serious look.

"Kim-un-kamuy falls in love absurdly easily. Have the boy take charge of the negotiations."

"I *totally* forgot!" I whispered. *How could I forget something so important?!*

I was aghast at the extent of my own stupidity. At the same time, I was getting more and more irritated.

In other words...this means...

Kim-un-kamuy wanted to keep the book with him in order to seduce women. In short, he was sparing himself the trouble of returning it and borrowing it again because he was spending all his time hunting for a wife.

To put it simply... We had been manipulated by the selfishness of this mountain man.

We went through all that because of him! I felt the blood rush to my head as my rage reached its peak. I glared sharply at him. "Kim-un-kamuy..."

Then Kim-un-kamuy, blushing slightly as if there had been some misunderstanding, held out the half-eaten bowl of ohaw.

It's a bit late to propose to me now!

He looked at me with eyes that sparkled with hope.

Expressionlessly, I pushed the bowl away with the back of my hand. I made a loop with my thumb and forefinger in the shape of a coin. "More importantly, Kim-un-kamuy, we still have something we need to do."

"Huh?" Kim-un-kamuy's face instantly stiffened.

I intensified my smile—then, in the next moment, I gave him a look colder than sub-zero as I delivered my verdict. "Shall we settle your late fees?"

"Hold on!" Kim-un-kamuy went suddenly pale. He straightened up as if he intended to run away, but without a moment's delay, Kapatcir-kamuy held him down by the shoulders.

"Three hundred and seventy-five days have passed since the scheduled return date," I said. "It appears that you made no response to Shinonome-san's repeated requests for you to return the books. Is that right?"

"W-w-well..."

"In addition, since we were obliged to make a trip to come and collect your late fees, we will also be asking you to pay travel expenses."

"Travel expenses?!"

"In order to get here, we asked an Oboroguruma to pick us up and drop us off. So the cartage fee will come to... Only joking. Right, let's see..." I took a calculator out of my bag and tapped the numbers in. Then, after checking that I hadn't made any mistakes, I nodded confidently and presented him with the total. "Here is the total of your late fees, including expenses and so on."

"Ough...!"

Kim-un-kamuy let out an agonized cry. Blinking furiously, he stared at the figure on the calculator as if he couldn't believe his eyes. At long last, he turned to me with a frightened look and said, a little shyly, "I don't suppose a discount might be..."

"That won't be possible, no," I declared with a smile. "Please gather the money together and make your payment."

My voice echoed through the dimly lit chise.

Sweating gallons, Kim-un-kamuy gave me an awkward smile. Just as I began to wonder what he was planning, he held the half-eaten bowl of ohaw out to me again.

"Don't tell me you're asking me to marry you and cancel your debt?" I asked, feeling my face begin to twitch and trying to put up with it.

Kim-un-kamuy gave me a timid smile—and a big nod.

This guy! Rage boiled up inside me, and I was about to lose it and shout at him—when the bowl in front of me disappeared.

Suimei, next to me, had snatched it.

"Wha?!"

"You."

Giving Kim-un-kamuy a look that was colder than the surface of a frozen lake, Suimei tipped the contents of the bowl back into the pot. "Marriage means being considerate toward your partner, supporting them, helping them, protecting them. Do you really think a man who can't even keep to a book return deadline could make someone happy?"

Kim-un-kamuy inhaled in shock. Then his shoulders slumped

dejectedly. "I'll pay," he said, drawing his big body in on itself to make himself smaller.

"Phew, it's over! I feel so refreshed!"

I had at last managed to collect the late fees from Kim-un-kamuy. As we were leaving the chise, I stretched.

In the end, he had paid his late fees in gold nuggets—and how heavy this bag packed full of gold nuggets was! It would certainly get us safely past the new year.

I let out a deep sigh of relief. "We can finally go home..."

Just then, Suimei appeared, pulling a sled fully loaded with our baggage.

On top of the sled was a huge pile of vegetables, dried salmon, and bear meat. Our baggage was bursting with a Hokkaido harvest. We had been given a share to make up for the shortfall in late fees.

"You're too lenient. Letting him pay the deficit in kind..."

"Ah ha ha ha... I wonder."

Suimei looked exasperated. Feeling a little awkward, I explained myself.

The truth was that we almost never got the full amount from customers whose debts had been piling up. Basically, we tried to be repaid the cost price of the book and leave it there. But Kim-un-kamuy was a repeat offender when it came to overdue books, and he had showed no signs of remorse, so this time I had decided to properly collect on his debts.

"If he had returned the books by the settlement date, he wouldn't have had to pay. I hope he does that next time."

Kim-un-kamuy's shoulders had fallen when he realized how much he had to pay, but when I had told him that we'd received a delivery of some new books of Ainu lore, his eyes had sparkled.

I hope he isn't too discouraged to come and borrow them. I don't want him to stop reading because of this. Never mind his motives; it would be a shame for all his enthusiasm in studying Japanese to go to waste. ...But I do hope he stops asking me to marry him.

As I walked along next to Suimei, I peeked at his face. "Thanks for before."

"For what?" Suimei looked as blank as ever.

I smiled broadly at him. "For getting angry in my stead. I hate yelling at customers. You really helped me out. I feel like I can depend on you, Suimei."

Before my eyes, Suimei's face reddened. "Wha... That's not true."

"Of course it is!"

All of a sudden, Kuro popped his head out of Suimei's bag. His red eyes twinkled. "Suimei is my partner!" he said, brimming with confidence. "Of course you can depend on him! That guy Kim—whatever his name was, he'll never find a wife, but there must be plenty of people who want to marry Suimei. Hee hee hee. If you're going to make a move, Kaori, you should do it while you still can!"

"Huh?! Make a..."

"Quit it, Kuro. Why are you in such high spirits?!"

"Huh? But..."

Marriage?! What does Kuro think he's on about?! I pushed their boisterous bantering out of my ears and began to walk quickly.

71

Now that Ape-huci-kamuy was no longer beside me, I ought to have been freezing, but my face was incredibly warm. I didn't understand why I was so agitated.

"We still have people to collect from," I declared, as if to dodge the thoughts that were all jumbled together in my mind. "We'll go home for today, but I'll see you again tomorrow!"

"Huh?!" Suimei protested as he hurried to my side. "You didn't tell me that Kim-un-kamuy wasn't the only one!"

"Isn't it obvious? There are loads left. We'll be collecting them until early in the new year."

"I *told* you! At least explain things in advance!" Suimei groaned in agony, glaring at me. "Who's next?"

"Let me see... I think it's a Namahage in Akita. They're about half a year behind with their payments."

"I can only see this ending in trouble! We're going to end up being chased around by someone wielding a knife!"

"I can't stand any more cold places!" wailed Kuro.

"It's a job, so we can't be picky," I said with an unflappable expression. "Besides, Kuro, you get to sleep in the bag! When the moment comes, we'll throw you."

"You haven't given up on the idea of throwing me?!"

Our lively banter unfurled across the snowfield, which glowed bluish-white under the light of the stars. It was so cold that my skin was tingling, but somehow my heart felt pleasantly warm.

I chuckled to myself. It must have been contagious, for even Suimei and Kuro burst out laughing.

Winter is a harsh season. But if you're with someone else, you can enjoy it, I thought, etching footprints into the fresh snow as I walked.

"Oh, hey!" Spotting the Oboroguruma who had come to pick us up, I waved enthusiastically.

CHAPTER 2

The Love Lives of the Bookstore

I N WINTER, the spirit realm was wrapped in complete silence, lending it an eerie quality. The spirits all shut themselves up in their homes and gave themselves over to idle slumber as they yearned for spring. This was winter in the spirit realm: as still as death, so much so that one hesitated even to breathe.

Illuminating this sleeping world was the winter sky, a sky as red as blood. This frozen sky, studded with flickering stars, painted a crimson glaze over a world dyed white by the snow.

"Ha ha ha ha..."

It was odd to get customers on winter days like these. Having settled the late fees for the moment, I was using the days when I didn't have to go to my part-time job devoting myself to working through my tsundoku pile.

A tsundoku pile is a stack of books one has bought and not had time to read, so they just keep accumulating. I'd just gotten my hands on the first new title in a while from a series of lengthy Chinese novels that I had been obsessed with as a child. I'd bought all the books in similar genres that I could get my hands on. Well, within the limits of my pocket money, of course.

Reading them all in order, starting with the first one... Oh, how happy it made me!

"Ahhh. What shall I do after this?"

Nibbling a rice cracker, I followed the characters on the page, totally absorbed.

Steam wafted from the kettle alongside the pleasant warmth of the oil stove, weaving seamlessly with the quiet... There was no better way to get on with reading.

"Kaori-kun. Sorry, but could you bring me some tea?" asked the gentleman who was reading next to me. He wore a high-quality suit, but it was all crumpled, and he sat carelessly cross-legged on the tatami. He still had his hat and leather gloves on although we were indoors, and his gray eyes sparkled brightly as he followed the story in his hands with rapt attention.

Without looking up from my book, I flatly refused. "I'm at a really good point right now, so please go ahead and make it yourself."

"Don't you think you're being too cold to me, Kaori-kun?" the gentleman said in a tearful voice. "I'm old, and you should be looking after me! Besides, I'm your employer! I'm only asking you to care about me a little...!"

Grudgingly, I looked up from my book to glare at him. "This is the spirit realm, and I'm not at work right now. If you want tea, Toochika-san, there's water in the pot. Can't you brew some yourself? I'm at a critical moment—I'm about to find out whether the protagonist's rival lives or dies!"

"Hmm, that is a matter of the greatest importance. All right, I'll make some myself."

This gentleman who had understood my plight so readily was Toochika-san, a kappa spirit who owned the place where I worked part-time in the human world. He hurriedly got to his feet and headed for the kitchen.

I heard him as he was making tea in the kitchen.

"No doubt about it, tea that a woman has made for you tastes twice or even three times as good. That sweet Kaori-kun gave me the test of making tea by myself. I'll show her that I can bear that kind of mistreatment. Ha ha ha, to think that I can even make tea... I'm perfect!"

He's a bit of a narcissist... Chuckling to myself, I called out to him. "What you just said is pretty much sexual harassment!"

"What?! How hard it's become to navigate this society! Gah, a life in which one cannot say what one thinks is as dry as sand," Toochika-san said, evidently astonished, as he came bounding back. He put his teacup down on top of the kotatsu and cheerfully reached for the book he had been reading: Edogawa Ranpo's *The Black Lizard and Beast in the Shadows.* It was first serialized in the popular magazine *Hinode.* The main character is a female thief who collects all the beautiful things in the world, and it's known for being a work in which the famous detective Akechi Kogoro appears.

"Ahh...the Black Lizard. No other woman is as beautiful, wise, cruel, and cunning as she. I want to meet her in the flesh—even if it's in a dream. My heart won't stop pounding as her loveliness radiates from the page!" He seemed to have slipped deep into the world of *The Black Lizard*.

It had to be said. Although Toochika-san usually tried to behave like a gentleman, when he got like this, it was extremely annoying. He started to get caught up in his own little world, making exaggerated gestures like an actor in a play.

"In any case, I'm sorry for keeping you waiting."

"Oh no, it's all right. I can read my favorite book."

In addition to employing me at his shop, Toochika-san was Shinonome-san's old friend and reading companion. He had apparently promised to have a drink with Shinonome-san today. The two regularly held parties where they each brought books they had recommended to the other and reviewed them together.

But as for Shinonome-san...

"Rargh! I can't write!"

Shinonome-san's annoyed voice filtered through from his room, which was next to the living room. As usual, his writing wasn't going anywhere. A few days ago, he had abandoned his manuscript in a sulk, so now he was struggling to meet his deadline. As a result, Toochika-san had come around to read at our house, but he had been left to his own devices.

"I like talking with Shinonome-san about books, but spending time reading all the books that happen to catch my eye is marvelous. Selecting from all the books put out by a publisher whose work I've enjoyed before... This bookstore has just as many books as any library. You can keep me waiting as long as you like."

Judging from his attitude, Toochika-san was enjoying himself anyway.

"You can get really absorbed, can't you?" an astonished voice cut in. It was Suimei. Sitting under the kotatsu, he was surrounded by a large pile of books just as we were, but he didn't seem very interested in them.

"You couldn't find a book you liked?" I asked.

He flipped through the book he was holding and closed it with a small sigh. "I don't really understand the attraction."

"Hmm, really?"

"Perhaps there isn't a book that suits me anywhere..." Suimei's shoulders slumped dejectedly.

I hated to see him like that. "It doesn't have to be a book, does it? How about a film, or a TV drama, or a game?"

Suimei shook his head. "No, it has to be a book," he insisted.

With a small sigh, I closed my book, thinking back to what had happened a few days ago.

On that winter's day, large snowflakes had fallen unceasing.

All of a sudden, Suimei had said to me, "I want to read a book."

By this point, it had been a little more than half a year since I had met Suimei. I was genuinely surprised that he would say such a thing, since up until then, he hadn't shown much interest in books. But from the way he put it, I got the impression that a certain incident had sparked his curiosity anew.

That incident had unfolded on an autumn day when the sky was painted a dark purple. Suimei had met his dead mother in the spirit realm.

Her death from illness had separated her from Suimei when he was only five years old. Anchored by the regret that she had left the young Suimei behind, she had been unable to reincarnate, and her soul had remained in the spirit realm. Mother and son had been reunited in a place where pained souls lingered, and although it had only been for a mere few days, they had been able to spend some time together.

"I'm bad at expressing my emotions. That was why my mother told me to read books. Read a lot, and study all kinds of feelings. That's why I want to read one," Suimei had said with great earnestness.

Luckily, our house was a rental bookstore; we were rolling in books. He had read nearly no books at all before, and I made him try out all kinds, from short stories to bestsellers that had sold a million copies.

Unfortunately, Suimei once again closed a book with a sigh.

"I don't really get this, either. How can a housewife be a detective? Doesn't this police detective know the words 'duty of confidentiality'?"

"It's just for entertainment! It's fiction! *Fiction!*"

"And that manga I read the other day... Don't you think the main character encountered murder cases too frequently, given that he was only an elementary school student? Dealing with dead bodies so often from an early age seems like it would have an adverse effect on the development of his personality. I feel like he might turn into a murderer when he grows up."

"What?! It's based on real events—I'm not comfortable with you saying that! Well, how about fantasy, then? Fantasy..!"

"What are all these elves and goblins? Spirits from somewhere?"

"Does that mean you'll have to start with Tolkien's *Lord of the Rings*?!"

"*Lord of the...* That doorstop of a book? *Me*, read *that*?"

For some reason, Suimei was struggling to find something he could really stick with. He wanted to read, and he had the ability to sail through long pieces of writing, but he couldn't genuinely enjoy them.

This troubled me.

"I just can't get used to it," Suimei said apologetically. "At any rate, I don't have any experience with stories. The truth is, my mother used to read them to me before I was old enough to understand what was going on...but I only found that out recently."

To a certain extent, Suimei's upbringing had been defined by a culture of purity. Everyone in the Shirai family who had been involved in raising him had, as a rule, intentionally kept him away from creative works. Consequently, he didn't really understand the attraction or the significance of fiction.

"My father and the old men of the Shirai family shut me away from everything, you see," he said. "When I was little, I was locked up in a pitch-black room. I didn't go to school. I was taught everything I needed to live by an old man. Knowledge, social etiquette, how to behave as an exorcist, how to wield a weapon, how to kill a spirit...

"To them, an education in aesthetics was nothing but a hindrance," Suimei said resentfully, all emotion wiped from his face.

Suimei was a former exorcist—and he had been born into a

tsukimono clan bound to an Inugami. He had been brought up being told: *You must not have emotions.*

When an Inugami is bound to a person and that person feels jealousy toward someone else, the Inugami is prone to hurting the object of jealousy. As long as Suimei was making his living as an exorcist, emotions were a threat, since there was always a small chance that he might hurt a client. Even so, I feel like forbidding emotions themselves was an overreaction. Then again, perhaps something had happened in the past...

Fortunately, Suimei was now released from that binding spell. The Inugami Kuro was still with him, though the magical connection between them had been severed. Now they were simply friends and partners.

With a sigh, Suimei gazed at the books he had piled up. "I haven't had much experience with fiction, so it might take me a while to understand the fun of books. Perhaps I just have to follow the usual path and get used to reading straightforward things like children's picture books first."

"That makes sense."

Suimei was trying to outgrow his old self and walk a new path. The first step on that path was studying emotions through reading. I sincerely wanted to help him if I could.

But...there seems to be nothing for it but to make him read books he's not interested in. I groaned to myself. "A book that you'd enjoy, Suimei? Perhaps there really isn't one..."

The kotatsu blanket bulged and wriggled, and all of a sudden, another person popped their head out from underneath it.

"I was listening, and... Well, no, I don't get it."

It was Kinme. He was one of a pair of raven Tengu twins, and a childhood friend of mine. His jet-black hair was tousled from being under the kotatsu, and although he usually wore a monk's clothing, today he was dressed very casually in a white turtleneck sweater.

As for why Kinme was at the bookstore without his twin brother Ginme, who he usually always accompanied? Ginme had gone with their teacher the Great Tengu of Mount Kurama to meditate under a waterfall, and Kinme had been lonely all by himself. He'd suddenly turned up and gone to sleep under the kotatsu, so I'd left him alone.

Now he grinned so widely that his drooping golden eyes partly closed as he turned to Suimei. "But hey, you're a boy of a certain age, right, Suimei? You'll want to read something sexy. A sexy book."

"No way, what are you—hey, Kinme!" Suimei protested, bright red.

Kinme cackled with laughter. Then his expression turned serious. "I think it's extremely natural for boys of a certain age to take an interest in sexual matters. Or rather, to have questions about them." Staring at Suimei, he tilted his head a little to the side. "How should I put it... How have you studied love, Suimei?"

"Love?" Suimei tilted his head, puzzled by Kinme's words.

"This is only a theory of mine, but...I don't think you can learn love from anyone else," Kinme went on. "For example, you could become aware of love by seeing the harmonious relationship between your parents, but you wouldn't understand anything about falling in love. That's because your parents went through the process of falling in love a long time ago. So if you think about where you learn how to fall in love, it must be from communal life at school, or books and television dramas and films... From creative works, right?"

"Oh... Maybe. Parents and teachers don't instruct us on how to socialize with the opposite sex."

"Right? That's because humans are animals. I think they learn sexual behavior through instinct. But when it comes to choosing what they should do next, they have to have something to refer to. Something cultural and rational. These days, though, if you pin somebody down 'because you love them,' you'll just get arrested."

"I get what you mean, Kinme, but you should say it in a more roundabout way."

"Huh? But that's such a pain." Kinme gazed at Suimei with keen interest. "That's why I had questions...about your love life, Suimei!"

What information is Kinme trying to get out of him? I looked at my old friend in astonishment. But on the inside, my heart was pounding. I, too, was curious about what Suimei's love life might be.

After thinking for a little while, Suimei frowned. "I don't really understand what a 'love life' is. The old man who gave me my education told me about the act of human reproduction."

"The...act?"

"The old man used these ancient books, bound in traditional Japanese fashion. He would stick brushstroke paintings of men and women intertwined with one another under my nose and recount his own experiences—"

"Eeeek! Wait! Stop right there, Suimei!"

I unthinkingly silenced him. Suimei looked annoyed, but this wasn't the time for me to worry about that.

What should I say... I kind of...kind of feel like running away!

"Heeeee...hee hee, hee hee hee hee... Wha...what?!... His *own experiences*? Eurgh!" Kinme had been the one to draw this information out of Suimei, but he clutched his stomach, laughing so hard he could barely speak.

I slowly took my hand away from Suimei's mouth and breathed a sigh of relief. Although I knew he wasn't, my whole body itched with shame as if he had been talking about *me*.

"Did I say something weird?" Suimei himself seemed to feel this was unreasonable. Frowning in displeasure, he glared at Kinme, who was still crouched there laughing.

"Don't worry too much, Suimei. Kinme's just horsing around, as usual."

"I'm not worried. Well, what it comes down to is that I don't really understand love. I don't understand the secrets of the emotions that normal people have in the first place."

As Suimei sighed out these words, one person in our little group instantly reacted.

"Oh! Very interesting." That was Toochika-san, who up until now had been sitting quietly, listening to us talk.

His handsome face shone like a teenage boy's, and he scooted over to Suimei. "So, in other words, you don't know anything of the promises and conflicts of love, right?" he asked with barely suppressed energy. "Oh, I'm so jealous!"

"Jealous?" Suimei tipped his head to one side.

"You're mentally mature, and you can enjoy stories without any foreknowledge," Toochika-san said with a faraway look on his face. "You can see both the great works of the past and new masterpieces through fresh eyes. All the stories spun in front of you will seem vibrant and revolutionary. If that isn't enviable, I don't know what is!"

Flushed with excitement, he gripped Suimei's hand. "Besides, there is some truth to what Kinme-kun said. Although we can't speak freely here about erotic books and the like, it's only natural for a boy your age to be interested in women. What you should be reading now are works that deal with youth and love... All the books that Kaori-kun has picked out for you seem rather light on romantic elements."

I instinctively recoiled at Toochika-san's words. "Ack... I just prefer adventure to romance!"

"Oh no, I like adventure too. I'm not saying that's a bad thing. Love that can be fostered in the midst of adventure is valuable, but it feels rather tacked on. I think it would be appropriate to try something new and experience the many works that choose love as their main theme. Though that has its advantages and disadvantages too... Well then, shall I introduce you to an acquaintance of mine who is well versed in matters of romance?!"

"O-okay..." Suimei said rather hesitantly to Toochika-san's excitement.

I, meanwhile, scowled at his eagerness. "Are you up to something?"

Toochika-san gave me an unnecessarily invigorated smile. "Ha ha ha. I couldn't possibly be. I just like watching platonically as young people, by turns irritated and bashful, close the distance between them little by little."

"What kind of hobby is that?" I forced a laugh. Toochika-san was puffed up with pride, clearly thinking it was a great hobby. *He's carrying his joke too far.* I sought agreement from Suimei, but...

"I understand. I am interested in romance. Please introduce me to this acquaintance of yours."

I was so shocked that my jaw almost hit the floor.

Shinonome-san's manuscript was nowhere near finished, so Suimei and I decided to go and visit Toochika-san's acquaintance straightaway. The squeaking of our feet treading down the piled-up snow echoed through the still and silent spirit realm, in which all hustle and bustle had been forgotten. Although it was winter, butterflies fluttered about us. These were glimmerflies, which inhabited the spirit realm in great numbers and were highly prized as sources of light.

Relying on the light of those butterflies, which danced about us as lightly as if they were playing, we journeyed through a world of perpetual night.

Suimei, Kinme, and I followed behind an exultant Toochika-san.

"Ooh, I wonder who it is. This is so exciting!" Kinme said in high spirits.

In contrast: Suimei. "Deliberately going out in the snow? What a bother."

He seemed to be fed up with the sheer amount of snow and wanted to go home already.

As I walked beside them, I covertly eyed Suimei.

"I'm interested in romance."

A question emerged in my mind: *Hey, Suimei, is there someone you've started liking?*

Biting back the urge to ask, I pulled my scarf up around my face. *What a change of heart...*

My own heart felt heavy.

At that moment, Suimei suddenly spoke up. "Are you cold, Kaori?"

"N-no, I'm fine."

"Okay, tell me if you are."

As he spoke, his eyes, framed by long eyelashes, partly closed in a gentle smile. As he looked up at the red-tinged sky of the spirit realm, he let out a white puff of breath. The snow fluttering down from the sky was reflected in his large eyes, and I found myself wondering what he saw.

"Ahhh." My heart pounded violently. My face felt warm. It was probably red.

Pulling up my scarf again, I bowed my head just in case Suimei saw. The only things in my field of vision were my boots, crunching through the snow.

I wonder why my heart is throbbing like this. I had been considering the reason for some time now, but no answer came to me.

It's strange. I wonder if I'm attracted to him, I thought absentmindedly. But at the same time, I thought it entirely possible that I was just baffled by how differently I saw him now from when we'd first met.

But there's no denying I find myself captivated by his expression when I least expect it. Having said that, there's no decisive way to confirm that this is love. The sigh I breathed out was dyed white by the chill of the air, then dissolved into nothingness before my eyes. *If only these gloomy feelings would disappear as well.*

At times like these, a desire flashed across my mind. I wished I had someone I could ask for advice without reserve.

Several candidates presented themselves. But my best friend, Nyaa-san, wasn't a human. And I would have felt embarrassed about going to Noname, who fulfilled the role of mother for me.

I should have made human friends.

The truth was that for a time, I had been allowed to go to a school that other humans went to. It had been Shinonome-san's idea.

"Don't you think you ought to try living in human society, just once?"

And so I'd disappeared into a school in Tokyo for three years. Toochika-san, who had a lot of influence even in human society, had taken care of the formalities.

And yet... However hard I tried, I had been unable to let my guard down among my human classmates.

I think those three years were pointless.

I'd studied just as well in the spirit realm, to the point where I hadn't had any difficulty in lessons. But I had been unable to make small talk with my classmates. After all, our values differed. Somehow, we remained definitively out of sync, and those differences created an unbridgeable gulf.

If only I'd faced up to my classmates properly during that time... If only I'd gained romantic experience during my school days...

But it was too late to worry about such things.

Perhaps Suimei and I are the same.

Suimei had spent his life isolated from everything. I had gone through life unaware of things that it was perfectly normal for humans to experience. Although I read books and watched characters fall in love, it had never seemed like something I would also do.

I'm similar to a human, but not the same. For me, "love" is like something from another world. Or rather...I wonder whether I can love normally?

"Hey, Kaori."

"Uh, wh-what?"

While I had been lost in thought, Kinme had appeared by my side. Golden eyes narrowing impishly, he peered at me. "Speaking of falling in love... Is there someone you like, Kaori?"

"What?"

The abruptness of the question left me greatly shaken. When I glanced at Suimei, he also seemed to be looking in my direction.

Looking here and there, I answered vaguely. "I d-don't know..." My voice trailed off.

"Oooh?" Kinme smiled meaningfully.

He was so interested in my reply, and I couldn't bear it. I turned the question back on him. "Wh-what about you, Kinme?"

With a look of surprise, he answered straightaway, "Love? Is it really necessary?" He tilted his head to one side and smiled innocently. "Love is just for weak-minded people."

Kinme threw those words out so casually. They pierced my heart like thorns.

"Here we are, ladies and gentlemen."

Thirty minutes after we had set out, Toochika-san stopped in a certain place.

"Oh! Toochika-san, is this really...?" Kinme exclaimed with delight.

"What are we doing here...?" Suimei asked, thoroughly confused.

As for me, I froze as soon as I saw where we were.

The Ohaguro Ditch was surrounded by a deep moat, alongside which ran a barrier of tall trees. There was only one place where people could get through, a great gate called a daimon (meaning "big gate"). As soon as we passed through the gate, I saw a small guardroom.

"Greetings," said Toochika-san.

The one-eyed spirit in the guardroom bowed his head as Toochika-san addressed him.

Returning the bow, Toochika-san strolled on.

"T-Toochika-san?! Shinonome-san told me never to come here!" Flustered, I chased after Toochika-san and held him back.

He gave me a sardonic smile. "I don't think we'll have a problem, You're an adult now, after all."

"But...! Is this really all right?" I asked miserably, looking at my surroundings again.

"Yeah, I'm sure it'll be fine. Now let's get on to Yoshiwara."

That's right, the spirit realm knows this place as "Yoshiwara."

In other words, the Yoshiwara that, from the Edo to the Showa period, was famous as a red-light district.

In the human world, its existence as a pleasure quarter came to an end after the passing of the Prostitution Prevention Law of 1956 (Showa 31), but as a matter of fact, it had continued to exist in the spirit realm.

The world of spirits was one in which things that had been lost in the human world still lingered. It was easy for places where many humans had spent time, and where many different emotions were jumbled together, to be restored to life. Even the tenement houses in which many spirits I knew lived had really existed in the Edo period; they had also been brought back in the spirit realm.

Nevertheless, there were parts of the Yoshiwara of the spirit realm that differed definitively from the Yoshiwara of the human world. Namely, although it had kept the townscape characteristic of Yoshiwara, it didn't function as a pleasure quarter.

The inhabitants of the spirit realm are, well, spirits. They don't share the human interest in hiring someone for sex, so red-light districts were deemed unnecessary.

"Well, in any case, let's go!"

"All right..." Although I felt uneasy, I followed after Toochika-san.

Passing under the great gate, we immediately came to a wide street. Smack-dab in the middle of the street was a mound of earth with cherry trees planted in it. But right now, it was winter. Their branches, blanketed in snow, looked bleak. I could nevertheless imagine how gorgeous this place was in brighter seasons.

Buildings jostled each other on both sides of the street, and paper lanterns filled with glimmerflies hung in rows from every eave.

In front of the shops, which had their trade names emblazoned on noren curtains, there were stands for hawkers to call out to potential customers. Beyond the noren, I caught glimpses of rooms of luxurious design. The sound of shamisen and hand drums floated from the second floor of the shops and echoed lightly down the street. The light that filtered from inside the shops was bright enough to illuminate the night sky.

As the world goes to sleep, day dawns in the pleasure quarters.

This was the nightless city such senryu poems spoke of.

The Yoshiwara of the spirit realm...

Even walking around and gazing at the townscape was interesting. There were tons of things I had never seen before; anyone with an interest in history surely couldn't help but be fascinated by it. But I kept walking along behind Toochika-san, shivering uncontrollably.

"Hey, niisan, niisan. Wait up. Won't you come and play with me?"

"Heavens, you're a pretty girl, aren't you?"

"If you think so... Come this way, come on."

The area doesn't function as a pleasure quarter. Or at least, it wasn't supposed to. But I could still hear the exchanges between prostitutes and their clients.

"He's running away! Chase him!"

"Whew...aahh...whew...aahh..."

"Catch him! Don't let him get away!"

"Whew...aahh...I'll definitely come back... Mother... Mother..."

Someone's rough breathing brushed past my ears, followed by the sound of many footsteps.

"Why! Am I not a regular? I'm here all the time, spending large sums of money! So why won't you see me?!"

"Go home. I don't like people like you."

"I love you. I fell in love with you at first sight. So why...?!"

"Please, go home!"

The man's voice was full of passion. In contrast, the woman's voice was cold.

Suddenly uneasy, I glanced about my surroundings. Just then, a woman's scream rent the air. At the same time, I heard sobs that made my whole body break out in goosebumps. However, although I could hear her voice clearly, the voice's owner was nowhere to be seen.

"What's going on? What's with this voice?!" Suimei was also looking around in consternation. One hand went to the pouch at his belt, preparing for battle.

Toochika-san and Kinme stopped and turned to me and Suimei.

"It's all right. They're just voices, so what's the harm?" With a gentle smile, Kinme put his hands over my ears.

I breathed a sigh of relief as the sound of my surroundings grew distant. But we couldn't do this for the whole time we were here. Lifting Kinme's hands away from my ears, I said, "Thank you. I'd heard about them, but they bothered me more than I thought they would."

I could still hear a woman's voice.

"I want to go back to my home, but I cannot..."

Her moans sounded as if they were coming from right next to me. Panicked, I shook my head to dispel them.

"Well... I guess it's pretty intense for humans. That's probably why Shinonome-san told you to never come here."

"Hey, Kinme-kun. I'm the one who's to blame for bringing her along. Kaori-kun's all right now. I just thought she shouldn't stay away from things like this forever."

There was a reason I could hear the voices of people we couldn't see.

The cries of the souls of people who once lived in places like this still clung to them even after they had been reborn into the spirit realm. Once these places adapted to the spirit realm, the souls' cries faded away, and the places themselves were transformed little by little from their original state. That was common knowledge in the spirit realm.

This was partly why Shinonome-san had ordered me never to come here. It would have been different were it a normal place, but he had decided that here in Yoshiwara, there were too many cries of sorrow and women's voices full of despair. He'd felt that, for me—as I was also a woman—the burden would be too great.

I couldn't see the women who had lived here. But when I thought about their circumstances, it brought such pain to my heart that I could barely breathe.

Kinme rubbed his finger in a circle between my eyebrows. "There's no need to empathize with invisible people. You really are a fool, Kaori." Then he laughed, looking intently at me. "That little wrinkle between your eyebrows... I don't care even if it is a bad habit of yours."

"Oof... I hate wrinkles. But it's because I can hear the voices."

"Hmm, that's just like you, Kaori. We told you: ignore them! No one is really sad or hurt, so just pretend you can't hear them. Okay?"

"Yeah... Thanks, Kinme."

Kinme glanced behind me and burst out laughing. As I was wondering why, Kinme threw his hands up as if in surrender. "Yeah, that's more like my old friend. I haven't seen you act like that in a while. All right! I'll feel bad if I get glared at anymore. Let's go now! Toochika-san, are we headed over there?"

"Someone's glaring?"

Kinme had instantly turned his back to me. I tilted my head to one side, then glanced behind me. But there was no one there except Toochika-san, grinning broadly, and Suimei, as expressionless as always.

"Ah, youth. Why, it's been a while since my heart fluttered

like this." With a spring in his step, Toochika-san followed after Kinme.

I looked at Suimei, who had been left behind. He easily turned his gaze away from me and followed behind Toochika-san.

"Eh? What's going on?" I tilted my head.

"Kaori? Come on, quickly!"

As if Kinme's voice had given me a shove in the back, I followed after the rest of them.

The place that Toochika-san led us to was one street over from the main avenue. It had once been a brothel known as Harimise. This area had already adapted to the spirit realm, and I could no longer hear the cries that had stopped me before.

The buildings of Yoshiwara, steeped in this world in which spirits lived, had taken on something of a magical air. The entire front of this lavish building was hidden by a cluster of Chinese lantern plants. Usually, summer and autumn were the best time to see these plants, but according to Toochika-san, here they bloomed all year round. The lantern-shaped calyxes, poking their heads out from under the white snow, looked freezing cold.

"Why are these here?" I asked as I cocked my head to the side.

Looking awkward, Toochika-san explained. "In the Edo period, they were used as an abortion drug... To a certain extent, they're very appropriate for a place like this."

"Oh... I see." My reply was interrupted by a gulp. Although Kinme had told me not to worry, a pang shot through my chest, and I stopped in my tracks.

Now that I looked at the building again, I could see that it was built in a way characteristic of a brothel.

When I heard the name "Harimise," the first thing that came to mind was a room facing the street with a wooden grille set in the wall. I'd come across images of such rooms in books that described Yoshiwara. Once, an establishment would have lined the women it sold along the interior of that grille, displaying them to customers walking past in the street outside. But here in the spirit realm version of Yoshiwara, something else occupied the space those women would have.

"It's beautiful."

Beyond the grille, as if enshrined there, grew a wisteria plant, its bluish-purple flowers like bells.

Those wisteria flowers were a symbol of refinement; they fluttered lightly every time the wind blew, and bravely withstood the snow that came dancing in through the grille. The sight of the glimmerflies flitting playfully between the flowers was beautiful, though it had an otherworldly air.

Hasn't wisteria been a symbol of women since ancient times? It seems that in the spirit realm, too, this place belongs to us...

"Kaori, you're gonna freeze if you just stand there. Come on, let's go."

As I stood there in a daze, staring at the magical scene, Suimei pushed me lightly in the back.

With a start, I resumed walking.

I trod down the narrow path, pushing aside the Chinese lantern plants that covered the entire face of the building, and entered the shop to see two small figures.

"Welcome. Please come in."

"The young mistress is waiting for you."

They were little servant girls, about five years old, with straight hair that fell all the way to their waists. One of them wore an ornate hairpin with a plum blossom design and the other one a cherry blossom design. They were dressed in matching kimono.

With sweet smiles, the two of them began to walk gracefully farther into the shop. We took off our shoes and followed them.

"Wow!"

The inside of the brothel was the very definition of extravagance. The pillars were lacquered with vermilion, and the transoms that demarcated the rooms bore exquisite designs. Wisteria in full bloom were painted on the fusuma sliding screens, making for a beautiful contrast between the elegant purple of the flowers and the vermilion furnishings. This went on for room after room.

However, unlike the Yoshiwara of the human world that had flourished as a working brothel, in this spirit realm Yoshiwara there was not a soul to be seen. An odd melancholy hung in all these magnificent, spacious rooms.

At last we came to the heart of the building. Here we found an atrium courtyard with a well crowned with snow and a great wisteria tree. Though blanketed with white snow, the tree's purple petals fluttered about, making it look just like a painting.

The two servant girls looked back over their shoulders at us.

"Please go up to the Winter Room on the second floor."

"There are drinks laid out for you."

We climbed the creaking stairs and came to a long corridor. Along the dimly lit corridor were several rooms, each one depicting a Japanese season. The two girls stopped in front of a fusuma decorated with a pine tree buried in snow and crouched down, one on each side of the screen, to reach out and touch it.

"Fuguruma-youbi-sama!" said one.

"Kami-oni-sama!" said the other.

"You have visitors," they said in unison.

The fusuma juddered open.

What waited for us beyond it? As I swallowed hard, I saw someone sitting on the other side of the screen. Two someones.

"Toochika!"

One of them was a stunningly beautiful young woman. Her hair, as white as the first snowfall of the season, spread out around her on the tatami, glossy in the light of the glimmerflies. Her skin was so pale, it was as if her blood was transparent. Because of this, her fingertips and cheeks, which were tinged with scarlet, really drew the eye. The effect was extremely erotic.

Her pale violet eyes, framed by long eyelashes, slanted upward, suggesting a strong-willed nature. Lipstick painted her soft lips scarlet, the same color that tinted the outer corners of her eyes.

The double-layered bridal robe she wore over her kimono was the white of morning mist infused with the hue of sunrise. At first glance, I thought it was plain, but when I took a good look at it,

I realized that it was embroidered with a thread that was a subtly different shade of white, picking out a delicate spread of wisteria flowers. From the look of it, the undercoat was of high-quality cloth as well, and the white wisteria flowers embroidered upon it were amazingly detailed.

"Come here, Toochika. Have you brought me another new book?!" Blushing attractively, she smiled and began to crawl toward him on all fours.

But her face twisted immediately. The person behind her had pulled her hair. With a bitter look on her face, she turned back to stare at the man.

"I'm in the middle of doing your hair, Youbi," he said. "Stay here in my arms."

"Waaah, you're so annoying! Hurry up and finish it!"

Unhappily, the young woman thumped the splendid pink obi tied in front of her stomach, clearly wanting to be next to Toochika-san. The man stifled a laugh and unhurriedly brushed through the woman's hair with the comb in his hand, as if there was no need at all for him to rush.

The man had a completely different air than the young woman. If she was the drifting snow, he was the shadow that fell across it.

His hair was so dark brown as to be almost black. It was long and piled high on top of his head. His tanned skin had obviously seen plenty of sun, and there was a large, tear-shaped mole under one of his clear eyes. His hooked nose was a little twisted, and the corners of his mouth were always turned upward. The clothes in which he was wrapped were jet black and finely patterned; from his obi dangled a tobacco pouch, made from the same cloth as the woman's bridal robe, and a pipe.

"Besides, dressing your hair is my job, Youbi. I want to be sincere in my work. I can't possibly rush."

"Then why are you wasting time talking? When are you going to finish my pompadour?"

"Well, now. I can't say for certain."

"Oh, come *on*, Kami-oni! Give me a break!" she pouted.

Chuckling, the man started to move his hands again. His eyes, the olive-green of a Japanese nightingale, were trained with rapt attention on the woman's hair. Every time he moved, his ornate hairpin—usually considered to be a woman's accessory—shook.

They're completely immersed in their own world...

I wondered whether it would be all right to say that. As I dithered in spite of myself, Toochika-san cleared his throat with a cough. That seemed to bring them back to reality. Letting out a little cry, the woman hastily straightened up and offered us zabuton.

"Forgive me for not greeting you at once. Apart from Toochika, it seems I haven't met any of you before. We are meeting for the first time. I am Fuguruma-youbi. And this persistent man who will not stop playing with my hair is Kami-oni."

"I'm not playing with it. I'm admiring it."

"Kami-oni, shush for a while. You're such a pain. Just be quiet."

"Hee hee. Your cold attitude is so amusing, Youbi! I'll concentrate on doing your hair, shall I?"

What characters they are... I stared at the two of them in a daze.

Meanwhile, Suimei frowned, and Kinme clutched his belly and laughed.

"You two are as interesting as ever." With a shrug, Toochika-san told us all about them.

Fuguruma-youbi was, in short, the spirit of a love letter. A spirit depicted in Toriyama Sekien's *A Horde of Haunted Housewares*, she had taken shape from the attachments dwelling within the love letter's undelivered sentiments.

As for Kami-oni, in truth, no one was sure how he'd come to be. In Japan, since ancient times it's been believed that hair possesses special powers. Many things, both good and bad, are locked up within each long, thin strand of hair. It was said that Kami-oni was hair itself that became an oni; it was also said that a woman's grudge had haunted a man and that, as a consequence, his hair had grown unceasing.

"So what kind of spirit are you really?" Toochika-san asked.

"Hee hee..." Smiling meaningfully, Kami-oni reached up and touched the hairpin on top of his head.

The hairpin uttered a single word. "Cuckoo!"

Apparently, he had no intention of giving a straight answer. After he made the little tin cuckoo cheep, he went back to stroking Fuguruma-youbi's hair, humming to himself.

Looking very small where she was sitting on Kami-oni's lap, Fuguruma-youbi let out a sigh. "Please forget about it. He's so weird about all that. Even I can't get an answer out of him."

"Ha ha... Is that right?" Toochika-san smiled uneasily at Fuguruma-youbi, who looked absolutely exhausted, and changed the subject. "As a matter of fact, I didn't come here today to deliver a book."

"Huh? Is that so? What a shame..."

"Sorry. When there's new stock in, I'll bring you something right away."

"That sounds wonderful! Now I'm looking forward to your next visit even more. Don't worry about the price, just bring me lots!"

I wonder what kind of relationship these two have.

As I was pondering the nature of their exchange, Toochika-san explained it to me.

"Fuguruma-youbi is an old friend. I sell love stories to her directly, wholesale."

"Oh, is that so?"

"She likes to keep the things that she wants with her. That's why she hasn't had anything to do with your bookstore."

"Parting with a book that you've come to love? What a horrible idea!" Fuguruma-youbi said irritably, turning away.

I'd expected there to be spirits who thought like this, but this was the first time I'd actually met one. "Do you have a great many books, Fuguruma-youbi?" I asked her, my interest piqued.

Fuguruma-youbi nodded proudly and exchanged glances with the two servant girls who were waiting behind her. They slid open the fusuma at the back of the room.

"Wow!"

On the other side of the screen, I beheld a vast bookcase that took up an entire wall. Everything from novels to manga and magazines was lined up along it.

As I sat there amazed, Fuguruma-youbi laughed. "This is nothing," she said, grinning boldly.

The servant girls, who had moved gracefully into the room, opened another fusuma.

I'm st-st-stunned!

"No way..."

As the screens were opened up one by one, new bookshelves appeared. It seemed we were sitting in the middle of what had originally been one enormous room that was now partitioned by sliding screens. There were bookshelves stuffed with love stories as far as the eye could see.

"I intend to get a hold of everything that bears the name of romance. I've been able to collect these so far, but I have a long way to go... There's such a lot of material..." Fuguruma-youbi let out a sigh, her cheeks dusted the pink of cherry blossoms. She really did seem to love romantic stories from the bottom of her heart.

In which case—she might know of a love story that Suimei could read!

I gazed at her expectantly. She tilted her head to one side with a wondering look.

Eyes sparkling, I made my heartfelt plea.

"Tee hee hee... I've been waiting for a chance to put my skills to use like this." Fuguruma-youbi gazed at the spines of her books, all neatly in rows.

"Please find something that Suimei will enjoy."

In response to my request, she picked out book after book.

"A little bit farther to that side, Kami-oni! Hurry up!"

"I understand."

"Whoa..."

However, I didn't know what to do about the scene unfolding before my eyes.

In the middle of my field of vision, a pair of white feet were kicking. They were lovely feet, with nails painted red. Above them, I caught fleeting glimpses of a deep crimson underrobe which I could see inside. I couldn't even see her upper body anymore. Every time she reached out a hand, her skirt loosened and her soft fair skin peeked through.

"Suimei!"

"I'm not looking. I'm not looking at her at all, so get off me!"

"No! Never!"

Frantically covering Suimei's eyes, I looked away from the lascivious behavior taking place right beside us.

"Toochika-san! What on earth is going on?!" I demanded, unthinking.

He answered as if it were nothing. "Fuguruma-youbi has a problem with her legs, so Kami-oni is carrying her."

"I'm not just carrying her. From time to time, I sniff the scent of her hair."

"Shut up, Kami-oni!"

"Ah ha ha ha ha ha! Amazing... This is too much fun. I should've brought Ginme along!"

Kinme was the only one who was just enjoying himself.

Fuguruma-youbi was pulling on Kami-oni's cheek, Kami-oni himself was rapt with pleasure, I couldn't move because I was covering Suimei's eyes... Frankly, it was chaos.

"I get it! You two are good friends! Enough already!" I shouted, unable to stop myself.

"I don't like him one bit," Fuguruma-youbi said in a chilly voice from within Kami-oni's arms, clearly annoyed.

"What...?" I gaped.

"Kami-oni seems to like me, but, frankly, I can't stand him."

Overcome, I stared at Kami-oni. He laughed, blushing faintly.

"You're so cold today," he said. "But that has its own charm. Feelings that fan the flames of my desire with all their strength... are good."

"So those are your tastes?" I asked without thinking.

His face as fresh as an unclouded sky, Kami-oni nodded.

What the heck is with this guy...? I slumped.

Fuguruma-youbi merely continued choosing books. "I just use him for my own convenience because he says he likes me. I've told him to hurry up and find a girl he likes and leave me, but he's still here."

"My heart will always belong to you. I mean, I'm not proud of it, but I'm not resourceful. If you weren't providing for me, Youbi, I'd wither away after a week."

"You want me to pay for your room and board, is that it?"

"No, absolutely not. It's because I love your hair more than anything."

"Eep!" Fuguruma-youbi suddenly went pale.

Taking advantage of her momentary lapse, Kami-oni breathed in a lungful of air.

He's really sniffing her hair, isn't he? This guy... I was getting a little bored, so I took my hands away from Suimei's eyes and changed the subject. "Well, never mind that! How about it? Have you found a nice book yet?"

Fuguruma-youbi stuck out her small lips in a pout and groaned. "As far as romance goes, if you don't *understand* the characters, you won't enjoy it."

"'Understand'?" I cocked my head, not following.

Suimei listened carefully as well, his interest piqued.

"It doesn't just apply to romance. Everyone does this unconsciously when they're reading a book—they entrust their own desires to the characters. Whether that's the thought that they want to be recognized by somebody, or the wish for mutual affection between them and the man they love, or the dream of adventuring in strange lands. They express desires that they are unlikely to satisfy in reality. Unless something unexpected happens, characters in stories are successful, aren't they? That's where people find the fun in stories." Fuguruma-youbi's gaze slipped along the spines of the books lining her bookshelves.

"Given that, whether you can lose yourself in a book and in the story within it...depends on whether the characters are worthy of being entrusted with your desires. No one would entrust something important to someone whose motivations they didn't fully understand."

Fuguruma-youbi flashed an impish grin at me, Suimei, and

Kinme. "I'm the incarnation of a love letter, right? People inscribe their very hearts upon me. The cries of their soul, their heartfelt prayers, their wishes. So I can understand people's hearts clearly. Take that girl over there, for example."

"Huh? Me?" Startled, I pointed at myself.

The red-tinted outer corners of Fuguruma-youbi's eyes turned down, and she said, as if rapt, "Isn't your mind saying that you aren't familiar with romance in the first place? Your heart can be charmed, but you don't know what to do with it... Hee hee, you're so innocent. Even as the years pass, your loving heart is still that of a babe. How *charming*! You would be well matched with a fresh young heroine who doesn't know anything. And then there's you, white-haired boy."

"What?!"

"It must be hard for you. Everything is unfamiliar. Thrown into a strange culture with nothing but the shirt on your back... Every time you shiver with cold, you realize there's something warm right next to you. You don't understand that it's all right to touch it, but day by day your attachment grows stronger."

"Stop." Suimei cut Fuguruma-youbi off, his face tense with alarm.

She let out a laugh like pealing bells. "Forgive me," she said sincerely. "For you, white-haired boy, it must be a tale of inter-marriage with strange beings. You would suit a hero who plunges into an unfamiliar culture."

Then she glanced at Kinme to size him up. "And you there, you're the most troublesome of them all. You consider your world complete. Every one of your smiles is transient. You might pretend to be easily flattered, but your emotions are the murkiest of all. How eerie! You're not similar to anyone at all, young man."

Maintaining a smile, Kinme looked intently at Fuguruma-youbi. "How disappointing. Am I really that murky?"

"Oh my. Don't you have any self-awareness? Heavens, that's even scarier!" Fuguruma-youbi buried her face in Kami-oni's chest. Moving only her eyes to glance our way, she said, "Well, there's just one thing that I want to say. Look for characters who are similar to you. Then entrust your hearts to them. If they're similar enough, you'll have a deeper *understanding* of them than anyone else, you see? If you choose books like that, it will work out. I'll help you."

Then she took a paperback from the nearest shelf and handed it to Suimei.

"Choosing books means confronting yourself."

We spent some time selecting books. Once I'd checked the one Suimei had started to read, I moved away to catch my breath.

Fuguruma-youbi's personal library was so extensive that I was worn out even though we'd just selected books. The main book collector herself, however, was full of energy as she enjoyed a drink with Toochika-san.

"Here's a drink for you," she cooed.

"Oh, thanks!"

"When can you swing by next?"

"Well, now... I'll drop by when work settles down for a bit. And I'll bring tons of new books."

"Hmph! Don't be so mean. Shouldn't you be saying 'I'll come tomorrow,' even if that's not true? Waaah, look at me! Toochika..."

As I watched them from a distance, for some reason I said what I was thinking. "She's a wily one. I really am 'innocent,' after all..." I grumbled to myself as I watched Fuguruma-youbi, mixed feelings stirring inside me. I understood that I was terribly obtuse when it came to matters of love. So why was I getting cross that somebody else had told me what I already knew?

"Oh, Kaori's angry! That's rare!" In contrast to me, Kinme laughed away. He seemed particularly unoffended.

"I *do* get angry, you know!"

"Hmm, really?" Kinme teased me.

I glared sharply at him.

Stretching his legs out on the tatami, he laughed loudly. "I'm 'murky,' right?" he said in his usual tone, and he gave me a flippant smile. "I didn't even mind a remark like that."

"'Murky'?" I asked hesitantly.

Kinme blinked rapidly in surprise. He tipped his head to one side. "Yeah. Did you hear that?"

Something in his words was more apathetic than usual. I swallowed lightly. But I was worried about him, so I gathered my courage. "But you didn't deny it just now."

"That's my old friend. You're a sharp one!" he teased me, then glanced over at Fuguruma-youbi. "My emotions are always murky.

I won't deny it, since it's true," he said in an uncharacteristically serious tone.

"You said you had no need of love. Does that have something to do with it?" I asked, choosing my words carefully.

Kinme smiled. "Yeah. I think it's a common mistake that people make. Humans are in heat all year round. It always ends badly for spirits who are attracted to humans. The same goes for spirit couples. I don't understand why two spirits who like each other would become a couple only to bicker all the time."

He played with his bangs, then let out a huff of air that blew it all over the place. "It's just like that woman said. Everything within me is complete. I don't need a partner or anything. I'm happy just going round and round the same places... I don't need new scenery. Sooner or later, everything gets mixed up together and becomes muddy—murky. Almost like churned butter."

The corners of Kinme's mouth turned upward cheerfully as he told me all this in a singsong voice. My mind immediately began to fill with questions—somehow I felt that, right now, he would tell me anything.

"Is there anyone else in your world, Kinme?"

With a lightness that suggested it was only common sense, he spoke a certain person's name. "Ginme. We're twins, so shouldn't that be obvious?"

Kinme and Ginme are raven Tengu twins. I'd first met the two of them when I was about five years old.

I'd found the twin chicks in the long grass of a beautiful springtime forest. Looking about, I hadn't see their mother anywhere; all I could see were the two chicks, cheeping pitifully. That, and the wreckage of their nest, destroyed by the impact of its fall. I picked them up and took them to the Great Tengu. Those two helpless chicks grew into raven spirits and then came back to me. Since then, we had spent our time together like siblings.

"When we broke through the shell of our eggs and were born into this world; when we fell to the ground and were abandoned by our mother; when we were starving and prepared ourselves for death, it was Ginme who was always there by my side. You should know that, Kaori."

"That's true."

"As long as I have Ginme, I'm fine. 'I want to fall in love, I want to find a partner...' Don't you think people think these things because they're lacking something? They want to make up for whatever it is they're missing. If they already had everything they needed, they wouldn't think like that. That's how it is for me."

Round and round, round and round...

Certainly, Kinme always frequented the same few places. That was his world, and he clung to it so very tightly. It hadn't changed since the time when he waited in that little nest for his mother to return. In his round, cut-off, nest-like world, with Ginme always by his side, Kinme was complete.

"But everyone tells me to find a mate someday. It's really stupid."

He screwed up his face in irritation. He almost never made a face like that.

Letting out a quiet breath, I told him my honest feelings. "For you, Ginme is the one and only, the most important person, isn't he...?" I murmured softly.

For just a moment, Kinme was lost for words.

"That's...right."

I paused, unable to read the expression on his face.

In a flash, his expression changed, and he said happily, "Speaking of Ginme... Recently, he's been trying really hard."

"Is that so?"

"Just today, he was so enthusiastic about going to meditate under the waterfall, even though it's so damn cold. He's been boasting about his six-pack. I think he's enjoying seeing the results of his hard work. He doesn't like making an effort, but despite appearances, he does well when he really tries..." Kinme's expression grew somewhat ambivalent. "You should go and visit him on Mt. Kurama soon. He's been saying that he wants to show you the results of his training, Kaori."

Kinme was returning, little by little, to his usual tone. I was bewildered, but I nodded.

He gave me a cheerful smile. "Ginme will be pleased. Thanks, Kaori."

Yeah. I let out a carefree laugh.

"Indeed..."

I suddenly realized that someone was standing behind me. Startled, I looked back and saw Kami-oni, nodding in agreement.

"How interesting!" he cried, sitting down between Kinme and me with a thump. Taking no notice of our scowls of annoyance, he looked at Fuguruma-youbi with half-closed eyes and spoke earnestly himself. "You've been thinking about this and that, but you're not in love. Finding a partner isn't necessary. There's no need to think so deeply about it."

"Why do you think that?" I asked, unable to stand his self-confident attitude.

Puffing on his pipe, he answered, "You can't fall in love and stay sane."

"S-sane?"

Kami-oni smiled at his own cryptic statement and thrust the pipe at me.

"It is easy to be single. Whatever you do, you're free, and there's no need to worry about someone else. But I am in love. I've taken the risk of letting someone else into my territory. And why? Because I was drawn to her. My heart was stolen by the fragrance wafting from that bewitchingly glossy hair of hers!" He tapped the end of the pipe against my shoulder. "I'm hopelessly caught up in her. I want to know more about her; I want to be by her side." He tapped my arms, my wrists, my thighs. "I want to touch her. If I could touch her, I'd be happy. I want her to touch me."

And then...he tapped his pipe in the center of my chest.

"I want her to know me, and to know my heart. The moment I thought that, it was love. It's useless to think about messy, difficult things. By that point, *you're already insane.*"

A shock ran through me. My heart began to race, and the blood rushed to my face.

Kami-oni gazed at me with his olive-green eyes, smiling in satisfaction. "Youngster. The time is now. Live impulsively. There's no reason to hesitate. Follow your heart! Who cares about logic? Throw it away. Step into the castle of madness."

When he had finished saying this, he put his other hand on Kinme's head to draw him close. "Young Tengu. Everyone thinks that fitting into the mold will make them happy. Sometimes we say painful things, thinking it's for the best."

"Will you give it a rest?" Kinme said with great annoyance from within Kami-oni's arms. "I hate being preached at."

"Ha ha. To me, you looked just like you were chirping from within your nest, desperate for someone to notice you."

"Agh!" Kinme shook off Kami-oni's hand and glared at him.

But Kami-oni deftly avoided Kinme's gaze. His face took on a cheerful expression. "I apologize for sounding preachy. The older I get, the more of a hopeless busybody I become." He combed through his hair with his fingers, looking philosophical. "Entrenched ideas sometimes transform into something else, and we bare our fangs at people who are important to us. It is very simple for affection to become a curse. Do not create something as warped as me."

Kami-oni was a spirit whose hair would never stop growing; he was haunted by a woman's hatred. As if he had just remembered this, Kinme listened patiently to what he was saying.

"Whoever the other person is, whatever kind of person they may be...there's no need to become subservient. No one can stop their heart being drawn to someone. So it is good to suffer. That's love; whichever point your emotions reach, that's love. Forget what others think about you!"

"Ha."

I realized that Kinme's shoulders were shaking.

"Ha ha ha ha..."

The shaking grew more pronounced as his laughter got louder, until at last he clutched his belly and roared with laughter.

"Ah ha ha ha ha ha! Just as sanctimonious as I expected. Oof, how ridiculous!"

"Huh? But I'm not kidding!"

"I don't need you to tell me that. More importantly than that..." Pointing to a certain spot in the room, Kinme asked in an amused tone, "Are you all right with *that*?"

"Uuugh!" As soon as he saw it, Kami-oni let out a distressed groan. He was looking at Fuguruma-youbi.

Perhaps she was feeling pleasantly tipsy... Or perhaps it was part of a cunning plan to win over a regular customer. I don't know which, but she was snuggled up against Toochika-san, spellbound. "Toochika..."

"Noo, that uncle's got me beat!"

Fuguruma-youbi seemed bewitched by the red-faced, drunken Toochika-san. A pinkish atmosphere floated about them that made one want to avoid looking straight at them.

This is bad! I trembled with fear as I foresaw the carnage about to unfold.

"Enough!" Kami-oni said, trembling.

"Come again?"

"Youbi blushing in another man's arms. I can't bear it!" Kami-oni's tanned cheeks were flushed. His attention fixed on Fuguruma-youbi and Toochika; he clenched his fist and suddenly got to his feet, glaring at them.

"Is this what turns you on?" I said to his back without thinking.

Looking back over his shoulder, Kami-oni flashed me a lively smile and gave me a decisive nod.

Kinme and I exchanged glances and both slumped at the same time.

"It takes all kinds of spirits, I guess..."

"I'm exhausted. Good grief..."

We giggled.

"This is tough, isn't it?"

"It sure is."

We shared an awkward smile.

Leaving Toochika-san to drink the night away, the three of us headed home. We went down the creaking stairs and out into the courtyard garden, where the wisteria bloomed in all its glory.

Even in the land of perpetual night that was the spirit realm, the temperature dropped as it got late. Perhaps because it was so cold that my fingertips were numb, the air felt clearer than ever. Crimson-tinted starlight poured down from the cut-out square of the night sky, beautifully adorning the bluish-purple wisteria flowers.

"Well, I never. He's dozed off and dropped his book."

Kinme wriggled to adjust the position of Suimei, whom he

was carrying on his back, as he trod carefully over the frozen floorboards.

I smiled slightly as I followed behind them. "He came all the way here for it, but I guess it didn't suit him after all."

Kinme and I had laughed when we caught sight of Suimei, who had fallen asleep with his book still clutched in his hand as he listened to the scene of small-scale carnage playing out between Kami-oni and Fuguruma-youbi.

"She might have told us to find characters who are similar to us, but that doesn't mean we're going to come across them straightaway."

"Right."

Encounters with both people and books can be once-in-a-lifetime events. Perhaps it's fate that brings us together.

"I hope that someday Suimei finds a book he can really get absorbed in." I peeked at Suimei's sleeping face as I spoke.

Fringed with long eyelashes, his eyes twitched, and from time to time opened slightly. As expected, he couldn't sleep soundly outside. He kept crossing back and forth over the threshold between dreams and reality.

"Huh?"

Just then, I met the gaze of Suimei's light brown eyes. Blinking slowly, he called my name and reached out a hand.

"Kaori..." He meaninglessly tapped me on the head, then fell asleep again.

"Eh?" Red-faced, I stared at Suimei, who slept peacefully on Kinme's back. *What does it mean? What does this behavior mean?!*

My head was all muddled, and sweat ran down my whole body. Crouching down where I was, I realized that Kinme was trying not to laugh.

"If you're going to laugh, just go ahead and laugh, damn it!"

"Ah ha ha ha ha!" Kinme grinned. "I wonder if it's love?"

"Who knows?!"

"I'd appreciate it if you and Suimei did get together, Kaori."

"Don't be selfish!" I yelled.

Laughing loudly, Kinme went on ahead of me, his steps light, leaving me there all alone.

I sighed.

Lifting my head suddenly, I found myself faced with the wisteria flowers that were blooming out of season.

The scene of petals fluttering down onto the white snow was profoundly unseasonal, and its beauty frightened me. With a small shiver, I tried to hurry after Kinme and Suimei.

"Why? Why can I not be with him?"

Then I suddenly heard a woman's voice.

Panicking, I looked around me, but there was no one there. In the meantime, the woman continued to whisper. Trying to calm my pounding heart, I moved gingerly toward the direction of the voice.

I came to a small well at the base of the wisteria plant. The wooden lid was down, and I couldn't see inside. But I was sure that this was the origin of the voice.

"Did someone throw themselves down here in the past?" As that horrible thought churned in my mind, my entire body broke out in goosebumps.

N-no no no. That can't be. It must be pretty deep, so it would have taken a long time to adapt to the spirit realm, that's all. There's no danger. There...shouldn't be any danger.

Covering both my ears with my hands, I tried to turn back...and gave up. The woman's voice had said something I could not ignore.

"Normal *love was impossible for me.*"

This woman, who was nothing but a voice to me, began to tell the touching tale of her misfortune.

"*I was raised in the red-light district. I should have lived my whole life within its walls. Normal love belonged to the outside world; it was something I could not have, something I could not reach for...*"

"Stop!" I cried out in spite of myself. But the woman's voice was ingrained in that place, and it continued automatically. Her heartbroken cries, growing closer and closer to sobs, flowed on, unaware that anyone was listening.

"*I thought I loved him. No, I still love him, even now. I adore him. I want to touch him. I want him to smile at me. I hoped to marry him, even though I was a prostitute, even though I was not a normal person!*"

"Stop..." I weakly implored the well, sinking to the ground. The snow was cold. The violent crimson of the starlight stung my eyes and made my vision begin to blur.

"*I had already given up.*"

I couldn't speak.

"*If I had only come to a decision more quickly, I would not have suffered so...*"

"Ohh..."

"I could never be like a normal person! And yet, I—"

"Shut up!" I screamed, trying to cut off the woman's voice.

Just then, a scene from my high school days floated into my mind.

Everyone else was happily enjoying their youth as I watched enviously from a gloomy spot. My excuse was always the same.

After all...I was brought up in the spirit realm.

Yeah, it was a real shame.

Being so wistful, not having the courage to approach the others, ending up passing those three years without making a move! I couldn't help feeling ashamed of myself.

I dragged the lid off the well with all my might and shouted down into it. "This time! I'm not going to run away!"

Then I set off running at a wild pace to catch up with Kinme and Suimei.

Kinme had been waiting for me in front of Harimise. As soon as he saw my face, his own face took on a surprised expression. "What happened? Are you crying?"

"Ack!"

Wiping away the tears that had begun to well up with my sleeve, I turned to Kinme—who was still carrying Suimei on his back—and said, "That was weird!"

"Huh?"

Clearly, he didn't understand what I meant.

Taking another deep breath, I pointed to Suimei, who was sound asleep. "It seems I've already lost my mind. I'm in love with Suimei."

For a second, Kinme looked dumbfounded. Then he exploded into laughter. "Is that so?" Smiling affectionately, he stuck his fist out in front of him. "I hope he reciprocates. I'll be cheering you on."

I nodded, my face serious, and bumped my fist against Kinme's. "Thanks for the support."

His face splitting into a broad grin, Kinme nodded. "Any time."

CHAPTER 3

Merry Christmas in the Spirit Realm

CHRISTMAS WAS APPROACHING in the spirit realm. Spirits don't care about Christianity, so it wasn't like the town was adorned with illuminations on the 24th of December or anything, but we did have Christmas in the bookstore. Since I knew about Christmas from books, Shinonome-san and Noname liked to throw a modest party.

"Merry Christmas!"

They would decorate the living room of the bookstore to the best of their ability and lay out a feast for the day itself. Chicken, well-cooked and glossy brown. Mounds of potato salad. Noname's special seaweed-rolled sushi. A whole homemade cake... And the next morning, when I awoke, there would be Christmas presents by my pillow.

That was the only Christmas party in the spirit realm, and it was held for my sake. When I was little, I had accepted it as natural. But looking back now as an adult, I saw that day as a miracle.

At any rate, there was no custom of celebrating Christmas

in the spirit realm. The parties I had so thoroughly enjoyed had been created from scratch, fumblingly, by the adults.

"Shinonome-san, Noname, Nyaa-san. This tastes great! This is so fun!"

I must have been the happiest person in the world then, smiling away, surrounded by all of them.

And now, this year, Christmas was approaching. In recent years, we had celebrated it on a smaller scale—I'd pick up a leftover cake on my way home from my part-time job or something. But this year, things looked very different.

The spirit realm had become so lively since welcoming Suimei and Kuro, and now, unlike previous years, it seemed to be approaching a holy day.

"So let's have a Christmas party!"

The living room of the bookstore was the same as ever. As Shinonome-san and I were sitting under the kotatsu eating winter tangerines, Toochika-san burst in, all high spirits.

"Huh? What do you mean 'so'?" Shinonome-san grumbled at his friend, who had not only broken in all of a sudden but had also started with a totally unexpected declaration. Shinonome-san was exhausted from working on his manuscript, and the dark circles under his eyes made him look worn out. He scratched his head and puffed away at his pipe as he spoke. "Don't be silly... A party? Have you eaten something weird?"

"Ha ha ha. I'm not kidding, you know. It's a completely serious suggestion."

With an excessively affected air, Toochika-san struck his chest with his fist. "Surely you haven't forgotten," he said quickly. "You keep breaking your promises to me, saying that you're busy with your manuscript. I've got high-grade sake and really controversial works that will get you all charged up and ready for our meetings, but you keep canceling on me! There are limits to even my patience. So you should make up for it by having a Christmas party!"

"I-I'm sorry...about that."

"Which is more important? Me or your work?!"

"Give it a rest before there's a weird misunderstanding," Shinonome-san said, his eyes cold.

Toochika-san shrugged pleasantly. "Well, I'm not just saying this on a whim, all right?" Turning gentle eyes on Shinonome-san, he began to speak with a slight air of melancholy. "Christmas is a day when everyone is allowed to be festive. Don't you think that, just for that day, you should forget about your work and do some of your favorite things? Balance is more important than anything. What I mean is, if you take a proper rest, then starting from the day after you can make good progress on your manuscript... Or maybe I'm just being a busybody. Right, Kaori-kun?"

Oh, Toochika-san is so kind! Touched by his consideration for his best friend, I nodded firmly. "You're right. I think so too. Shinonome-san, you've been working too hard recently."

Shinonome-san had a small appetite to begin with, but recently, he'd been eating even less, even though he was so busy.

Because he was a spirit, it was hardly as if he was going to die, but I was certainly a little worried.

"I think you might be pushing yourself too hard. Don't you want to relax?" I asked.

Shinonome-san's eyes grew slightly red. Looking about uneasily, he rested his chin in his hands and said quietly, "It might be nice from time to time."

"Oh, yay! Toochika-san, it looks like Shinonome-san's going to be okay," I said happily.

As I did, Toochika-san's face took on a somewhat ambivalent expression.

"What's wrong?" I cocked my head to one side, puzzled.

Toochika-san scratched self-consciously at his cheek. "Oh, no, I was just thinking how easily you got him to agree... Well, what else would I expect from you, Kaori-kun? You're super-effective on Shinonome. Looks like I was worrying for nothing."

I blinked. "What do you mean?"

"Because it's Shinonome, I thought you'd have more of a fight on your hands."

"Who do you take me for?" asked Shinonome-san, exasperated.

Toochika-san laughed dryly. Then he glanced anxiously at the sliding door that connected the living room to the shop.

Toochika-san was acting oddly. Just as this thought occurred to me, Shinonome-san raised an eyebrow.

"I've got a bad feeling about this. Toochika... What the heck are you—"

At that moment, we heard loud voices outside. No sooner

had the sound of clattering footsteps reached us than the door burst open with great force.

"Shinonome, let's have a Christmas party!"

It was Kinme and Ginme. They rushed into the living room without hesitation and came over to Shinonome-san.

"Treat us all to a glittering Christmas tree! Doesn't that sound fun?"

"You have a small party every year with Kaori, right? This year, we're gonna join in too!"

The twins sat down on either side of Shinonome-san, and each put an arm tightly around his shoulders, grinning.

"What are you two playing at?" Shinonome-san was flustered by their sudden approach.

I wonder why Kinme and Ginme would suddenly bring this up? As I was puzzling over their timing—it must have been planned— someone else appeared.

"Hello! We heard Shinonome was being selfish, so we came over." It was Noname, along with Suimei and Kuro.

"I heard you were refusing to throw a party, even though the kids were asking for one?" Noname said, taking a good long look at Shinonome-san's face.

"Huh? Who said—"

At this point, Suimei broke into the conversation. "A Christmas party? What's that? I've heard that it begins with the extermination of a spirit dressed in red..."

"And if you steal his treasure, then you get to keep it!" Kuro declared. "What fun!"

"Stop! Why are you here? What have you come for?" Shinonome-san shouted, half-desperate.

Suimei and Kuro looked at each other, then pointed at Toochika-san. "He told us to," they said simultaneously.

Jumping on the bandwagon, Kinme and Ginme nodded vigorously.

"Ah ha ha ha ha! You gave me away so easily!" Standing up straight, Toochika-san took off his hat and tapped it against his chest. "Them coming here was all part of my plan. A plan to make you want to throw a Christmas party, Shinonome!"

Turning on his heel, he winked performatively and smiled. "Sorry, everyone. I had plenty planned for you as the rear guard, but it seems like we don't need any of that now. Thanks to Kaori's persuasion, the Christmas party will be going ahead. Rejoice!"

Kinme, Ginme, and Kuro all cheered.

"Hooray, a feast!" they crowed.

"Yay!" I paused. "By the way, what are you stealing, and who from?"

I didn't really get it, but we were all going to have a party. I was as excited as a little kid.

Shinonome-san began to slowly move. As I watched him, I realized that Toochika-san was trying to sneak out of the room. My father crept up behind Toochika-san, and as Toochika-san put his hand on the sliding door, Shinonome-san swiftly immobilized him with a headlock.

"What's the meaning of this? Were you just going to throw my home into chaos and leave? You've got guts!"

"Ha ha. Didn't your partner ever tell you to be gentler when you're embracing someone from behind?"

"Sorry. I've never had any luck with romance."

Shinonome-san squeezed his arms even harder, and Toochika-san's face began to grow pale.

"Erp! I surrender. I'll properly explain my reasoning. I *said*, I'll explain!"

"It's your own fault for coming up with this weird scheme, you moron!"

Released at last from Shinonome-san's arms, Toochika-san coughed violently and looked up at him with a half-smile.

"So, then, why did you do this?" Shinonome-san asked.

"Well, ah..."

Noname, who had been watching all this unfold, called out from behind them. "There must be a woman involved. Don't you think it's weird that he'd be free at Christmas?"

"Whoa, are you serious? Did you get dumped, Toochika?" Ginme asked.

"Don't, Ginme," said Kinme. "You mustn't poke at the emotional wounds of a mature gentleman."

"Kinme, you're being just as harsh... But I could say more!"

In spite of myself, I smiled awkwardly at them. They were all saying everything that came to mind.

At that moment, Toochika-san collapsed where he stood. His handsome face crumpled, and he began to cry. As I froze, Toochika-san started to speak between sobs. "Please listen. Fuguruma-youbi was the only one I was seeing, and she went and dumped me!"

"You only have yourself to blame!"

"'Oh, Yoshiko, come back to me!'"

It seemed like Noname had hit the nail on the head. Having been dumped right before Christmas, Toochika-san was afraid of spending that romantic night all by himself.

"Christmas. A cold futon. Sleeping alone... No! I can't bear it! Hey, Shinonome! Don't leave me all alone! You're all I have left!"

"I keep telling you, there's going to be a misunderstanding! Stop talking like that!"

Toochika-san clung to him; Shinonome-san kicked him away and heaved a deep sigh. Then he smiled tiredly. "You really are hopeless. I've known you for centuries, after all. All right, we'll have a Christmas party."

"Really, Shinonome?!" At once, Toochika-san's eyes sparkled, and he grabbed Shinonome-san's hand, tearfully pressing his cheek against my father's "I'm truly in your debt! I won't let you sleep the whole night, dear friend!"

"I *told* you, stop talking like that!" Kicking Toochika-san away again, Shinonome-san looked around at everyone...this time, with a wicked grin. "All right, you lot. We'll have a party at Toochika-san's expense."

"Huh? Hey, I never said anything about paying—" Toochika-san paled at this unexpected development.

But, paying him no heed, Shinonome-san started briskly giving out orders to everyone. "Let's call Tamaki too. Noname, I'll leave the feast up to you."

"Got it. Hee hee hee, I'll put all my skill into it!"

"What about lighting and decorations?"

"Have Toochika do them. He runs a shop in the human world, so they're his specialty. I'll just get hold of a fir tree. Right, Toochika?"

"Y-yeah."

At last, Shinonome-san had brightened. He got close to Toochika-san, his stubbled face breaking into a grin. "This year, we'll enjoy that holy night to the fullest, my dear friend!"

"A...ah ha...ah ha ha ha ha ha..."

Crestfallen, Toochika-san fell prostrate on the ground.

We couldn't help laughing at him.

From the next morning onward, we were running all over the place getting ready. It wouldn't be a Christmas party without a host of sparkling decorations. As for the food, Noname was preparing it. She was an excellent cook and would give us an absolute feast; I was already looking forward to it. We would also be throwing the party in the living room of the bookstore. It was a bit small, but it would be all right.

That just left the decorations.

It was the end of my shift. After making sure that all the other shop assistants had gone home, I met up with Toochika-san—the owner—and we headed to the shop's storehouse. We were going to fetch some things we could use for illumination.

"Well, I never expected this would happen..."

Toochika-san had been a bit gloomy before, but his mood had already improved. He had turned defiant and was now enthusiastic about throwing a grand Christmas party.

"I'm sorry Shinonome-san was so unreasonable," I apologized, but Toochika-san roared with laughter.

"It's fine! It's not that unusual—I've known him a long time, after all."

"Now that you mention it, he did say you'd known each other for centuries, didn't he?"

"Yeah, that's right. I looked after him just after he became a Tsukumogami."

As we walked along the path to the storehouse, Toochika-san told me how he and Shinonome-san had met.

"He was in a terrible sulk when I met him. His eyes were full of hostility; he glared indiscriminately, as if he didn't trust anyone anymore. He wouldn't let anyone get close to him... I remember that feeling fondly."

Shinonome-san was the Tsukumogami of a hanging scroll. What's more, it was a cursed scroll that was supposed to bring luck. From time to time, powerful people had fought amongst themselves as they tried to get their hands on Shinonome-san's scroll. Shinonome-san hated this; he'd abandoned the human world and come to the spirit realm.

"At that point, Shinonome-san couldn't live a normal life, what with the mental state he was in. So I put him in someone else's care."

"Who was that?"

"The bookstore's previous owner. The greatest book collector in the spirit realm—oops!" Toochika-san interrupted his story with a pleasant chuckle. "I shouldn't go any further than that. It's not for me to talk about."

"That's easy for you to say! You've got me on tenterhooks now."

"Now, now, just forget about it. I'll get yelled at if Shinonome-san finds out."

I glared at him, but he just laughed. He clearly had no intention of telling me any more than he already had. A sigh escaped me as I looked up at the frozen sky of the human world.

"You two are as close as ever... I'm jealous. You know a lot about Shinonome-san that I don't know, Toochika-san."

Toochika-san peered at my face with an expression of great interest. "Aren't you best friends with that black cat?"

"Yes, but... We're still not on the level as you and Shinonome-san. Knowing each other better than anyone else, being able to talk to each other without holding back... I admire you two."

Blushing shyly, Toochika-san immediately arranged his features into a serious expression. "Do you want to know the secret? If you do, why don't I take you out to dinner at a restaurant with a good view...?"

"No thanks."

When I turned him down straightaway, Toochika-san burst out laughing.

"Such disdain! You're so similar to Shinonome—sometimes it startles this old man."

"Perhaps if you didn't say such flirty things, I'd think you were normal."

"Normal, huh? I give up!"

Bantering back and forth, we made our way through the town, wrapped in the freezing air of winter.

This human town sparkled so prettily as it waited for the approach of Christmas. Even the people walking through it seemed happy, as if the whole world was in high spirits. Everyone was waiting expectantly for that special day, and it made the atmosphere so pleasant.

"I'm really looking forward to the Christmas party. Is that weird at my age?" I asked as I looked cheerfully up at Toochika-san.

With a tender smile, Toochika-san struck his fist against his chest with an air of confidence. "It's not weird at all. I'm going to do my best to make sure that excited pounding of your heart never fades away."

Just then, some women who were passing by let out shrill cries of excitement. They happened to have seen Toochika-san's exaggerated expression. Immediately, he turned to them and waved. He didn't neglect to hand over business cards for his shop, either.

What else would you expect from this old womanizer? He's a shrewd one...

"Jeez, you never change, do you?" Forcing a smile, I bowed to my adoptive father's dependable friend. "I'm counting on your help."

After that, weighed down with luggage, I returned to the spirit realm, where I was stopped by Kinme at the entrance to the bookstore.

"Come over here for a second." Kinme led me into the darkness and whispered stealthily in my ear, "Hey, Kaori. Suimei's present... Have you decided what you're going to get him? It's your first time spending Christmas with the person you like. What are you gonna do?"

"Erk! I don't know, I'm not Santa. I didn't know about that at all!" I cried out in a hysterical voice.

Kinme shot me an impish grin. "You idiot. Use this opportunity to lessen the distance between you. That's one of the old tricks of romance, right?"

"You seem to know all about it."

"I might not feel the need for love, but I do enjoy reading romances."

A present for Suimei. My face grew warm. I felt fidgety and restless. *I wonder what he'd like to be given? I wonder what I could give him...that would show him how I feel?*

"Honestly, I don't have a clue." I despaired at my terribly low romantic intelligence.

Kinme clapped a hand on top of my head. "Didn't I say I'd support you? If you're at a loss, talk to me about it."

"Thanks... Hey, are you going to give anyone a present, Kinme?"

"Me?" Pointing to himself, he gave a flat, lazy smile. "I'm going to give a present to Ginme, naturally. Christmas isn't just for lovers. It's for family too, you know."

"Family... Huh. Yeah, you're right!" My face shone. I turned to him with a serious expression. "Say, Kinme. I've got a small favor to ask you..."

"What is it? If it's something I can help with, ask me for anything."

The twenty-fourth of December. That special night came to the spirit realm too. All of those things that are necessary for a Christmas party: a feast, and decorations, and charming invitations...and thoughtful presents.

With all of these in hand, we would be ready for Christmas.

Christmas Day arrived. Unfortunately, the sky over the spirit realm was cloudy. The wind died down, and large, fluffy snowflakes drifted down into streets that were even quieter than usual.

Such was the scene as we gathered in the bookstore and each got on with our own preparations.

"Jingle bellth! Jingle bellth!"

"Jingle all the way!"

Umi and Sora, young raven Tengu twins training under the Great Tengu, sang away in high spirits. They wore reindeer costumes as they happily put up decorations. It seemed the Great Tengu had made those cute costumes for today.

"Kids, stop singing and get a move on!"

"Look, someone's hanging up stockings!"

Kinme and Ginme were supervising the boys. They often looked after the younger twins, so they knew how to take good care of them.

"How's this, Suimei?"

"Shouldn't the taste be a bit stronger? We're having it with alcohol, right?"

"Me too! Let me taste it too!"

Noname, Suimei, and Kuro were in the kitchen, preparing the food. Well, in truth, Kuro was just scampering about, getting under their feet. Ignoring Kuro's frantic pleas for a taste, the other two silently finished their cooking.

"Well, then, that just leaves..."

The tree. We didn't have the crucial fir tree. Shinonome-san had said he was *just off* to get it ready, but...

When I think of Christmas, a tree is the first thing that comes to mind, and yet... Is it really going to be okay?

I stepped through the glass door of the living room into the courtyard. Although I had gone to the effort to shovel the snow, it had just kept on falling, and just like that it had covered everything, creating a little snowfield.

It was so pure and white that it seemed a shame to trample it. But I had to cross it. Despairing at my own inelegance, I walked on, etching my footprints into the snow.

Three people were waiting for me on the other side.

"Let's go!" I called to them. "The preparations in the party venue are going well."

"I don't mind whether they're going well or not," said the first to respond in his usual somewhat cynical tone. Yet he carried on with his own usual eccentricities of speech. "If this were a story, I'd want you to be bluffing when you said that. I'd be hoping wholeheartedly that everything beyond this point was in an up-roar, and that all of today's plans were in truth ruined."

"I see you talk as much as ever..."

"I see you've allowed yourself to be captured by that boy who used to be an exorcist, no questions asked. You're inviting your own displeasure." He let out a deep sigh.

This was Tamaki-san, the story-seller. He looked differ-ent than usual; because he was outside, he was wearing a black Inverness cape and boots, and a thin layer of snow had built up on top of his fedora. He must have been waiting for some time.

"I'm sorry that you'll be seeing Shinonome-san while his manuscript is still incomplete." I bobbed my head in apology.

Tamaki-san avoided my eyes, self-conscious. Instead, he scowled in annoyance at the person standing next to him. "In which case, can't you pester this fool a bit more? You're not an imprisoned heroine, and I can't afford to just to wait around."

The person standing next to him laughed, not looking the least bit guilty. "Ba ha ha! That's life, eh?" said Shinonome-san. "I'm just not making any progress. When something clicks into place, it goes quickly, but at the moment..."

"And when is that 'something' going to click? When, exactly?!"

"Hell if I know... Achoo!" Sniffing, Shinonome-san wrapped his hand towel tighter about his neck. Perhaps because the others were dressed in Western clothes and Shinonome-san had chosen Japanese clothing, he looked extremely cold.

"You didn't bring your scarf?" I asked. "You'll catch a cold!"

"Huh? That one Noname knitted? I hate it. A guy knitted it, after all."

"Rude!" I scolded. "...But if *I* knitted you one, you'd wear it?"

Shinonome-san avoided my gaze for a second. Then, blushing, he said somewhat curtly, "I-In that case, I'd think about it."

"How sweet!"

I wasn't the one who let out that shrill cry.

"Wow... You're so sweet, Shinonome! You've got this old geezer's heart pounding!" The one cheering like a schoolgirl was Toochika-san. He patted Shinonome-san on the head with a soft smile. "I wish I had a daughter. Mm-hmm. I wonder whether my wife will give me one."

"You've been saying that for half a century. If that's what you want, get on with finding someone."

"My love isn't the kind that can be tied down to any one person. But never mind that—hadn't we better start soon? If we stay here any longer, we'll freeze. I'll leave this to you, Tamaki."

Tamaki-san said nothing as he glared resentfully at Toochika-san from behind his sunglasses.

"What is it, Tamaki? Are you still not happy?"

"Be quiet, Shinonome. I did what I did before because I had no other choice, but this is just Toochika being selfish. I don't want to."

"How stingy of you! Stop being such a cheapskate."

"Shinonome. Are you serious?" Tamaki-san asked in a voice that was deeper than I'd ever heard from him before.

But Shinonome-san shrugged lightly, seemingly unperturbed.

"Are you going to keep fixating on the past? That's not like you. Isn't the new and the revolutionary *marvelous*? Rid yourself of the ancient ways!" Shinonome-san teased, turning Tamaki-san's pet grudge back on him.

Tamaki-san sank into sullen silence. He heaved a great sigh and abruptly started out across the snow.

I wonder what that was about?

Tamaki-san was a pretty mysterious spirit. His background was unclear; I didn't even know what kind of spirit he was. At the same time, I was pretty sure Shinonome-san and Toochika-san did know and just weren't saying. But Tamaki-san didn't have horns or claws or a tail. So at first glance, he just seemed like a normal human.

As I was pondering his true nature, Tamaki-san stopped in the middle of the courtyard. Then, scowling up at the sky, he took something out of his breast pocket.

"A brush?" I could see at a glance that it was a high-quality paintbrush. It was clearly out of place here.

Shinonome-san called out to him obsequiously. "Good luck, my dear friend. This is something only you can do. We're counting on you!"

"Ahhh, good grief. I decided not to create anything now that I'm the story-seller..." Tamaki-san grumbled.

Shinonome-san sniffed as he called out to him again. "Copying something you created in the past isn't creating something new."

Tamaki-san said nothing, only glared at Shinonome-san

with his clouded right eye. But Shinonome-san just flashed him a broad, toothy grin and rubbed his reddened nose.

"Given how long I've known you, the way you treat me is especially irritating," Tamaki-san spat, taking the paintbrush in his left hand. "This is my non-dominant hand, so don't expect much," he muttered, staring fixedly at the tip of the paintbrush without doing anything.

I was surprised to see what looked like ink oozing out of the end of the bristles. Blinking in astonishment, I watched as Tamaki-san slowly drew something on the surface of the pure white snow.

Tamaki-san's brush danced over the snow with swift, flowing movements. His hands were more slender and sinewy than Shinonome-san's. Although his blue veins stood out, giving him a high-strung air, his movements were free and uncontrolled, as if his consciousness were in his instrument. The point of the brush never stopped in one place, instead wafting playfully over the surface of its uncanny canvas.

As the fluid brushstrokes stained the immaculate snow, the lines it drew were by turns fine and powerful—and strangely, they didn't sink away into the white. Rather, the ink-stained brush tip etched verdant leaves into winter itself.

At last, the arc of Tamaki-san's clouded right eye drew a twisted trunk that his brush followed. Before I knew it, a pine tree had appeared there.

It stretched its branches proudly toward the heavens, its pointed leaves spreading out as if puffed up with self-satisfaction.

The tree's silhouette was the very image of magnificence, and its tall trunk was bent and rugged, as if it had been powerful enough to withstand long years of wind and rain without collapsing.

"Huh?"

At that moment, a sense of déjà vu came over me, and I racked my brain to remember where I had seen this before. But though I frantically searched my memory, I couldn't explain it.

I could hardly bear the pent-up feelings in my heart, but even as I struggled, the situation was changing around me.

"This is the final touch." To top it off, Tamaki-san wrote some words in the snow.

"Spirits/ Are said to appear/ In ancient trees."

The characters were beautifully formed. For some reason, those words alone sank into the snow.

Scratching his beard with his left hand, Tamaki-san narrowed his eyes as he looked over the whole drawing.

"Kodama," he called out.

Who on earth is he talking to...? I wondered.

Someone suddenly replied. "It has been a long time since I last saw you, Master. How may I help you?"

"Hah...?" I let out a gasp of surprise. The voice seemed to have come from right next to Tamaki-san...from *inside* the picture.

Shinonome-san came to stand next to me and pointed cheerfully at the picture that Tamaki-san had drawn on the snow.

"Look, Kaori. See, there's a wrinkled old man."

"Gaaah..."

I found myself at a loss for words. Inside the picture of the pine tree that Tamaki-san had drawn, I could see the figure of a person moving about.

He was an old man, withered as a dead tree. Because he had been drawn in ink, I couldn't tell what color he was supposed to be. However, I could guess that his rather depleted topknot was white, and that the kimono wrapped around his bent body was a somber color, perhaps the dark orange of persimmons. In a hand so frail it looked like the bones might break any second, he clutched a rake. He waited, motionless, for Tamaki-san to speak.

Tamaki-san turned to him and said in a matter-of-fact voice, "The same as before, please."

The old man's already wrinkled face creased even more as he smiled happily. "Yes, I understand. Most certainly. With pleasure. Absolutely! Hey, Aunty!"

Bobbing his head furiously, the old man called out to someone behind him—an old lady who looked to be about the same age as him. When she saw us looking at her, she gave us a leisurely bow.

"For one night only: your Christmas tree. Let us prepare for you the tree of your dreams, with branches more splendid than any other." The old lady swished the broom in her hand back and forth a few times.

At that moment, the tree changed dramatically. Like the surface of water into which a single droplet had fallen, the ink-drawn lines rippled... And with a strange burbling sound, something black began to appear from within them.

"Stand back. It'll swallow you up. If you don't want to become like the unnamed hordes who die obscure deaths in stories, get out of its way."

Looking extremely displeased, Tamaki-san dragged me and Shinonome-san off to the edge of the garden. My feet caught in the snow, and I thought I would slip. I knew it would be fine as long as I kept looking forward, but I just couldn't tear my eyes away from the scene.

"Ah ha ha! How splendid!"

In the end, Toochika-san clapped his hands together happily. Shinonome-san smiled as he saw the final product. Sniffling from the cold, I looked up at it, dumbfounded.

An enormous, black, ink-covered fir tree towered above me. Having said that, it wasn't all black. Within the blackness, there were different shades, and some of it faintly reflected the snow light, standing out bluish-white against the black background.

That's right, it was *made out of ink, after all.* I thought. "I feel like...I might have seen this somewhere before."

I stared up at the fir tree. There was something eerie about this jet-black tree in the gloomy world of the spirits.

Shinonome-san stood next to me, gazing up at the tree. "The winter of the year when you first came to the spirit realm, I had Tamaki-san make you a tree like this one."

"I don't remember that at all. But why did you stop doing that the next year? We've celebrated Christmas many times, but until now we never had a tree again."

"Well..."

Tamaki-san had been sunk in silence until this point, but now he opened his mouth. "Just who was it who started bawling and saying it was too scary?" he said sulkily.

The normally tough, sarcastic Tamaki-san was pouting like a child.

"Pfft..." At that moment, I felt a certain sense of foreboding, but I couldn't help my outburst. "No way. *That's* why...?"

"Yeah. Tamaki-san fell into a sulk and said he'd *never* do it again, the scoundrel."

"Because of that, all the decorations we'd made went to waste. It really sucked," said Toochika-san, bringing over an old wooden box. Inside, there was an incredible amount of tree decorations. They were a little dusty, but otherwise they looked as good as new.

"What's that? You taking a trip down memory lane?"

Noname, dressed in a frilly apron, poked her head out of the glass door to the living room. She glanced at Tamaki-san's sulky face and let out a pleasant laugh. "You were expecting her to be happy, so you were really disappointed, weren't you? You'd helped make the decorations too."

"Who did he make them with?" I asked wonderingly.

"You, of course, Kaori."

Noname stepped nimbly down onto the snow and went over to Toochika-san. After rummaging through the box of decorations he was holding, she handed something to me. "You can look at this any time, as a keepsake," she said earnestly.

The thing in my hand was as golden as if all the glittering things in the world had been concentrated within it.

It was a large, gold, origami star. It reflected the light that filtered out of the living room, illuminating my surroundings with flashes of brightness. Several sheets of paper had been stuck together to produce paper of this thickness. It was slightly bent... but somehow it held a gentle warmth. That warmth spread at once through my chest, making my heart tremble.

"What a pretty star..." I murmured.

Through his round sunglasses, I could see Tamaki-san's gaze wandering about. He scratched his head moodily. "What about... this tree?"

"Huh?"

"You're not scared of this tree?"

I broke into a grin at his awkward question and shook my head. "I'm not scared. I'm...an adult now."

"Huh." That was Tamaki-san's clumsy way of being kind.

Feeling a lump forming in my throat, I spontaneously embraced him. "I'm sorry about last time. Really, I am! And thank you!"

"Hey, stop that. Let go of me! I'm sweltering!"

"Oh, that's nice. I tried really hard with the decorations too, Kaori-kun."

"Okay, you too, Toochika-san!"

"What are you lot doing?! You shouldn't touch a girl of marriageable age so casually!"

As the clamor of our voices filled the courtyard, other merry voices joined in.

"Look at the garden, everyone! Isn't it amazing?"

"What?"

"What is it?"

"Are we going to play outside? I don't like snow..."

The voices of the children chorused—Umi, Sora, and Kuro. At Ginme's urging, they gathered by the glass door, their faces shining as they saw the fir tree that had suddenly appeared.

"It's a treeeeeeeeeee!"

Bursting with energy, the twins rushed out into the garden, their cheeks as rosy as apples.

"This is gonna be our Christmas tree, right? It's awesome!"

Cheering and whooping, they both began running in circles.

Kuro, left alone in the room, called out to Sora and Umi, "Huh? Is that going to be our Christmas tree? That sparkly thing? How? Hey, hey, hey, hey, tell me!"

As if they were grown-ups, the young raven Tengu twins schooled themselves.

"We'll decorate it. With twinkling lights."

"Shiny gold apples. Fluffy snow. Dolls. And of course, right at the top..."

"A big, big star!"

The hands that they suddenly threw up into the air looked like little stars themselves.

With their younger counterparts looking so merry, Kinme and Ginme glanced at one another. Then they, too, hopped down into the garden and raised their fists.

"All right, decorating squad! Time to put the finishing touches on this!"

"One final push!"

The children's cheeks grew even rosier at Kinme and Ginme's words, and they cried out eagerly.

"When we've finished, we can feast to our hearts' content!"

"Yeah!"

With cheerful shouts, they crowded around the wooden box that held the decorations.

I winked at them all, and we began the decorating.

After about an hour, a pretty Christmas tree had appeared in the gloomy world of the spirits.

We looked admiringly at one another, our hearts glowing with satisfaction at what we'd achieved. Ornaments of all colors stood out against the inked fir tree. When the decorative lights (connected to a generator) began flashing on and off at intervals, glimmerflies started to gather around us, unhindered by the insect-repellent incense that we were burning.

I think they're happy too...

As I watched the glimmerflies, enchanted by their playful fluttering, someone tugged at my sleeve.

"Let's go, Kao-chan! The feast is waiting!"

It was Sora and Umi. Faces shining with anticipation, they pulled me back toward the living room. As we walked, they began to sing.

"Jingle bellth! Jingle bellth!"

Listening to the children lisping their way through the song, I instinctively broke into a smile.

"Umi, Sora. Are you looking forward to this?" I asked.

"Yeah!"

The boys beamed up at me. The illuminated stars on the Christmas tree twinkled in Sora's eyes as he said, "Me and my brother will never forget today!"

As if he didn't want to waste even a second more, he took off at a trot and hurried back inside.

I suddenly stopped in my tracks and looked up at the tree.

It glittered away so prettily. And displayed at the very top, there was a slightly crooked, handmade star.

The towns of the human world must be as merry as this now. I felt a stinging pain in my chest. As the thought crossed my mind, I got a little choked up. "I wonder if I also celebrated Christmas every year before I came to the spirit realm... Who did I look up at a Christmas tree with?"

My muttered words melted into the white winter sky and disappeared.

"Kaori? Come quick! The food's getting cold," Suimei called out to me.

Shaking my head a little to put those feelings behind me, I set off with light steps toward the warm living room.

The Christmas party finished as a great success.

Once we had all eaten our fill, we gave the children their presents. Umi, Sora, and Kuro, who had been in such high spirits, wore themselves out with playing and fell asleep. And it wasn't just the children; Shinonome-san and the other two old geezers tired themselves out too. I thought they were going to drink and discuss books, but before I knew it, they'd drunk themselves into a stupor.

"Nothing to be done about it," said Noname, dumbfounded. She and Suimei spread futon out in Shinonome-san's room and started to put the three old men to bed. I decided that I would go and see off Kinme and Ginme.

Carrying a sleeping Sora on his back, Kinme whispered happily to me. "Good luck, Kaori."

"Huh? What for?"

"Handing over your present, of course!"

My face flared red.

Kinme smirked at my blush. "You're really riled up, aren't you?"

"Of course I am. We worked together on it, so I want it to be a success."

Kinme thumped me hard on the back and laughed. "Good luck," he repeated.

"What? Why are you wishing me luck?"

"Because I'm keeping it a secret from Ginme," he giggled.

Ginme shot him a suspicious look.

After watching the two of them soar up into the wide, open sky, I cooled my warm cheeks in the outside air before I returned to the living room. Finding Noname and Suimei ready to go home, I hastily called out, "Oh, are you leaving already?"

"Yeah," Suimei nodded. "It's pretty late, and look at the state Kuro's in."

Kuro was sleeping snugly in Suimei's arms. I smiled at how happy Kuro looked. Then I said, "Wait a moment!" to hold them back.

I hunted through the cupboard, took something out, and brought it back over to them.

Oh, I think my heart is going to explode... Giddy with nerves, I stopped in front of Suimei. "Here you go."

"What's this?"

"A p-present." I managed. *Uh-oh, my voice is shaking!*

Although I was aghast at my own lack of courage, I looked down so as not to see Suimei's expression. I felt a secret sense of relief when Suimei accepted the present from me.

"Can I open it?"

"You mean now?! I don't really mind, but..." As I panicked at this unexpected development, I heard the rustling sound of wrapping paper. *I w-wonder if he'll like it...*

My anxiety mounted to the point where I wished I could just run away.

"A picture book...?" Suimei murmured.

The book I'd prepared as a Christmas present for Suimei was one of my favorites. It was a bestseller about mouse brothers who made a giant pancake; I had adored it for years. I didn't really understand why, but whenever I read it, I felt more peaceful. So, I loved it so much that I read it time and time again, until it had grown so worn out that I'd had to buy a new copy.

I had kept the one I could no longer read tucked away safely in my closet.

"You said it before, didn't you, Suimei? When you were having trouble finding a book you liked. You said maybe you should start from the beginning, with picture books, the way a child does. I thought you might be right... So I decided I'd give you my favorite story."

I sneaked a glance at Suimei. He was looking at the book as blankly as ever.

I wonder if he likes it? Or if I've let him down? The feelings in my pounding heart as I handed over his present. Hope—and a little bit of fear. Those feelings relentlessly roiled in my stomach, and large droplets of sweat prickled on my back.

Still he said nothing.

Argh. What does this mean? Does he like it? Hate it? If you're going to do me in, at least get it over with!

As I was tying myself in knots over Suimei's lack of a response, I suddenly heard someone laughing.

"Hah...ha ha ha ha..."

They sounded as if they were frantically trying to suppress their laughter. The owner of the voice was, of all things, Suimei.

"I-I'm sorry for giving you such a childish present, okay?!" I wailed.

Suimei's shoulders were shaking with laughter. The fear that I had given him a strange gift circled round and round in my brain.

"I-If you don't like it, you can just give it back..." I held out my hand despondently.

Suimei hugged the book to his body like it was something

precious. "No. I was just thinking how perfectly like you this is, Kaori. Thank you. I'll accept it gratefully."

He gave me a gentle smile that was quite unlike his normal blank expression. My chest tightened painfully, but at the same time I let out a sigh of relief.

"Oho. Should I excuse myself...?" Noname asked in a teasing tone.

I looked up with a start to see Noname watching us, smirking and covering her mouth.

"Oh, no! Noname, wait!" Shaking my head vigorously, I held out the other parcel in my hands to Noname.

"Huh? There's one for me too?"

"Yeah. I realized that I'd never given a Christmas present to you or Shinonome-san. It's not much, but it's something to show my thanks."

Yes, for the Christmas party I had bought a present not only for Suimei but also for Noname and Shinonome-san.

Christmas is a special day for lovers. At the same time—it's also a day to spend with one's precious family.

A human girl, all alone, had tumbled out of the human world. Furthermore, she'd been a mere child of three. It's doubtful that this child had even been able to logically understand her circumstances. But these people had taken good care of her. Instead of eating her, they'd kept her alive. They'd watched over me and brought me up.

I'll never forget how thankful I am to all of them. That gratitude is something I have to share with everyone who's raised me up till now. So I thought I should repay them, even if only in a small way.

"It's a new color of nail varnish, like you said you wanted, Noname. Please use it if you like!" I smiled.

Overcome with emotion, Noname embraced me. "Yes... You've grown up to be such a lovely girl! Oh, I can hardly take it!"

"That tickles, Noname!" I laughed, trapped by her strong arms.

"You bought something for Shinonome-san too, right?" she asked me abruptly. "I'm sure he'd be happy if you gave it to him."

I opened my mouth.

"Huh? Why have you gone quiet? Did you forget to buy him anything?"

"No..." I avoided Noname's gaze and let out a sigh.

The next morning, I heard a shout from my father's room.

"Whoooooa?!"

At the same time, there were violent footsteps and a shriek as if someone were being crushed. I paused in my breakfast preparations.

The sliding screen clattered open and someone appeared, their face flushed red with excitement: Shinonome-san.

"It's amazing, Kaori! Santa came to me!" He was clutching a small parcel in his hands.

Sitting at the tea table, he began to rip off the wrapping paper. Soon, rubbish lay scattered all about, but—to my frustration—he took no notice. As soon as he saw what was inside the parcel, his eyes shone.

"It's a fountain pen!"

But seeing him as excited as a child, I couldn't help a small smile.

Just then, two people appeared out of Shinonome-san's room, looking exhausted.

"Shinonome, you stepped on me. You could at least apologize."

"You've been bouncing off the walls since this morning. Are you a clown or something?"

Their faces were puffy from having drunk too much. When they saw the delighted Shinonome-san holding a fountain pen, their expressions turned as sour as if they'd just bitten into pickled plums. Then, exchanging smiles of satisfaction, they rushed over to Shinonome-san and began making a fuss.

"That's nice! Your present from Santa. Ooh, it's amazing, isn't it? Right, Tamaki?"

"Yeah, you must have been well behaved. I couldn't be more jealous."

"Yeah... That must be it! Ba ha ha ha ha, you've got us beat!"

Shinonome-san glanced at me and flashed a delighted smile.

Then Toochika-san and Tamaki-san grinned wickedly, and each put an arm around Shinonome-san's shoulders.

"Well, I'm glad you got such a lovely present," said Toochika-san. "You should be able to make good progress on your manuscript now!"

"How about we move the deadline forward, Shinonome?" asked Tamaki-san. "Wouldn't that be good?"

"Wh-what are you talking about?! I don't understand. Hey, Kaori, say something! You're the one who gave me this, right?"

I turned back to my cooking.

"Why are you ignoring meeee?!"

As Christmas came to an end, the sky of the spirit realm rang with Shinonome-san's cries.

Feeling secretly guilty, I continued ignoring him. But why?

A woman of marriageable age mustn't be moved so easily by her father.

The Meaning of Happiness and Where It Can Be Found

THE FOOTSTEPS of the new year gradually approached.

Lively voices echoed through the front of the shop.

"Congratulations!" Kaori congratulated the other woman.

She smiled shyly. "Thanks. But I haven't reached the crucial moment yet."

She nevertheless looked happy as she fidgeted bashfully with the horns protruding from her forehead. Her gestures were full of joy, and Kaori's face seemed to itch with envy.

"So what does it feel like at the moment?" she asked as she pestered the woman. "You're going to give birth soon, right? Can I touch your belly?"

"I'm due in three months. Go ahead, say hello to the baby."

The woman was Otoyo, the onibaba who lived next to the bookstore. She smiled gently as she patted her belly.

Otoyo had been married for two hundred years, but she hadn't been blessed with children until now. Pregnancy for an oni was a long haul—it lasted ten years. I had also heard that oni were more likely to miscarry than humans, which was why Otoyo hadn't even told us, her next-door neighbors, until right before she was due.

Otoyo sat in a chair in the shop. The heating was on, and it was warm enough to make me sleepy. She smiled gently as she gazed down at her own belly. "The baby's very energetic. It kicks my stomach a lot, which wakes me up in the middle of the night."

Now that she was finally able to tell us that she was having a baby, Otoyo seemed relieved.

"Hey, Nyaa-san. It's amazing that there's a baby in here, isn't it?" Kaori said.

"Hmm."

Smiling at me, Kaori cautiously touched Otoyo's swollen belly. She *looked* delighted, but was she really all that happy? As I cocked my head, Otoyo giggled.

"Cats have lots of children, don't they? Babies are nothing special to them."

"It's not that. I just wasn't sure why you were in such high spirits," I sighed.

At that moment, I heard clattering from behind me. Getting a bad feeling about it, I looked back. There was Kuro, his red eyes wide as saucers.

"C...cat? H-h-hey, cat."

"What is it? More to the point, what's a mongrel like you doing, swanning around the shop as if you belong here?"

"I'm j-just accompanying Suimei for his nap! Anyway, you were talking about *having lots of children*, right?"

I blinked several times and stared at Kuro. "So...you understood pretty well, even though you're a mutt? Those words have a lot of strokes in their characters."

"D-don't look down on me! Even I've been reading recently. I can understand this much! Anyway, cat. Cat..." Kuro swallowed, and his face took on a somewhat serious look as he asked me, "Have you...had children?"

"Yes?" I answered immediately.

Kuro froze, his mouth open so wide that his jaw almost hit the floor.

"Why are you reacting like that?" I tilted my head, puzzled. Hearing someone giggling behind me, I frowned and looked back; it was Otoyo and Kaori, frantically trying to stifle their laughter.

"An Inugami and a kasha? That would be pretty complicated, huh?"

"I wouldn't mind seeing Kuro try to walk that thorny path..."

"Hey, could the two of you please not decide that for yourselves?" I said with a touch of irritation.

They both apologized sincerely.

With a look of surprise, Kaori said, "In any case, I think this is the first time I've heard that you had children." She gazed at me curiously.

"That's because I didn't tell you. I didn't need to. It's in the past."

"What do you mean by that?"

I blinked slowly and fixed my eyes on Kaori. "If you're content now, there's no need to look back on the past, is there?"

"That makes sense." Seemingly content, Kaori stroked my back, and I reflexively purred.

Otoyo smiled as she watched us. "You two get along well, don't you? I wonder if my child will be good friends with you too..." Otoyo's eyes were full of affection. She patted her belly and began to speak as if to her child. "I want this child to be happier than anyone. Will I really be able to be a good parent...? I'm full of anxiety, but I intend to try my hardest to do a lot for them."

"That's lovely. I'm sure your child will be delighted too."

"Ha ha... If I'm struggling, will you give me advice, as an old-timer?" she asked me.

I blinked. "But I don't think cat parenting and oni parenting has much in common, do they?"

"No, I'm kidding. That aside, I'd like you to choose books for me to read to my child..." Otoyo smiled as she suggested this to Kaori.

But Kaori only stared vacantly at Otoyo's swollen belly and did not reply.

"Kaori-chan?"

"O-oh... Sorry! Um, books, right? Wait a moment!"

Kaori rushed over to the shelf of picture books.

Staring at Kaori's back, I let out a secret sigh.

That night, as always, I was sleeping with Kaori. Slipping out of the futon, I jumped nimbly up onto the windowsill.

The moon was very bright tonight. Because of that, the breath from my damp nose was so cold, I thought it would freeze. They say that on cloudy days, it's like there's a lid on the earth, so the warm air can't escape. That means fair days are especially cold in winter. I supposed it was no wonder they would be.

Settling down, I gazed out of the window. It was a moonlit winter night. The sight I could see from this window was a special one.

It wasn't that the view was amazing. It was just the view from the second floor of a run-down, shabby house. But on clear winter nights like this, it left a different impression, as if touched by magic.

A big moon shining on a spirit realm town. Everywhere blanketed in white snow. When the moonlight struck the snow, the light was reflected, making the snow itself shine brilliantly. This is called snow light.

Both the sky and the snow were shining. The tiny, tiny snow crystals twinkled as if breathing. Yet everything was shrouded in a silence as deep as that of the grave.

Nothing moved. It felt as if I was the only creature in the world.

"Pretty, isn't it." Kaori had been standing behind me, unnoticed. She wore a short hanten coat over her haori. Screwing up her eyes as if dazzled, she gazed outside. "You love sleep more than anything else, Nyaa-san. This is unusual for you, isn't it? Being up at this time of night."

Turning only one ear in her direction, I said reproachfully, "It's because *somebody* kept squirming about."

"Argh... Sorry. For some reason I couldn't get to sleep. Please accept this as my apology." Smiling awkwardly, Kaori let me inside her hanten.

I slipped inside it quickly. It was warm and pleasantly snug, and I settled myself down, instinctively flicking my three tails back and forth.

"You seem satisfied," Kaori grinned impishly.

"N-not really... I was just cold, that's all."

"Yeah, whatever."

I poked my head out of my best friend's sleeve and glared at her half-hearted response.

She giggled.

"Anyway, why are you feeling down?" I asked as if I were just chatting normally.

At once, her expression clouded as she flinched. She blinked her chestnut eyes several times, her gaze wandering all over the place. For a while, she was silent, but finally she let out a long sigh of resignation. "So you found me out?"

"For ages now, when you've been worried about something, you struggle to get to sleep. That's how I know."

"I'm no match for you, Nyaa-san..." Kaori's nose had turned red from the cold. Scratching it with her finger, she turned to look out of the window. "Isn't it pretty outside?"

"It is."

"I wish my heart was as pretty as that."

I stayed quiet and waited to hear what she would say next.

She was on the verge of tears. "I was...jealous of a child that hasn't even been born yet. What a fool I am."

Tears quivered in her eyes, and her eyebrows drew together a little. She hugged me closer to her.

"I'm content with the situation that I'm in now. I have Shinonome-san, and I have friends. But out of nowhere, I'll suddenly find myself thinking about them... My birth parents."

Kaori closed her eyes. Her expression, which had lost all its usual vigor, was despondent, and my chest tightened to see it.

"You're not genuinely happy, are you, Kaori?" The words just slipped out.

Kaori immediately shook her head, denying it. "No, I *am* happy. I can say that with confidence. I'm only thinking about them because...I'm very greedy."

She said that as if she ought to be ashamed, and I couldn't help laughing.

"Hah...ha ha ha. Silly you. What's wrong with being greedy? Greed is a human characteristic. It's how humans have enriched their lives. Cats don't have that."

"That's because it was a trait necessary for survival, right? This is different. I can survive without knowing anything about my birth parents."

"You're a strange girl. That just sounds like an excuse to me." Stretching out my body, I bumped my nose lightly against Kaori's. "I think, when I'm happy, I make myself into a circle."

"A circle?"

"The sun, which provides me with warm spots... Cushions, which are comfy to sleep on... Tasty tinned food... They're all round, aren't they?"

Round things are packed full of happiness. That's why I curled up into a circle to sleep. In order to get close to happiness itself, I mimicked its shape, and then I had dreams full of warmth.

"Circles are a pretty shape, so I can stay a circle. But if I get even a little crooked, or if I'm missing something, then I'm no longer a circle. I get the feeling that you're not a circle right now, Kaori." Slipping out of her hanten, I sat on the windowsill and looked up at her. "So, shall I tell you?"

When Kaori tilted her head to one side in puzzlement, I smiled, my differently-colored eyes closing slightly. "Something that might make your heart round again, Kaori. About when you came to the spirit realm. Everything that I saw, and everything that I know about the human world."

Bringing my face up to Kaori's ear, I whispered, "Do you want to know? Do you want to hear it? I don't know whether you'll really be able to return to being a circle after you've heard this, Kaori. I'm a cat; we do as we like, and we take no responsibility for the messes we make. But if you have the resolve to hear it, I'll tell you."

Kaori was fixated not on an unborn child but on her own past. If she wasn't unhappy with the way things were now, then her mood ought to improve once she learned that past. Theoretically.

It wasn't so simple for a human. If she found out *too* much, it might make her life difficult in the present. ...But if she never found out anything, she would stay at this standstill, no matter how much time might pass. If that didn't sound like happiness to her, there was nothing for it but to make a change.

My heartfelt wish was for Kaori's happiness. For her to be able to go on smiling... And to keep the promise I made that day.

"I don't know what will happen. Nevertheless, if you want to move forward..." I spoke bluntly, taking no responsibility, as was my feline right, and I smiled suspiciously, as was my spirit's.

Kaori swallowed, then nodded, her expression earnest.

The fire in the brazier had been raked out, and the charcoal replaced. I gazed at the redness of the flames.

It was a relief when the warmth returned to the freezing room. Kaori entered my field of vision, looking a little nervous. Her features were mature now, quite different from that time when she had sobbed in the middle of the forest, and for just a second my eyes went wide with astonishment.

She's come to resemble you. She really has. ...Don't you think so? The similarity is startling.

I spoke to that person inside my mind. Then, a moment later, I opened my mouth.

"It was a summer when the cicadas cried insistently."

At that time, a series of typhoons hit the human world, and there was terrible flooding everywhere.

The river completely forgot its normal, elegant flow and

bared its ferocious fangs. A number of humans lost their lives. That night, many shooting stars flew through the sky of the spirit realm.

Enma, king of the world of the dead, must be extremely busy.

In the midst of this, two spirits had met in the spirit realm bookstore and were groaning about the situation.

"What are we gonna do about this?"

"What do you mean, 'what are we going to do'? If you're not going to eat her, then give her to someone else."

"Yikes! You say surprisingly awful things, don't you, Noname?"

"It's not awful for a spirit to say that about a human. What are you on about?"

It was Shinonome and the apothecary, Noname.

After I had picked Kaori up in the forest and scattered the spirits who had been enticed there by the glimmerflies, hoping to feast, I took the little girl to Shinonome's place. I had been unable to just leave her where she was, but I also had no intention of looking after her myself. I had decided that was too much for me to handle.

Shinonome was known even within the spirit realm town as an eccentric. Although he was a spirit, he collected books that humans had made and lent them out.

I always wondered why anyone would even come to borrow such things, but surprisingly he seemed to be doing well. Spirits commented on books to their friends, saying "this one's good" or "this one's bad," and they enjoyed the worlds that humans had created. That was why I chose Shinonome; I thought that, if he liked books, then at the very least he couldn't bear any ill will toward humans.

I judged correctly. It seemed that Shinonome had no intention of eating Kaori.

"W-waaaaahh!"

"Hey, hang on. Don't rub your snot on that! It's my only good kimono!"

Kaori seemed to sense that instinctively. Although she kept bawling away, she stayed on Shinonome's lap, looking very small, and held onto his sleeve, refusing to let go. Shinonome tried his hardest to peel her small hands away, but he couldn't bring himself to treat her roughly, so he was at a complete loss.

Good grief. If he's like this, it looks like she's going to be okay.

Once you've become attached to something, even for a moment, the idea of someone tearing it to pieces makes you feel sick. It looked as if Shinonome was going to treat the child well, so I decided to leave the bookstore as soon as possible.

"Oh, no you don't, cat. That's too irresponsible of you."

But all of a sudden, someone roughly caught hold of my tail, and a thrill of fear ran through my whole body.

Reflexively, I tried to claw at them, but they easily evaded me. I ground my teeth in frustration.

The person responsible—that is, Noname—flashed me a bold smile. Taking me by the scruff of the neck, she returned to Shinonome and flung me carelessly onto the child's lap.

"Meeooow?! What are you doing?!"

"Oh my, what a pretty voice you have!"

"I'll kill you, apothecary!"

I hissed threats at that strange person; it was hard to tell whether she was a woman or a man. Irritatingly, she didn't seem to think anything of it. She just watched me coolly.

"No, you mustn't!" Then a small voice came from over my head, interrupting my threats. "Mama always told me not to argue. It makes people sad."

Kaori earnestly begged us to stop fighting. But her body was trembling, and tears continued to gush from her round eyes as if from a broken tap.

Noname and I looked at each other, and we both heaved a deep sigh,

"You're an apothecary, and you made a child cry?" I sniffed. "You're the worst."

"You're the one who picked her up, and yet you're taking no responsibility for her, cat?" she snapped. "*You're* the worst."

The apothecary and I glared at each other, then pointedly looked away.

"Cut it out, you two," Shinonome said, exasperated.

I glanced back in disgust at this man who spoke so glibly despite having done nothing while he watched what unfolded.

Shinonome sighed deeply. "I understand. At any rate, I'll hold on to this human child temporarily."

"What do you mean by that, 'temporarily'?"

I thought I'd handed her over to him. I peered suspiciously as he spoke this nonsense.

Shinonome tapped a still-bawling Kaori on the head and gave

me a tight smile. "Her Mama or whoever will be worried about her. You'd better find them quickly."

"Hang on. What are you..."

This blockhead was giving me a headache; I glared up at him. But Shinonome only grinned idiotically and, not taking my feelings into account in the slightest, continued. "You're not being honest with me, are you? Surely the reason you brought her here is so I could return her to her parents. If not, then you must be saying I can eat her."

"Huh? I *told* you, bookseller, hang on a moment—"

"It's because I'm known throughout the spirit realm town as an oddball, isn't it? But your judgment was correct. I'll look after this child until she can be returned safely to her home. So go and do your best to find her people. Don't waste your act of kindness!"

Ugh, this guy never listens! I've completely lost my appetite! To Shinonome, I was a kind, human-loving kitty. *You've got to be kidding me. Don't go too far with your misconceptions...*

"Oh? Is that so?" Noname said, sounding surprised; she seemed to understand that Shinonome had the wrong idea. She winked at me with a malicious grin. "In which case, I'll help too. It will be terrible if you only have this man to give you a hand. And I'm interested in finding this 'kindness' of yours."

"What? Give it a rest, you two!" I cried.

Crouched down in front of me, Noname gave me a look that said, *I can see right through you.*

"You picked her up, so you take responsibility for her," she said. "That is, unless...are your limbs so short that you can't wipe your own behind, Miss Cat?"

I'm gonna hit the roof! You piece of crap! In a flash, my anger reached its peak, and I saw red. Unsheathing my claws, I tried to scratch the idiot in front of me...

"Stop fightiiiing!"

I froze as the sobbing child held me tightly.

Ugh, be quiet... I sighed. Her cries were so loud that my eardrums were vibrating fit to burst.

"Waaaaaahhhhhh..."

"Oh no. You two made her cry. How immature of you."

"Ugh, it wasn't my fault—argh, shut up!" I shouted, unable to bear the noise. "Don't scream so close to my ear!"

"Waaah? I-I'm scaaared! Mamaaa..." Kaori only cried more and more.

Completely fed up, I wailed in despair. "I get it, okay?! I'll find your Mama! So please stop crying!"

"That's right, leave it up to the cat. Now come on, isn't it about time for good children to go to bed?"

"Don't wanna sleep! I wanna sleep with Mama! Waaaaaaah!"

"Are you going to go to bed, or aren't you?!"

Ugh, I've really drawn the short straw! Looking up at the sky, I heaved the deepest sigh of my life.

That was how I got stuck with the task of searching for Kaori's parents in the human world.

The charcoal blazed quietly in the darkness. As I paused in my storytelling, entranced by the faintly gleaming colors of the charcoal, I realized that Kaori was holding her head in her hands.

"You weren't friends..." She seemed genuinely surprised by the truth of our relationship back then.

"That's normal. Shinonome and Noname had been friends for a long time, but we only knew each other by sight. When a spirit meets somebody, they quarrel."

By nature, spirits are solitary creatures. They don't meddle in each other's business and go about their own lives as they please.

To be frank, the current state of affairs in the spirit realm was abnormal. Altered by Kaori's existence, the spirits had become close to one another as if they were...humans.

"Even if that's the case, isn't that very different from the way things are now?" she asked.

"I had no choice but to compromise. You should be thankful."

"Wow. How generous of you, Nyaa-san..."

Kaori slumped, but the next moment she lifted her head cheerfully. It looked like there was something she wanted to ask me. She gazed at me intently. "That reminds me. What about my name?!"

"What about it?"

"Where did you find it out?! I was three, so I could probably say my own name, but I wouldn't have been able to write the characters for it! Did you just pick appropriate characters? Or..." Kaori suddenly brought her face close to mine and asked excitedly, "Did my parents tell you?!"

"No."

I swiftly denied it, and Kaori immediately crumpled. Unconcerned, I groomed myself and continued my tale.

"Your name was written on your underwear. The kana reading was neatly added to the kanji. That's all."

"Oh..." Kaori's shoulders sagged in disappointment, and she urged me to go on with the story.

After that, I believe it was from the next day onward, I went around contacting the cats I knew in the human world. I told them I'd found a missing child called Muramoto Kaori, and I was looking for her parents.

At first, I didn't take it very seriously, thinking I would find them straightaway. Obviously, a small child going missing is a matter of the greatest importance. However...

"After several months of searching high and low and finding nothing, I was at a loss. Because of the typhoons, there were far fewer feral cats about. Toochika might have been able to find them immediately from the lists of missing people kept by the police, but back then, I didn't even know that kappa existed."

I think that was careless of Shinonome and Noname. If they'd turned to spirits who knew more about the human world than I did, it probably wouldn't have taken so long.

That's right. If I had met that person earlier... I might have made a different decision.

For a little while, I fell silent. When I looked up with a start, I found Kaori watching me anxiously. I hurriedly schooled my expression and picked up the story again.

"While I searched everywhere, summer passed and autumn came. It was just when I had begun to doubt that your Mama existed at all, Kaori..."

As the heat of summer died away and the sky over the spirit realm was tinged a purplish-red, a cold autumn wind began to blow.

Exhausted from my search for "Mama" in the human world, I listened to the dry sound of the fallen leaves by the roadside as I returned home. The moment I stepped into the living room of the bookstore, my face creased into a scowl.

"Waaaaahh!"

Someone was crying noisily. It was as if they had carefully calculated the volume to make it as unpleasant as possible. I swiftly turned on my heel, but at that moment—much to my disgust—I was seized by the scruff of my neck.

"Perfect timing! This is a big help, cat. Come here for a minute!"

It was Shinonome. He looked very strange. Although he had the kind of elegant look that women liked, he was wearing a bandana with a motif of little bears on his head. Right in the middle of his apron, which was made from matching material, was a patchwork bear with a stupid expression on its face.

"You've taken on her style..." I sighed.

In an instant, Shinonome's face became serious, and in a voice as deep as those of the devils of hell he growled, "Stop it."

Just as I was giggling at the terribly funny sight, I was dropped somewhere with a thump. I stiffened when I realized where that was.

"Nyaa-chan!"

I was directly in front of Kaori, who was in the middle of eating.

She was seated at a little desk made for a child, eating a lunch of spaghetti. It was smeared all around her mouth, as if she were a wild animal feeding on entrails, and the dress that Noname had proudly hand-picked looked like evidence in a murder case.

At some point, Kaori had stopped crying; she smiled and reached out a hand in my direction, as if she were about to stroke my head.

"Stop. Don't touch me with your dirty hands! And besides, what do you mean 'Nyaa'? You can't just give me a name of your own accord. And don't call me '-chan.' Show a bit of respect for your elders—at least use 'san'!"

"Nyaa-cha...Nyaa-san."

"Clever girl! You're a good girl, aren't you?" Shinonome cooed.

Kaori let out a shy giggle at the compliment and scratched my head with her dirty hand.

Averting my eyes from her brownish hair, which was decorated with meat sauce, I gave Shinonome a look of great displeasure.

"So, why did you put me here?" I asked.

"Kaori settles down when you're around. Please stay here just for a bit."

Shinonome had a mountainous pile of laundry in his arms. *Is this how much you end up doing when you add just one child to the mix?* I wondered, watching absentmindedly as the clothes hung up in the courtyard fluttered in the wind.

"Humans are a lot of bother..." I muttered.

"Bother?" Kaori asked.

"It means 'please grow up and become independent quickly,'" I said snidely.

As if she hadn't understood at all, she cheered. "I'll do my best!"

"So, how did it go?" Shinonome asked me as he stretched out a clean white sheet.

Looking askance at him—he seemed to have become adept at what he was doing—I informed him that I'd had no success.

For just a moment, Shinonome stopped. "Is that so?" he replied laconically.

"What's with that attitude? If you're not happy, say so clearly! After all, you must think I'm useless, not finding anything after all this time!"

I was exhausted from coming and going between the spirit realm and the human world all the time, and I was annoyed that I hadn't found a single lead; I took this jumble of feelings out on Shinonome. Bracing myself for whatever he might fire back at me, I was surprised by the timidity of his reply.

"I don't think that. But..." Beating the sheet all over, he picked up a clothes peg. "It's already been three months since she came here. I was just thinking, I've grown used to living with a child. That's all."

I stared in silence at his back as he hung out the washing. Irritated, I looked away from him and curled up.

What?! What on Earth do you mean? Have you grown attached to her? The way you're talking, it sounds as if you don't care if I never find them!

"Are you...fighting?"

I heard a worried voice. Kaori was watching us, looking ready to burst into tears at any moment.

"No. So hurry up and eat."

"'kay. Shimomome's not cross, is he?"

"He isn't. This is business as usual for that idiot."

"Business?"

"It means 'normal'!"

As if she'd finally understand what I'd said, Kaori nodded in satisfaction. "Uh-huh!" Clumsily, she picked her spaghetti up with her fork.

Good grief. It's not just Shinonome. I'm taking on her style too. I was astonished that I was participating in a child's conversation—that I was willing to compromise like this.

Just then, I heard the noisy clattering of footsteps. The spaghetti that Kaori had scooped up so painstakingly spilled out of her mouth, and tears sprang into her eyes. As I willed her not to cry, the owner of the footsteps burst into the living room.

"Oh, there you are, Nyaa!" It was Noname. Her unusually bright green hair was disheveled, and she held out a flier to me. "Look at this! Come on, quickly!"

"Don't *you* start calling me 'Nyaa' too!"

Cursing her, I reluctantly looked over the flier. My brain froze suddenly as I saw the information printed on it.

"I am looking for a child. Muramoto Kaori. A three-year-old girl. At the time of her disappearance, she was wearing…"

"For a long time now, I've been letting my customers know that we're looking for Kaori's parents. One of them brought me this. They said an acquaintance of theirs gave it to them."

They had probably found it lying on the ground somewhere and picked it up. The flier was slightly dirty all over, and the crucial contact details were so smudged that they were unreadable. But the girl in the photo that was printed on it was unmistakably Kaori. Noname and I looked at each other and nodded decisively.

"The spirit that gave you this, where are they from?"

"Akita. It's Kawa-akago. They said that one of the children in their neighborhood had gone missing."

With a gasp, I swung around to look at Shinonome, who was standing at the foot of the clothes-drying platform.

He seemed to have heard what Noname had said. He gazed at Kaori, grappling with the spaghetti by herself, with an expression I didn't really understand.

Kawa-akago is a spirit who appears in Toriyama Sekien's *Illustrated One Hundred Demons from the Present and the Past.*

In Toriyama Sekien's pictures, Kawa-akago can be glimpsed hiding in reeds at the edge of rivers, his face the only visible part of him as he lets out a cry similar to an infant's. But the legends don't record what kind of spirit he really is. In that same book, Toriyama Sekien states that he may be a Kawatarou, a variety of Kappa.

I decided that I would travel through hell all the way to Akita to meet Kawa-akago.

Kawa-akago's den was deep in the mountains. A primeval beech forest stretches around Lake Tazawa, and in the middle of that beech forest, where all the leaves were tinged yellow in the autumn breeze, the calm Sendatsu River flowed. At different spots along the river, fish such as char and masu salmon could be found, and Kawa-akago survived by catching and eating them.

"In the past, I lived a little closer to human settlements, but recently I've been dwelling quietly deep in the mountains, not frightening anybody."

"Have you been around here for a long time?"

"Yes, since my parents' lifetime. So I recognize the people who live in these parts," the spirit said. His serene voice didn't fit his name, but as his name "river infant" suggested, he had the small body of a child. He was wearing nothing but a red apron. Although his head was disproportionately large, he walked through the thicket as adroitly as an adult.

The beech leaves fell gently on us, hinting that winter was almost here. As that gold rain drifted down, dazzling my eyes, Kawa-akago arrived at a particular spot and stopped.

"There it is."

Kawa-akago was pointing at a rustic inn. The single-storied wooden building, which had a historical feel, bore a sign reading: Yume no Yu—the Hot Spring of Dreams. Apparently, it was a hot spring inn. The smell of sulfur permeated our surroundings, lending the inn a peculiar atmosphere.

"So, is the woman who was handing out those fliers here?"

"Sometimes, to pass the time, I come here to watch humans. I've seen her heading out with the fliers many times. But recently, I haven't seen her daughter at all."

"You know a lot about this situation, don't you?"

"All the spirits around here have too much time on their hands. We love people-watching. Why, the Kodama-nezumi even crawl under the floorboards of the guests' rooms—"

"I don't care about that. Thanks for guiding me here."

Cutting him off in the middle of his story in bad taste, I set out toward the inn.

I brushed off his careful warnings not to let anybody see me and continued on my way, though I didn't forget to disguise my three tails as a single tail.

Well, even if I did get discovered by a human, I could probably dispose of them on the spot, I thought to myself. But if the worst happened and I accidentally killed one of Kaori's parents, this would all come to nothing.

The Hot Spring of Dreams was a fairly small inn. As far as I could see, there were no other buildings around it. This was in the area known as Nyuutou Onsen, where hot springs are dotted all over the base of Mount Nyuutou. However, the Hot Spring of Dreams wasn't included in the extensive list of hot springs within Nyuutou Onsen. According to Noname, it's still known as the best secret hot spring amongst true enthusiasts, but...

"Maybe it's just not thriving," I whispered to myself, gazing up at its roof, which seemed to bend under the weight of the snow piled on it.

The Hot Spring of Dreams was obviously run-down. The spirit realm's bookstore had seen the rough end of many winters as well, but this disrepair went beyond that.

I walked the grounds, avoiding the places that looked as if they might collapse at any moment, and searched for any sign of humans. But I was already losing heart.

"It *stinks*. I think my nose is going to stop working. I hope I can go back soon..."

The smell of sulfur was almost unbearable; it was so powerful that the inside of my nose hurt, and I winced as I walked. Just then, I sensed people nearby, so I hid myself. Peering out from my hiding place, I saw a woman and a man who appeared to be a couple past their prime.

"Tsk... So what if service is bad, or the towels in their rooms smell? They should stop complaining."

"They really should. I *told* them, if they have complaints, they're welcome to go somewhere else. They went bright red and left. I wonder what they'll do. The nearest inn from here is a pretty long walk away."

"I don't give a damn! I hope they run into a bear."

Unbelievable...

I listened, stunned, as they fired these remarks back and forth; I couldn't believe they worked in hospitality. I'm a cat—and a spirit—so I don't understand human feelings that well, but I could tell that they had a uniquely awful attitude.

How disagreeable.

Having seen this dark side of humans, I sighed. But I shook my head and quickly put those feelings behind me. I was going to find Kaori's parents without delay and thereby free myself from this search for "Mama." I didn't have time to think about anything else.

The mature couple probably weren't Kaori's parents; they were too old to be the parents of a young child. That meant there had to be someone else about. Turning around quietly so that the couple would not notice me, I headed off to look for them.

"Akiho-san?! Our guest has left. Hurry up and clean their room!"

"Okay!"

I stopped as a lively voice reached my ears.

"Be quick about it. We have a new guest arriving in the evening."

"Understood."

A woman came running over. Tucking her brownish hair behind her ears, she turned to the couple and bowed deeply. When her head bobbed up again, I saw that her face was somewhat pale.

The instant I saw her, I recognized traces of Kaori in her features. I realized that my search for "Mama" was over.

After that, I carefully collected information.

Kaori's mother's name was Muramoto Akiho. Judging by her conversations with the other employees, she was a single mother, as well as a blood relative of the couple who ran the Hot Spring of

Dreams—the older man of the couple I'd first seen was her uncle. She had started living at the inn a year prior, following the death of her husband.

She had been staying in a room for hot spring employees along with Kaori, her only daughter, who had been two years old when they arrived.

However, her daughter had gone missing several months ago. It had happened while the road to Nyuutou Onsen was blocked off by a fallen tree that had come down in a huge typhoon, the scale of which had rarely been seen in recent years. Kaori had suddenly disappeared while Akiho was repairing the windowpanes that had been shattered by the storm.

Akiho had asked the police to search for her, but the damage from the typhoon had been so great that, as one problem led to another and another, the police had kept putting off the search effort.

They conducted a search once the road had been reopened, but they had found no trace of Akiho's daughter.

These were all the details I could gather on the incident.

"I see..." I nodded to myself as I secretly watched Akiho laboring away.

The day the typhoon struck, the spirit realm and the human world must have become connected by rare chance. In other words, Kaori had been "spirited away."

The spirit realm and the human world are separated by a single, thin wall. In many cases, humans have accidentally stepped into the spirit realm and gone missing. When this happens, the human world says they have been spirited away.

Famous legends of such incidents include Samuto no Baba of Iwate, who disappeared as a young girl and returned thirty years later as a Yamauba mountain witch... Oh yes, and speaking of Akita, there is the tale of the peasant Saku no Jou. A Tengu said it would show him the future and promptly returned him to the human world eighty years after the point from which he had been taken. Neither outcome was satisfactory.

That kid really was lucky.

Thinking of Kaori and remembering how, right about now, she was being pampered and snuggled, I flicked my tails.

Well, never mind her. That child is being protected by Shinonome. Her safety is guaranteed. That means she's less of a problem than... her mother.

"Where on Earth have you wandered off to, Kaori-chan?" one of the other employees of the inn suddenly murmured as she was washing tableware in the sink.

Akiho, who had been chatting with her, stopped what she was doing and gave her a sweet, invigorated smile. "It's all right. Kaori's alive! She's just a bit lost, that's all."

With that, she returned to her work. Her colleague smiled vaguely and went back to washing dishes too.

My heart hurts. What's with this woman?

Did she have proof that her daughter was actually safe? Even though the girl had been missing for months now?

She's not acting like a normal person. I wonder if she's gone a little crazy from the shock of losing her daughter?

At any rate, this woman was certainly Kaori's mother. Even to a cat, it was clear that her brownish hair and chestnut eyes were the spitting image of Kaori's. *So what I should do now is bring Kaori back here, I suppose. But...*

"Ack...ack, hack..."

"Are you okay? Do you want to take a break?"

"I-I'm fine. My uncle will just get mad and tell me not to be such a baby."

"But..."

Akiho's colleague gazed sympathetically at her as Akiho continued to work, still coughing away.

This doesn't look good.

It would have been so very easy to bring everything to a close at this moment. But I couldn't bring myself to act.

"I have to make absolutely sure," I muttered to myself.

Letting out a sigh from the depths of my being, I leapt nimbly down from the tree.

When the inn's guests had eaten, and the employees had finished cleaning up, it was finally their break time. Akiho had worked without stopping since sunrise, and it seemed she was in the habit of returning to her own room for a light meal and a nap until it was time for her to clean the baths.

I followed stealthily behind her, deep into the innermost part of the building. Akiho's room was several steps down from ground level; that had probably been arranged so it couldn't be seen by guests. Concealed by a partition screen, it looked more timeworn than the rest of the building. The paper stretched across the sliding screen door was black with mold; the steps were warped and looked as if she might put her foot through them at any moment.

I don't think that door was fitted right. And she's left it open—how careless.

Slipping through the door, which was slightly ajar, I entered the room. Inside, it was terribly musty. I thought the tatami might be rotting too. There was too much give in it, which made it extremely hard to walk on.

"Strange."

I stopped in a place that gave me a full view of the room, which wasn't terribly big. It was a six-tatami-mat Japanese-style room. It had no other nooks apart from a closet, but I couldn't see Akiho.

My fur stood on end as a feeling of discomfort ran through me. Just then, I sensed a presence behind me, and I whipped round.

"Kittyyyy!"

A figure filled my field of vision. It was Akiho, swooping down on me, her eyes so full of greed that they were practically spinning in their sockets. I was thrown into confusion—and completely forgetting that I was in the human world, I let out an undisguised shriek.

"Eeek! You weirdooo!"

This was how I encountered Kaori's mother, Akiho. And this was my first impression of her: that she was a strange woman.

"My head hurts..."

"I bet it does."

This was the first thing anyone had told Kaori about her mother. At first, Kaori's eyes had sparkled, but as I went on with my tale, she looked more and more unwell.

"My mother... You're certain that was my mother, right?"

"I haven't checked the family register or anything, but I'm pretty sure."

Kaori's shoulders slumped in disappointment, and she began to pick at the tatami. She seemed to have created her own mental image of her mother; she couldn't stomach the gap between that image and the reality.

"Well...it's too bad that Akiho was a bit strange," I said.

"Isn't it terrible to talk about her like that?!"

"It's a fact, so there's no way round it," I chuckled, watching Kaori. "But she wasn't a bad mother."

"O-oh?" Kaori flushed slightly at my words. She clutched her knees, burying her face in them. "So my father died? That's a shame. But my mother..." Kaori whispered, as if she was digesting the news. She closed her eyes.

Kaori's own roots were becoming clear. They would have a profound effect on her.

Humans change easily. The Kaori who knew about her mother would be a different person from the Kaori she had been until yesterday. I wondered how the information I was about to give her would transform her.

It will be all right, won't it? She's an adult now. She'll be fine, even if I tell her everything, I persuaded myself, trying to dispel the anxiety swirling about in my mind.

Slowly, Kaori opened her eyes. "Nyaa-san? Um... If I had a mother, why didn't I know about her?" she asked me hesitantly. "Perhaps she's still alive somewhere? Or..."

Her lips tightened as if she were bracing herself for something, and she asked me one more question.

"Did something happen to my mother?"

Looking down at the brazier, I slowly picked up the story again.

"That was careless," I scolded myself, holed up in the midst of a pile of zabuton in a corner of the room. Akiho was peeping through a gap in the zabuton, waving a cat toy to try and lure me out.

"Kitty... It's amazing that you can speak! Won't you talk to your big sister?"

"You're not my big sister, you're more like my aunt. In age, at least."

"That's harsh! But I get it."

Tired of hiding, I turned defiant and started talking normally. Akiho cackled, drawing back the cat toy and holding something else out to me.

"Here you go—shrimp tempura. How's that?"

I said nothing, but as the pleasant aroma wafted into my nostrils, I remembered that I hadn't eaten in a while. At that moment, my stomach growled. I heaved a sigh. "That's not fair..."

"You shouldn't make fun of a human's intelligence, you know."

Although I was irritated by Akiho's proud tone, I stuck my head out from the pile of zabuton. In front of my eyes was a small plate with tempura on it. I sank my teeth into it without hesitation.

But I immediately screwed up my face. "It's cold."

Having the tongue of a cat, I don't eat piping hot food, but naturally I don't go for cold tempura either.

When I complained about the hard coating and the oily texture, Akiho giggled and apologized. "It's a guest's leftovers. I'm sorry it's not freshly cooked."

"They make their employees eat food scraps at this inn?"

"Oh, no. It's my choice—it saves on food expenses, you see. I'm a freeloader."

Akiho bit into an even tougher-looking piece of sweet potato tempura. It didn't look like it tasted very good. After eating a few bites, she put down her chopsticks.

"Don't you have any money?" I asked pityingly.

Akiho gave a light laugh and shook her head. "I'm economizing. For the future."

"All the same, what are you doing eating leftovers? Your husband died, right? Didn't you get a life insurance payout or anything?"

"You know a lot about me, don't you? Well... I did get quite a large sum. But a good friend of mine was having money troubles, so I lent it to them."

"Have they paid any of it back?"

"No. We lost touch. I'm sure they're busy."

She's such an easy mark... I was beginning to feel sorry for her instead of exasperated.

As I gazed at her, Akiho suddenly brought her face close to mine. Her eyes sparkled with all the curiosity of a child who had just discovered a new toy. "Hey. Never mind me—tell me about yourself! A talking cat? That's amazing. And what's more, you know about life insurance and everything, so you must be clever."

Nimbly dodging the hand that Akiho stretched out toward me, I tried to change the subject. "There's nothing much to tell."

But Akiho didn't give up. She sidled toward me. "If you don't tell me, I'll make up my own wild ideas. Ooh, perhaps you're an extra-terrestrial? If I reported you to NASA, I'd get loads of money!"

A strange light shone in Akiho's eyes. I broke out in a cold sweat. She'd just told me she didn't have any money. I could hear her heavy breathing in my ears.

"Hey...wait. Calm down. You won't get that money."

"I could at least sell you to a circus. Right? Don't you think?"

"Don't ask me to agree with you! Are you stupid?!"

Akiho reached a hand toward me. I didn't know what was going to happen if I didn't do something. But she was Kaori's mother; if I carelessly hit out at and injured her—

My thoughts went round and round in circles. My judgment was thoroughly unsound. Completely forgetting that I had sharp claws, I closed my eyes like a weak little kitten.

"Ack. Gack..."

But her hand never touched me. I could hear her coughing painfully. At the same time, a sweet smell drifted toward me, and I slowly opened my eyes.

A vivid liquid, the hue of ripe pomegranates, trickled through the gaps in Akiho's fingers, dripping down and staining the worn-out tatami. Blood.

"Ack. Sorry, I got too excited..." Still coughing painfully, Akiho gave me an earnest smile.

I had no idea what kind of expression I should make.

Akiho lay down on the damp futon and flashed me another smile. "I'm sorry I startled you."

"It's okay," I said, washing my face with my front paw.

"Any way you look at it, you just seem like a normal cat," Akiho said curiously. "It's strange. What are you, really?"

"Are you still thinking of selling me to NASA?"

"That was a joke. Or rather..." Akiho's chestnut eyes half-closed as she smiled and said lightly, "I just wanted to check whether you were a shinigami."

A god of death? Sucking in my breath, I looked hard at Akiho.

She's awfully pale. And she looks gaunt, somehow. Kind of unappetizing. I bet she's really thin underneath those clothes. She wouldn't make a filling meal.

"Are you dying?" I went ahead and asked her.

Akiho looked straight at me. "Yes. I'm dying. I have terminal cancer."

She said it so indifferently. A silence fell between us.

Akiho had lost her husband and been cheated out of his

life insurance payout, and then—to crown her already dire cir-cumstances—her daughter had gone missing. And she would be conscious of all this misfortune until her final hour.

What an unhappy, luckless, wretched life.

So why, despite this...are her eyes the only parts of her that aren't dying?

I saw in them a fear that I didn't understand. "Sorry, but I don't do the tasteless work of collecting the souls of those who are about to die." I said it jokingly, so she wouldn't guess how my heart quaked.

Akiho looked disappointed. "That's a shame."

I cast a sidelong glance at the children's toys that had been tidied away neatly in a corner of the room. "I'm just a spirit," I said. "A cat spirit. Even so... There must be something wrong with you if you're looking for a shinigami when you have a child."

"I don't think it's that strange. I know that I'm dying, so I just wanted to know how long I have. I want to leave as much as I can for my child."

"But I heard she'd gone missing?"

"You know a lot about me, don't you?"

"Weren't you handing out fliers?"

"Wow, so those fliers even reached monsters... That's amaz-ing!" Akiho suddenly brightened. Then she looked off into the distance and stroked her belly. "My daughter... She went missing the day the typhoon struck. You'd think I'd be in utter despair. Even my uncle got angry with me and told me to face the facts. But I know...she's alive, somewhere, still."

"Why do you think that?"

Akiho grinned, showing her white teeth. "Mother and child are connected by their bellies from the time of pregnancy onward. That's how I know. The link between us hasn't yet been cut."

So, Akiho was absolutely confident that she would return.

"Instinct? You're relying on something so uncertain?"

"The world is overflowing with more wonders than you could ever dream of. Look, even here." Pointing at me, Akiho smiled impishly, like a child. I faltered, unsure of what to say; Akiho grinned proudly.

"You're a strange woman..."

"I get that a lot."

I had accidentally let my real feelings slip, but Akiho didn't seem offended; she just coughed again.

Then, glancing at her watch, she began to grudgingly get up. "Oops, I was enjoying talking to you so much that I forgot. I have to go."

"Where?"

"I've got cleaning to do. The baths, specifically—so the guests can have a nice dip first thing in the morning."

"But you're ill. Can't you ask someone else to do it?"

"No. This is my job. If I slack off, they'll dock my pay. My uncle's very strict in that regard." Akiho put on a hanten emblazoned with the name of the inn and staggered out of the room.

Seeing her so pitifully exhausted, I couldn't help asking, "Look, if you try your hardest and then die straightaway, what's the point of that?"

Akiho paused with her hand on the doorframe and turned to

look back at me. "I don't care whether I live or die. I'm a mother. I'm earning money solely for my child's sake. She'll never be happy without money in today's world…" She smiled. "Hey, kitty. Will you come back again? This is the first time I've ever had a monster for a friend. It's fun."

Then, without waiting for my reply, she left the room.

Slipping out of Akiho's room, I returned at once to the spirit realm.

A dry wind blew as I made my way through the town. I stopped in front of the bookstore, where the lamps were glowing. Pushing open the badly fitted glass door, I entered the shop and heard lively voices coming from the living room.

"Read more, Shimomome!"

"Okay, okay! Hey, sit down!"

"Kaori, would you like a treat? I bought sweet dumplings."

"Yes! Thank you, Momame!"

When Kaori had first come to the spirit realm, she had done nothing but cry; but once I brought her here, she'd seemed to finally grow accustomed to it. Her innocent laughter betrayed not the slightest trace of gloom.

Heart sinking, I padded slowly into the living room.

Kaori spotted me at once and came rushing over. "Nyaa-cha—san!"

I swiftly stepped out of the way before she could hug me. Her chubby cheeks swelled up like a balloon.

"Why won't you let her hug you?"

"Shut up, apothecary." Glaring at Noname, I picked the softest, fluffiest zabuton and curled up on top of it.

As I did, Shinonome said nervously, "So, how did it go?"

"How did what go?"

"Finding Kaori's mother!"

I cast a sidelong glance at an irritated Shinonome and let out a long sigh. Just as I made to inform him that I'd located Akiho, I was surprised by the words that came out of my mouth. "I haven't found her yet. I'm still investigating."

"O-oh, I see..." When Shinonome heard this, he relaxed, his expression softening with relief.

What an idiotic face he's making. It's really annoying—almost as if he's glad *that I haven't found her.* Normally, I would have yelled at him, but this wasn't the time.

Wait—what am I thinking?!

If I reported that I'd found Kaori's mother and took the kid back with me, all of this bother would be over, so why was I delaying? I couldn't for the life of me understand it, and the confusion made my head spin.

"Hey, Shimomome. The book..."

"Gotcha. Which one should I read?"

Taking no notice of me, Shinonome lifted Kaori onto his lap and began to read to her. As I listened to his soothing voice, I frantically analyzed my own feelings.

It's possible that I don't want to give her back to her mother.

I was conscious of my attachment to Kaori. I wasn't in as deep as Shinonome, though. So why...?

"I'm a mother."

At that moment, I recalled Akiho's words, and all at once I understood.

Say that I was Kaori's mother—I'd want her to come back to me, wouldn't I?

I remembered my own children, with whom I had parted a long time ago. That had been back before I became a spirit. There had been three of them, black kittens who were the spitting image of me. I believed that, as a parent and as a cat, I'd drilled the rules of survival into them. In my own way, I'd taken great pains to ensure that my children would have an easy life.

A mother's children are her pride and joy. Although Kaori was not my child, I saw the traces of my own children in her, and I cherished her to the extent that I unconsciously wished for her to be happy.

So, those thoughts had come from the part of me that was a mother.

It was precisely because I had come to understand Akiho's thoughts and decisions as a mother that I was now disinclined to return her little daughter to a place where she would certainly end up unhappy.

Where on Earth does happiness wait for this human girl?

Realizing this, I spontaneously threw a question Kaori's way. "Hey, Kaori, Are you happy?"

Kaori tipped her head suddenly to one side. "What does 'happy' mean?" she asked, entirely uncomprehending.

"Being able to eat your fill—or have a good sleep. Enjoying yourself. That kind of thing."

That was what happiness was for cats, anyway.

"Hmm." Kaori tilted her head, still puzzled. The next moment, her expression brightened suddenly. "The rice here is warm and tasty. You don't have to add tea to it."

"Tea? Why would you have to add tea to your rice?"

"Well..." In clumsy words, Kaori explained to me.

Apparently it wasn't just Akiho who'd eaten leftovers at the inn. At that place, their meals were almost always cold, and if too much time had passed, they often solidified. In order to make them pleasant to eat, Akiho used tricks like pouring hot tea over the rice.

"And when I'm sleeping, cold wind doesn't come through like *whoosh*. I love having tons of books to read. But...I get lonely sleeping without Mama." Kaori's shoulders drooped dejectedly, and she dragged her toes over the floor. Tears welled up in her eyes. She was trying desperately not to cry.

"What kind of environment was this child brought up in...?" Noname murmured.

"It sounds awful..." Shinonome agreed.

They cast their eyes downward, their faces grave.

Sighing, I asked Kaori another question. "Do you...love your Mama?"

Kaori beamed like a flower bursting into bloom, and said clearly, "Yep. Very much!"

"Uh-huh." Bracing myself with that single word, I left the bookstore.

"Hey, what's going on? What was with those questions? That's not like you," Shinonome called out, frantically rushing after me.

Glancing behind me, I saw Kaori sticking her head out of the bookstore's porch, looking worried.

"That kid will catch a cold. Humans are much frailer than spirits. Go back to her."

"But..."

I clicked my tongue at the flustered Shinonome. Turning my back on him, I said as if delivering a monologue, "Leave everything to me, and you look after her. Everything I'm doing is for the best."

Shinonome was silent for a few moments before finally opening his mouth. "I'm counting on you."

At the sound of his profoundly frail voice, I instinctively looked behind me. My eyes went wide with astonishment.

What's going on?

Shinonome was bowing his head.

A single, carefree spirit who does as he pleases, emotionally invested in someone enough to bow to them?!

"Good grief." Smiling slightly, I shook my head. "You're quite moved, aren't you. Despite being a spirit."

He stiffened. "Th-there's nothing I can do about it. I've become fond of her."

I turned my back on Shinonome again and looked up at the sky. "You're just like her father, you know."

Then I headed off toward the human world. Who knows

what expression Shinonome was making at that moment, but I thought idly that it was probably absolutely pitiful.

A week after that, I was once more in northern Akita Prefecture, around Lake Tazawa, where winter had come early. In a flash, the trees that had been dyed by the reddening of their leaves finished their preparations for winter; white snowflakes began to flutter down from the sky, and it became so cold that to be touched by the air outside was painful.

In the midst of this, deep in the mountains at the dead of night, when the breaths I sighed out froze in the air, I met with Kawa-akago.

"Thanks to you, Cat-neesan, I haven't finished preparing for winter yet... Good grief."

"Never mind that. Just tell me."

"Yes, yes. You're scary when you get angry, Neesan, so I'll inform you right away."

At some point during our many meetings, Kawa-akago had branded me "sister," and it had stuck. He rubbed his hands together, which looked like autumn leaves, and began to speak.

"I had a Kodama-nezumi look into the Hot Spring of Dreams."

Kodama-nezumi are another kind of spirit from Akita. They take the round form of a house mouse, and they're said to explode with a pop when the mountain gods are angry. It's also said that some Matagi hunters turned into these spirits. They're quite good at acting in secret.

Kawa-akago shook his head with a look of disgust. "The couple who run it aren't human. They're demons. Demons!"

"What do you mean? Don't tell me they're actually spirits."

"It would be more fitting if they were! That woman, Akiho or whatever her name is, is ill, and she doesn't have long left. The managers have already put in the paperwork to officially adopt her missing daughter."

"Isn't that natural? Someone needs to look after her once she's found."

"Well, that would be fine. Except they've taken away Akiho's bank book on the pretext that they'll be looking after her daughter after she dies. What's more, they've already started using her accounts."

"What did you say?"

Kawa-akago gave me a bitter smile that didn't suit his round face. "It seems the business of running the inn isn't going well," he said, disgusted. "They're making up their debt with Akiho's savings."

"That's outrageous."

I was already speechless, but Kawa-akago wasn't finished.

"I want you to check this yourself, sister... I have a feeling that they were involved in the missing child case too."

"Really?!" I pressed him, agitated.

Flinching slightly, he gave me a tight smile. "Check it yourself. Your complaints are going to be unbearable if I'm wrong."

"Check it? What should I do?"

"According to Kodama-nezumi, on the day when that typhoon

wind was howling, the woman was absolutely beside herself. Look—it was a day like today."

At that moment, a wind so violent that it almost choked us gusted past. The trees shook, and everything around us grew turbulent. The silhouettes of the trees, illuminated by the starlight, writhed like monsters and seemed to sneer at us for being in the mountains in the dead of winter.

I gulped and listened intently to what Kawa-akago said.

"Go and look from under the floorboards in their bedroom. I bet you'll get a nasty surprise."

Nodding quietly, I rushed off through the howling wind toward the Hot Spring of Dreams.

I'm glad the snow hasn't settled everywhere yet.

Crawling beneath the floorboards, enduring not only piles of dust and rubbish but the cold air that threatened to freeze me solid—and hardly able to bear the fact that the fur I was so proud of was getting dirty—I got into place and slowly closed my eyes.

Directly above me was the room where the couple who managed the inn lived. At present, it was a scene of complete carnage.

"Cut it out! It wouldn't help even if you died!"

"No... Please don't stop me! I can see the child. She's coming for me!"

"There's no one there. Get a hold of yourself!"

My face stiffened at the painful sound of a sharp slap. The man had hit his wife, perhaps to bring her to her senses. But far from stopping, his wife's wailing only grew more intense.

"Arghh! I *told* you I hated it. Having a dying woman with a kid sponging off us. Scheming for the sake of a little money. This is all your fault. You're the one who dragged me into it!"

"B-but we had no choice. This inn is all we have. If it went bankrupt, we'd be out on the streets. I did it because it was the only way for us to survive. Even you should be able to understand that!"

"But...a *child*...!"

"Shut up."

As soon as the woman spoke that word, the man lowered his voice.

"What would happen if someone overheard us? We have guests, you know."

"I-I'm sorry, dear..." the woman apologized timidly, seemingly coming to her senses. But unable to bear everything that was stored up in her heart, she began to cry bitterly. "I can't forget pushing that child in. She was only three! She was too young to understand what was happening, and she struggled so fiercely. I-I put my hands around her slender neck...and I let her fall. Her small body, buffeted about by the wild river—until she disappeared from sight."

"Never mind that. Get some sleep. You must be tired, huh?"

"I can still feel her in my hands... Oh, my dear, what can I do to be forgiven? Listen to how the wind howls. I can hear her screams in the sound of the wind..."

"No one's going to forgive us. Not me, not you. Raising a child costs money. We couldn't look after her. We just sent her on ahead to where her mother's going. They'll live quite happily in the next world..."

"Adopting her, even though we had no intention of bringing her up... What an unlucky pair they are."

Once I'd heard all this, I left my spot under the floorboards.

Unbearable nausea surged through me, fueled by a dreadful rage.

Dashing through the garden, which at some point had been covered by a thin layer of snow, I crouched at the base of a tree. Everything in my stomach came roiling back up, and I vomited then and there.

What did I hear just now? Was it the truth? Calling those two "human" is a joke. Evil spirits, or man-eating rakshasa... I'm sure there's been a mistake, and they're one of the two.

I gasped.

Oh, I get it now.

In that moment, a question I had pondered for many years was answered.

Amongst the spirits, not an inconsiderable number were once human. The reason for this was a mystery to me. How could any human, who had lived in such a bright world up until the moment of their death, become a spirit?

But now I was sure of my answer. If you tore through the thin layer of a human's skin, no matter what kind of human they were, you would find them packed with something dark and sticky. Muddy, thick. Every one of them carried within them a substance that no light could pass through.

And if for some reason a human became completely steeped in that ichor...they would be forever transformed into something else, something even uglier than a demon.

"Kitty?"

"Gah!"

At that moment, someone called out to me, startling me so much that I almost jumped into the air.

After schooling myself, I looked slowly behind me. I saw a face I recognized—but when I thought of how she must be struggling, I honestly wasn't thrilled to be reunited with her.

"Have you come to visit me again?"

Yeah, she's even thinner than she was a week ago.

Akiho stood before me. She was still steadily advancing toward the abyss of death, and she shone dimly pale in the starlight, wearing a faint smile.

Beckoning me into her musty room, she looked relieved as she told me that there were no reservations at the inn the next day. "That means I can do building repairs. There's a lot that needs reinforcing before the snow really starts to pile up. I have to eat lots to keep my strength up—so that I'll be all right whenever Kaori comes back."

Akiho didn't seem to get any days off. It was pitiful to see her chewing on a slightly bigger portion of cold rice than usual, telling me that she had to do manual labor come sunrise.

"I'm glad I got to see you again. There are so many mysterious things that we only get to encounter once, aren't there? I did worry that we might never meet a second time."

I stared at Akiho in silence as she spoke happily to me.

She stopped trying to pick up a piece of daikon radish and put her chopsticks down. "Hey, kitty."

Her next words were terribly quiet. Yet her eyes, underscored by circles that were even darker than before, were as peaceful as a waveless ocean.

"I think there's a meaning to our meeting." Akiho turned so that she was facing me directly, and she peered straight into my eyes. "Forgive me if I'm wrong... But you know where Kaori is, don't you?"

At that moment, the wind howled. As if in response, the worn building trembled, and the windows rattled loudly.

I sighed. "How did you find me out? Did I say something weird?"

Akiho frowned, troubled, then spoke with great anticipation. "You...didn't deny it. That's how. I think you know where Kaori is, and that's why you came to see me."

"Give up. Face the facts."

The people around Akiho had cruelly flung those words at her. Because of that, she had realized the truth simply from the fact that I deliberately hadn't denied them.

I let my guard down.

I was pained by the thought of my own stupidity, but when I remembered that I had come with the intention of telling her about Kaori, my attitude shifted. It was just coming out a bit sooner than I had planned.

"You're right. Kaori is...with an acquaintance of mine. In the spirit realm—a world crawling with monsters like me."

The sparkle returned to Akiho's eyes. Her ashen face regained its color; she opened and closed her mouth as if she couldn't properly form words, and her eyes blurred with tears. "I-I knew she was alive! Is she well? Is Kaori well?!"

"She's alive. She's living a happy life in a much better environment than this."

"Ohhh...God...!" Akiho trembled with joy.

In contrast, my heart felt totally frozen. Then I said the cruelest possible thing. "Sorry, but I'm not giving her back."

"Huh?"

"She was given to me. I've taken a liking to her. She's mine."

Akiho's expression suddenly changed, suddenly furious as she shouted. "Why?! What for?!" She pressed me frantically, flaring up as if she'd quite forgotten my uncanny appearance. There was no trace of her former calm. "Kaori is my child, my precious, only daughter! So give her back. Please, kitty! Give her back to me... She's not a toy. She's not something you can be *given*..."

As Akiho pleaded with me through tears, telling me that Kaori was her reason for living, her treasure, I stared coldly at her.

"I don't want to," I said. "It wouldn't be good to bring her back here."

"Wh-what?"

"What do you intend to happen to your child after you die?" I asked.

Regaining a little of her composure, Akiho glared at me. "Of course I've made preparations. The couple who manages this inn will look after her. I've even given them money for it. And my life insurance payout... That won't amount to much, but they'll use it for Kaori's sake. So she'll be all right. Now please, give Kaori back to me."

"Hmm. Hey, have you checked the contents of the bank accounts you left them in charge of?"

"What?" Akiho blinked, staring at me in puzzlement.

I ground the point home. "I said, have you checked your balance?"

"Um... Well, I handed my cash card and my bank book over to my uncle."

"So you wouldn't know if they've taken money out of your accounts, then."

"What do you mean?" Akiho went pale before my eyes.

"That couple. They're embezzling your savings," I said mercilessly.

"You're lying. That's impossible..." Akiho's gaze roamed frantically, unable to settle.

I stretched my body and whispered ominously in her ear, as if to deliberately stir her unease. "So you don't want to believe it? What a fool you are, trusting monsters like them. If you're a mother, face the facts. Look..." I glanced around the little room and let out a sharp sigh. "Given the way those two treat you, you don't seriously think they care about you, do you?"

"Um..." Akiho swallowed her words.

I flicked my tail from side to side. "Your husband is dead, and the only relatives you have to rely on are those people. Your best friend is never going to pay you back. You're going to die any day now. I'll ask you one more time: What do you intend to happen to Kaori?"

"Look…" The shock of the truth about her uncle and his wife had smashed Akiho's confidence to pieces.

But I don't think I'll reveal who's responsible for Kaori's disappearance.

That would be too dangerous. I had a feeling that if Akiho found out the truth, the tranquil woman I knew would vanish, and she would transform instead into some kind of wrathful deity like a Shura.

A child is more important than anything to a mother, and if she finds out someone has hurt them, she cannot remain as she is.

I looked up at Akiho, who was white as a sheet as she hung her head. We had only just met one another, but for some reason, I liked this human.

"This is the first time I've ever had a monster for a friend. It's fun."

Akiho had spoken those words with such nonchalance. Perhaps she had even been happy.

Well, Akiho. Have you thought about it? Have you realized what you need to do in order for Kaori to be happy? The biggest obstacle in her clear path to happiness…is you, her mother.

Akiho still stood there, pale and silent, her eyes downcast. Her tightly clenched fists trembled slightly, and she bit her lip so hard it had gone white.

I began to speak to her, careful to use a gentle tone. To an onlooker, it would probably have seemed like the murmurings of a devil. But I *am* a spirit—an inhuman monster—so they wouldn't necessarily have been wrong.

"There are entities in the spirit realm who've grown fond of the child. They can take care of all her needs without a problem. They can give her warm rice to eat instead of leftovers, and they can prepare a bed for her that isn't cold. Hey, Akiho, you're Kaori's *mother*. What do you think?"

I deliberately emphasized the word.

Carefully thinking through my next words, I asked, "Despite all that, do you want to spend the short time before your death with your child?"

If I do return Kaori to Akiho... The time leading up to Akiho's death will be irreplaceably precious. Maybe Akiho will even be able to die without regrets.

But what would become of Kaori when she was left behind? What could Akiho bequeath to her? The only thing left for that sweet, innocent child would be her mother's cold corpse.

At that moment, I realized that Akiho's shoulders were shivering slightly. The tremors grew bigger and bigger until at last they were joined by a laugh that startled me.

"Ha...ha ha..."

"Akiho?" I asked, concerned that she had finally lost it.

In the next moment, Akiho looked up with a gentle, exhausted smile. "Thanks for everything, kitty."

"Why are you thanking me? Idiot," I snapped. *That's not what you say to someone who's trying to steal your child!*

Akiho was such a soft touch, it was disconcerting.

She picked up a book in the corner of the room. "I've loved books for a long time."

I cocked my head at this abrupt, meaningless statement.

Akiho stroked the cover. "This book is Kaori's favorite," she said as she showed it to me. "She loves stories, just like me. I've read it to her over and over..."

It was a children's picture book, a famous one about mouse brothers who work together to make a pancake. The cover depicted two mice who looked like they got along well.

The book was slightly dirty all over, and it was crawling with fingerprints. The cover was ripped, and I could see where it had been repaired with tape. Many of the pages were torn as well. I could tell that it had been read many times.

"I used to imagine it all the time before I got married, you know—reading my child all sorts of stories, and putting together fine bookshelves for her, and choosing books together with her before she went to bed..."

A single tear dropped onto the book.

Akiho's lip wobbled, and she continued in a hoarse voice. "But then my husband died, and money became tight. I couldn't afford to buy books. That...was when I realized it for the first time. Books are a luxury. Here, deep in the mountains, we can't even go to a library. Reading itself became difficult..."

She gripped the book tightly. Perhaps it was a side effect of her medication, but her nails were ragged and black, as if they were stained with ink.

"When I'd read the same book to her over and over, even

Kaori said she was getting fed up with it. She wanted a new one. But I couldn't buy it for her. I couldn't...buy her anything at all."

Crouching down, she let out a tearful wail. "Why am I so useless...?!"

Akiho's face screwed up in pain, and gazing up at the empty sky, she continued through her tears. "Even my late husband used to say that to me. *You're too trusting,* he told me. But I can be suspicious of people too. The best friend who started talking to me as soon as I received the payout... I thought she might never pay me back. And I thought it was suspicious when my uncle and his wife wouldn't return my bank book. But..."

Her chestnut eyes were wet. In an instant, there were more tears than her eyes could hold, and they slipped down her gaunt cheeks and onto her clothes, where the drops burst and disappeared.

"I knew how kind, how good they could all be. So I didn't want to think that they might be tricking me. But people change when money is involved. I understood that, even though no one told me. It was obvious."

At that moment, Akiho began to cough terribly; merely breathing seemed to hurt her. When the cough subsided, she gazed at the hand that had been covering her mouth and muttered, "I'm alone, going around in circles, wringing my own neck, and there's no way out. I'm such a fool. I always make the wrong choices. Before I became a parent, I used to think that I wasn't fit to be a *person*. Argh..."

Akiho looked at me with a feeble smile. "I wanted to have

been born a cat, you know. Lying in a sunny spot, napping to my heart's content... To curl up and sleep in what seemed to be the symbol of happiness. Not having a trace of worry..."

Akiho's hand was brightly stained with blood. Her expression tightened, and, as if she were at her wits' end, she asked me, "My child really...really is living a good life, without too much or too little of anything, isn't she?"

I nodded vigorously. "With an eccentric but trustworthy guy," I reassured her, speaking with conviction.

But Akiho looked like a lost child. "No. I don't believe any of it. I'd hate myself." She crouched down, clutching her knees.

I frantically suppressed the laugh that was about to burst out of me. "Idiot. If you start talking about believing me in this situation, there's no help for you."

"I-I guess." Akiho gazed at me, her eyes overflowing with tears, and sighed. "Kitty, you're so kind and gentle. If I can, I want to trust you."

"What's that supposed to mean?" My gaze darted about, and I hastily turned my back on Akiho. My heart felt restless. A faint warmth was spreading out from my stomach, and my head was light. *Come to think of it, this is probably the longest I've spent with a human in a long time.*

My heart suddenly ached as I realized that it felt like returning to the time when I was just a cat.

At some point, I had started living separately from humans.

In the past, I'd harbored genuine affection for the people who looked after me, and I'd enjoyed being pet. But once I became a spirit, I'd forgotten that before I realized it, and I'd become convinced that I had to live alone.

That sensation of entrusting someone with my heart and being entrusted with theirs. I had missed it so much.

As I woke once more to this curious kindness, I turned to Akiho.

"I guess I have no choice." I shook myself lightly, letting power flow through my whole body. Then, with a creaking sound, I grew. I grew and grew until I had transformed to the size of a tiger and was wreathed in flames. In that shape, I loomed over Akiho and brought my face close to hers. "In which case, I'll let you trust me. Come with me."

"Kitty... You really *were* a monster..." Akiho blurted out stupidly.

As my pins and needles wore off, I brought my body low to the ground and urged her onto my back. "My moods shift quickly, you know. Get on quick, before I change my mind."

"B-but... The bathroom cleaning..."

"Listen, is there really any need for you to fulfill your duties toward the pieces of crap embezzling your money?" I glared sidelong at Akiho.

"Pfft," she snorted, supremely amused. "There isn't, is there?" With that, Akiho excitedly put on her coat and wound her scarf about her neck. She spoke eagerly, her eyes shining with childlike curiosity as she climbed onto my back. "Come to think of it, riding on the back of a giant animal was a dream of mine."

"I'm glad your dream came true, then."

I sighed inwardly at how light she was in comparison to the size of my body, then flew out of the open window.

"Whoa. We're flying!"

Kicking the air, I raced through the winter sky. As the freezing air wrapped itself around my whole body, I found myself longing for a warm room. But Akiho didn't seem to care.

"It's like swimming in an ocean of stars..." she murmured as if she were dreaming, and she gazed in fascination at the winter sky, totally absorbed in the sight.

The whole time we were on the move, Akiho was in high spirits.

As we passed through the scorching heat of hell, she yelled, "It's hot!" and waved at each of the demons we passed. When we reached the spirit realm, she stared in wonder at the glimmerflies who flocked to her, and she let out a sigh at the old townscape that emanated a sense of history.

"Come to think of it, I haven't even been on any trips recently..."

I don't really know whether or not Akiho understood the situation that she was in, but she seemed to enjoy the journey.

We landed on the roof of the building in front of the bookstore, and I made the flames around my body flicker so as to hide Akiho's presence.

"Here?"

"That's right, this is where Kaori is."

Akiho's expression grew serious, and she hid in my shadow as she gazed at the building, which seemed more worn than its neighbors.

"Books for loan..." She stared at the sight beyond the glass door. Seeing the rows of books all lined up, she let out a hot breath of surprise.

That's when it happened.

"Waaaaahhh…"

The voice of a child crying emerged from the bookstore, along with the extremely flustered voice of a man. No sooner had we heard a hurried clattering than Shinonome stumbled out of the shop, dressed in a large hanten.

"Kaori!" Akiho gasped at the sight of her daughter crying in Shinonome's hanten, and she started to climb down from my back.

"What do you intend to do?" I asked as I stopped her.

Frowning in pain, Akiho reluctantly sat down again, resigning herself to intently watching Kaori and Shinonome.

"Waaaugh!" In the meantime, Kaori continued to cry, red-faced. She seemed to be throwing a tantrum. "Mamaaaaaaa! Mamaaa!"

She missed her mother. She stretched out her little hands and screamed.

As she watched, Akiho clasped her hands together so tightly it looked painful. "It's no good. When she gets like this, there's nothing to be done. If I don't hug her, she'll cry forever. Aaghh…"

Akiho wanted to hold Kaori right that instant. She fidgeted, unable to settle. But if she went over to Kaori now, everything would be ruined. She had to hold on.

Kaori's cries echoed through the silent spirit realm town. It seemed as if she would go on crying forever. Just as I was growing irritated, Shinonome finally moved.

"Argh, damn it. I'm sorry, I'm lousy at comforting you." With clumsy movements, Shinonome hugged Kaori tightly and patted her on the back. "Was this it? Let's see…"

Clearly nervous, he started to rock her rhythmically.

To and fro, to and fro. To and fro, to...and fro, to...and...fro...

Had someone taught him how to comfort a baby? Rocking her irregularly, he brought his mouth close to Kaori's ear. "Don't cry," he said gently. "Don't cry, it's all right." Closing his eyes slowly, he continued to speak to her, all quiet and calm. "There's nooothing to worry about. I'm here. I'm here..."

But she wasn't going to stop crying all at once. As Kaori sobbed, he kept on talking to her, ever so patient.

It went on like this for a good while.

At last, Kaori stopped crying and looked up at Shinonome, her eyes sore and red. He seemed sincerely relieved. The corners of his eyes crinkled as he smiled, overjoyed.

"Good girl. You're a good girl, Kaori."

As he turned and walked back toward the bookstore entrance, he spoke in a lively tone. "How about I read you a book? I'll tuck you up in your futon and read you any one you like. How about it?"

Kaori's face brightened at once. "The mouse book!" she said energetically. "The one where they bake pancakes."

"That one, huh? You really love that book, don't you, Kaori?"

"Yeah!"

Smiling at each other, they disappeared back inside the shop. The sliding door banged shut behind them, and the spirit realm returned to silence once more.

The glimmerflies flitted lightly around us. I followed them with my eyes as they gave off their bright light, and I nestled close to Akiho, whose shoulders shook silently. Akiho hugged me tightly to her. Hot tears dripped down her face and slid off my coat.

As I turned my gaze up at the red sky over the spirit realm, I said, as if to myself, "My children became independent more quickly."

A frail voice replied. "We're not like cats... It takes longer for humans to become independent."

Smiling a little, I continued to talk to myself. "There's no need to be the same as everyone else. I don't really mind. What's certain is that Akiho, a human, did a splendid job of raising that child until now. You really did your best."

Akiho gasped, upset. She hugged me even more tightly and said in a shaky voice, "Even so, I wanted to be a mother... I still wanted to watch over her..."

Lifting her head, she looked up at the red sky, so different from the one over the human world.

"I wanted to be at her side when she was having a rough time. I wanted to praise her when she did well. I wanted to rejoice as she grew. I wanted to cook her delicious meals. Whether we were laughing or crying, even if we were suffering or sad, I wanted to be with her!"

Tears fell from those eyes, which looked so like Kaori's.

"My life has been nothing but mistakes. Why...do I have to die? Why do I have to die and leave behind my lovely daughter...?!"

Akiho wailed over her own misfortune. With a desperate expression, she turned to me and pleaded. "Kitty, become her mother in my place."

"Akiho..."

"Look, *please.* Make her happy. Protect her. It might be absurd for me to ask this of you so soon after meeting you, but there's no one else I can ask... I'm begging you!"

Distracted by her fleeting tears, which disappeared as they fell, I shook my head slightly.

"I can't. I'm a cat. She's a human. There's no way to change that."

"That's a stupid way of looking at things. I'm desperate! Why?! Surely you can grant the wish of a dying woman?!" Akiho threw a tantrum just like Kaori had before her.

I sighed and licked her face.

"Ack!" At the touch of my tongue, which was not only rough like any cat's but significantly larger, Akiho's whole body broke out in goosebumps, and she froze, her face stiffening.

I put my forehead against hers and spoke slowly. "No one else is her mother. You are."

Flinching, Akiho drew into herself. "Then what should I do?" she asked, her voice shaking slightly. "I want to do something for her, but I'm good for nothing!" She hung her head.

I nuzzled my forehead against hers. When she looked up, I gazed straight at her and smiled. "I'll...become Kaori's friend."

Akiho's eyes went wide with surprise.

"When someone has neither parents nor siblings, the closest person to them is a friend. I'll be by her side." I blinked slowly. "It's all right—I'm a spirit. Unlike humans, we're not dazzled by money."

When I alluded to the people who had betrayed her, Akiho looked at me in amazement for a moment before immediately crumpling back into tears. Burying her face in my fur, she said weakly, "Really?"

"I don't lie."

"You have to promise me!"

"I promise. I'll be by her side until the day she dies. So that she isn't unhappy. So that she can always wear a smile like a ray of sunshine. Because that child..." I hesitated for a moment and looked away. "...Is the precious child of my friend."

"Huh?!"

When I'd said what I wanted to say, I took Akiho by the scruff of the neck and tossed her up onto my back.

"Eep! Wh-what? What's this?"

Checking to make sure that Akiho was clinging to my back, I soared up into the night sky, brooking no argument.

The ground fell away, and the stars grew closer. Accompanied by the glowing butterflies that had gathered around us, attracted by Akiho's human scent, I rushed up through the sky. At last, when the houses of the spirit realm were no larger than grains of rice, I stopped climbing.

"Kitty? Wh-where are we going?!"

"Who knows?"

"Are we going back to my uncle's inn...?" she asked in a frightened voice.

I grinned impishly. "Oh, did you want to go back?"

Akiho shook her head vigorously. "Now that I've made sure

that Kaori's safe, I never want to see those thieves ever again."
Drawing in a great, deep breath, she yelled, "I won't stand for
being exploited anymore! I'm not a slave!"

"That's the spirit!"

Smiling, I steered to the south and began to fly in that direction. "Hey, Akiho. In that case, let me spirit you away."

"Huh?" she said stupidly.

"If you haven't got long left, I'll keep you company until then.
You haven't been on a trip recently, right? Don't you want to go
somewhere you've never been? I'll take you with me. I'll stay with
you on your deathbed. And..." I paused for a moment, considering. But I'm a spirit, so I soon picked up where I'd left off. "I'll eat
your remains."

"Agh!"

I could tell Akiho was perturbed, but I carried on, as if
indifferent.

"Did you know? There's only one way spirits can hold a funeral
service for someone. While mourning their death and looking
back over the time we spent together, we take their remains into
ourselves. By eating their bones and flesh, we carve their feelings
into our own. That's why I'll eat you. That way, your thoughts and
wishes will be by Kaori's side."

She might refuse. I had said it all in the space of one breath,
and I felt a slight sense of regret.

I knew that, according to human sensibilities, such an act was
unthinkable. Although I had done my best to choose pleasant-
sounding words, there was a high chance that Akiho would be

viscerally unable to accept. If that happened, there was nothing I could do. I let out a slightly self-deprecating laugh and awaited Akiho's reply.

But she confounded all my expectations. *I'd forgotten. That's right—this woman is strange!*

"That's amazing! All right!" Akiho cried excitedly, throwing her arms around my neck with all her strength. "I was so angry with my uncle and his wife. Seeing how they've been carrying on, I'm sure they're planning to steal my own life insurance. I'll be spirited away. That way, they won't be able to confirm my death within the seven-year limit, and there won't even be a payout! Serves them right!"

Akiho scrambled up onto my back. Climbing up toward my neck, she dangled down, almost covering my face. Just as I was about to complain that what she was doing was dangerous and she needed to stop, Akiho entered my line of sight and smiled as brightly as the sun.

"This way, no one will mourn my death. Kitty, you've done nothing but help me. Thank you so much..."

Once again, she began to cry big round tears. As they were blown away by the cold winter wind, her tears took in the light of the glimmerflies flitting around us and reflected the red sky of the spirit realm. They gleamed a deep scarlet and looked just like rubies. Those tears, which held within them blood and heat and all the radiance of life, shone more nobly than any tears I had yet seen as they streamed out behind us on the wind.

Aahhh! How—how pretty they are...!

In a wink, I found myself fascinated with them. I smiled. "No need to thank me. Well, shall we go? We don't have much time. There must be many things in this world that you've never seen before, Akiho."

"Yep!"

We flew against the whistling wind through the spirit realm sky. Kicking at the air, I aimed for the stars and the moon as I bounded along. With each leap, Akiho smiled, and I triumphantly leapt even farther next time.

Akiho gazed ecstatically at the scene below us and at the butterflies that surrounded her. "Kitty, the world is beautiful... It's so lovely! I want to show it to Kaori too, someday!"

"It's all right, just leave it to me. I'll absolutely show it to her."

"Hey, kitty. Come to think of it, what's your name?" Akiho asked me merrily.

I pondered for a moment before I told her. And when I did...

"Nyaa! What a lovely name. It might not be for long, but I'm looking forward to spending time with you, Nyaa-chan!" Akiho said, gazing happily at the moon that hung suspended in the sky.

It's a cold, cold winter's night. Being a cat, I've had enough of the cold.

But that day alone, the cold was surprisingly pleasant.

We were feverish with excitement about all the things we hadn't yet seen. The sky through which I flew, my irreplaceable friend on my back, helped to cool us down.

Oh, Kaori's crying.

She wept in a manner that was much more mature than she had as a child. She knew her mother's fate now.

What had Akiho said then? Oh, right.

"If I don't hug her, she'll cry forever," she had restlessly told me.

I wonder if Kaori can stop crying by herself these days...

This reaction was probably from the shock of her mother's death. When Kaori had finished listening to my tale, she had suddenly hugged me and begun to cry. To a certain extent, I'd expected this—I was speaking about her mother, after all—but it seemed like she was going to need some time to accept my words as fact.

The warmth of her body heat enveloped me as I continued in a matter-of-fact tone. "After that, I went on a journey with Akiho. We traveled all over the place. In the spirit realm, and in the human world too. Akiho's condition wasn't good, but we didn't stop until the end."

In the meantime, Akiho told me about herself: her memories of her childhood, the things she had studied at school, what she liked these days, what she had liked in the past, things she enjoyed, her first love, how she met her late husband, the time she had first held Kaori...

That had been Akiho's life. A warm, happy, painful, lonely, very normal life, with all its ups and downs. I'm sure those were the parts of herself that she had wanted to leave to Kaori, and they'd come from the heart. Everything Akiho said to me in those days was for Kaori.

As soon as I realized that, I engraved it all in my memory so that I wouldn't forget even a single word.

"Akiho told me...that someday, when you were an adult, Kaori, and your heart had grown strong enough to accept such things, she wanted me to tell you about her." I smiled awkwardly as I spoke to Kaori, who was still crying. "I'm sorry for not saying anything until now. I stole your mother from you."

I'd meant well. I'd thought, at the time, that this was the right answer. But now, I thought my judgment might have been mistaken. I'd never guessed how much it would trouble Kaori to know nothing about her birth mother.

It's all my fault. I should have returned you to the human world, even if it was only for a while. That way, Kaori might have had some memories of her mother. If my intuition had been a little more human, I would never have made such a mistake.

In the end, however hard I might try to change my ways, I was still a spirit. And Kaori was a human.

"It's all right for you to resent me," I said. "I don't even mind if you hate me. But even so, I can't stop watching over you, Kaori. I'm sorry. I made a promise to my friend."

An important promise, one I couldn't break.

Whatever Kaori might think of me, I have a duty to protect her until her dying day.

Slipping out of Kaori's arms, I tried to leave the room; I thought that the two of us would need some time to reconcile.

But she immediately embraced me from behind, stopping me in my tracks.

"Kaori?"

Until this point, Kaori had only cried and said nothing. Now she finally spoke. "Nyaa...san. What did...my mother say?"

"Huh?"

"At the end...did my mother leave any words for me?"

My chest clenched painfully as I remembered Akiho's last moments.

Her life had only lasted for a few months after that fateful night. She'd passed away before the spring arrived, and as I'd promised, I ate her. Because of that, Akiho's feelings still slept within me.

I sat down where I was. Outside the window, a great moon hung in the winter sky. Gazing at it, I released the feelings that drifted in the depths of my being as if in a tranquil ocean.

"Kaori," I said, speaking the words my friend had spoken at the moment of her death. It was as if Akiho herself were calling the name of the daughter who was more precious to her than anything.

She'd spoken gently, infusing each individual word with love, like the wind that invites the spring into the chilly winter.

"Kaori...be happy."

In the back of my mind, I could see Akiho's face, peaceful in death. She had breathed her last as if she were sleeping. She had been so thin that, in comparison, her sorry state when I first met her had been the bloom of health. But she had kept smiling until the very end.

"Please, be happier than anyone..."

*I'm not asking for much. I just want her to live a life of content-
ment.* That was Akiho's last wish. And now...it was my wish.

"Uh-huh," said Kaori, and nothing more. Sniffling, she hugged
mc tightly and rubbed her check against mine.

"Hey, Kaori. Aren't you angry?" I asked.

"Why should I be angry? I don't really see the need." Kaori
wore an ambivalent expression that could have been either laughing or crying, and she shed lovely tears, like gemstones. "All I
know from what you've just told me is that I've been loved by
many, many people."

Her face looked far too much like Akiho's. I asked her automatically, "Kaori, are you happy?"

Kaori replied without pause. "Of course. I'm definitely happy."

"Okay."

I waved my tails slowly back and forth and looked up at the
sky. It was identical to the one through which I had flown with
Akiho back then. I let out a single meow.

The Man in the Fox Mask Gets Drunk Alone

"How ugly," the man murmured as he was buffeted by a howling wind fit to pierce his skin.

The man stood on a fire watchtower, looking down over the spirit realm town. The watchtower was made of wood, and of a kind rarely seen nowadays. Standing on top of the roof to which the fire bell was fixed, the man observed the crowds of spirits coming and going.

The man's appearance was pretty strange for the spirit realm. He was clad in a British-style three-piece suit. Its silhouette, which snugly fit his slender body, emphasized his gentlemanly air. The black coat around his shoulders was made of leather. He seemed somehow out of place in the spirit realm, with its rows of Japanese-style buildings.

Strangest of all was his face. From his build, one would have guessed that he was a middle-aged man, but a crucial identifying feature—his face—was hidden and could not be seen.

The thing that hid it was a fox mask. The eyes drawn onto its white base were as thin as threads, and it was painted here and there with scarlet patterns. The fox's face seemed to be laughing, lending it a celebratory air.

"Ugly, ugly, ugly, ugly... Argh, everything is so ugly. They're disgusting. They're repulsive!"

However, at odds with the expression on the fox mask, the man continued to hurl insults at the spirits walking about below him. His persistent rebukes coupled with his needy tone made clear his strange personality.

"Nevertheless..."

As soon as he spotted a certain person amongst the spirits, the man's mood instantly improved. He took a skillet out of his breast pocket and, shifting his mask slightly to the side, gulped down its contents.

Letting out a sigh of satisfaction, he wiped his mouth, which was damp with sake. Spreading his hands as if he were an actor on a stage, he declared, "There are some things that look beautiful precisely because they are in the midst of ugliness."

He was gazing at two figures making their way through the jostling crowds of spirits coming and going. One was a young woman who carried a black cat on her shoulders; she smiled in a relaxed manner as she walked. The other was a young man with white hair. He carried a black dog in his arms, and for some reason, his face was faintly red.

The two of them stood out more than any of the spirits below. Butterflies that emitted an unearthly light had gathered about them. This, more than anything, was proof of their humanity. But even here in the spirit realm, where many spirits loved to eat humans, no one attacked them.

From the man's point of view, this was an unusual sight indeed. By nature, spirits didn't possess the power of reason; they gobbled up humans just like wild animals driven by the need for blood. They also lacked the propensity for sophisticated society, choosing instead to take up primitive lifestyles. As far as the man was concerned, spirits were inherently inferior creatures.

So how were these two humans getting away with not being hunted down in this realm?

"What's the meaning of this? What can it mean? How curious it is..." the man murmured in a singsong tone as he crouched on the roof and rested his chin in his hands.

At that moment, the watchtower swayed unsteadily. At the same time there came the sound of shoving and pushing and some sort of scream. Thrown slightly off-balance by the shaking, the man leaned over and peered under the roof.

"How long do you intend to keep me waiting?" the man asked icily, and silence fell at once.

"My apologies. I'll be with you in a moment," a hoarse voice replied. It was impossible to tell whether it belonged to a man or a woman.

Shlurgh...crack. Crack...crack...crack. Shlurgh.

Sounds so vividly grotesque that they would make anyone want to block their ears filled the air at the top of the tower. But the man seemed unbothered. He listened silently to the sound that echoed up into the sky, but which didn't reach the hustle and bustle below.

Finally, something moved within the watchtower. A hand, covered in a sticky black liquid, caught hold of the edge of the roof. The person to whom the hand belonged vigorously hauled their body up, exposing a pair of plump breasts to the starlight.

"How's this? I think it's pretty good quality."

It was a woman, naked from the waist up. Her jet-black hair, glossy under the moon, adorned skin so pale it was almost transparent. But in contrast to the bewitching beauty of her top half, the lower half of her body was ominously covered by a bloodspattered kimono. After looking down for a moment, the woman turned to look toward the fox-masked man; like him, she wore a mask, though hers was of an old man's face. She tipped her head to one side.

The man didn't even glance at her, only brought his lips to the skillet again. "Whatever," he said coldly. "Hurry up and go."

"Yes, sir."

The woman seemed not the least bit intimidated by his forbidding attitude. As if this happened all the time, she launched herself off the watchtower. In the next moment, a loud flapping sound echoed through the night air; the woman had transformed into a bird, and she soared high up into the air.

When at last the figure of the bird had been swallowed up by the darkness, the man muttered to himself. "A child cannot become independent just as they please, not without the permission of their parents."

Chuckling low in his throat, he happily watched the two humans and their butterfly attendants walk on for as long as he could.

CHAPTER 4

The Mother and Child from Adachigahara

FOR SOME TIME after hearing Nyaa-san's story of my mother, I was unable to concentrate on anything.

Joy that I had found out about her. Pity for her situation. Shinonome-san's struggle to look after me. The things Nyaa-san had done for my sake. And, more than anything, the wish my mother had cherished.

"Kaori, are you happy?"

I wondered how many times Nyaa-san had asked me that question. I'd thought it was simply a pet phrase of hers; I'd had no idea that her inquiry contained my mother's feelings.

Besides, there was the fact that Nyaa-san had eaten my mother's remains. I knew it was how spirits mourned, but the fact that it had happened to a family member gave me a slightly odd feeling.

"Hey, Kaori, could you forgive someone who ate one of your parents?"

Suimei had said those words to me not long after I met him.

If I were a normal person, I suspected I would probably harbor negative feelings, the way Suimei had. But I had been brought up in the spirit realm, and I felt only gratitude toward Nyaa-san for giving my mother a proper funeral. As you might expect, my feelings were out of sync with those of the average human.

Ahh. My mother loved me...

Now that the suspicion I had nursed for so long had been swept away, I was exhausted. Perhaps this was why, although I did go out to my part-time job, I ended up shutting myself away in the house a lot.

That suspicion I had harbored was that my mother had abandoned me.

Shinonome-san, Noname, and Nyaa-san had watched over me, and I had grown up wanting for nothing, but this suspicion had always followed me—to the extent that I had been jealous of a baby who was yet to be born.

There was no feeling as desolate as being unable to honestly rejoice at someone's birth, so I was grateful to Nyaa-san for telling me the truth. I also felt as if my best friend had at last recognized me as an individual adult, which made me happy.

But then there was the fact that I had no blood relatives left in this world. That would take some time for me to accept. At the very least, I spent whole days gazing distractedly at the garden. For some reason, I needed to be with Nyaa-san; she sat right next to me. Although she usually hated to be touched any more than necessary, she stayed by my side without saying anything, her concern evident in her generosity with her time.

"Akiho said she loved big snowflakes. They looked tasty, she said."

"Whaaat?"

I spent time with my best friend, watching the snow, my heart growing warm at the occasional memories of my mother that Nyaa-san shared with me.

That winter was like it always was, and yet it was completely different.

Meanwhile, New Year's arrived in the blink of an eye.

Around this time, the spirit realm's winter slumber began to break as the spirits who lived in town held a humble festival to celebrate the new year. They would play flutes, thump taiko drums, and prepare amazake, sweets, and dango dumplings. Spirits told one another of the dreams they had during hibernation, and they laughed about how much they yearned for the spring... New Year's in the spirit realm was very peaceful.

Ordinarily, I would have gone to the festival with Nyaa-san. But this year, I didn't feel like it, so I planned to stay at home.

"Hey, Kaori. Wanna go out with me?"

However, to my amazement, when Suimei came to wish me a Happy New Year, he invited me to head out into town with him.

I was so shocked that I couldn't reply straightaway.

"You've seemed kinda down recently," Suimei continued, his face still turned away from me. "Why don't you have a bit of fun?"

"Have you been worrying about me?"

"It's only that every time I come here to sleep, you're in an annoyingly gloomy mood."

He's not being honest. I let out a laugh. Suimei was the same as ever.

Blushing right up to the tips of his ears, Suimei turned his back to me.

Oh. I can feel my heart pounding. ...Oh yes, that's right—it's because I'm in love with Suimei.

I was so happy that the person I loved had shown consideration toward me that my body felt as light as if it had sprouted wings.

How self-interested of me. I was down in the dumps until just a minute ago.

Just then, I suddenly thought of my mother. My father had died before Nyaa-san and my mother met.

Before they got married—when they were dating—did my mother's heart flutter like this, I wonder? I wish I'd been able to talk to her about it.

All at once, I felt deflated, and my shoulders sagged.

Suimei peered at my face. As I glanced up at him, he said with a sullen expression, "Do you hate the idea of going out with me that much?"

He'd grown tired of waiting for me to accept his offer. I shook my head vigorously at his look of discontent.

"N-no! I was thinking of something else, that's all!"

"Then hurry up and get ready. Kuro's waiting outside."

"Okay, hang on a moment."

Running to fetch my coat, I peeked next door into Shinonome-san's room. My adoptive father was thoroughly drunk, clutching a tall sake bottle. I couldn't help sighing.

"I'm just heading out with Suimei!"

"Huh?! Okay... Take Nyaa with you," he slurred.

I glared sharply at him. "You shouldn't drink too much. I told you, Tamaki-san might come round to collect your manuscript."

"Ack!" Shinonome-san choked.

"Just kidding!" I told him with a smile, and I headed out to the entryway.

As I was putting on my shoes, Nyaa-san leapt nimbly onto my shoulders.

"Wow. You're coming with me willingly, even though it's so cold? That's unusual."

"It's just that even resisting would be too much of a bother."

Laughing, I left the bookstore.

When the sound of merriment struck my ears from afar, I stopped in my tracks.

The lively song of flutes, the thumping of taiko drums, smiling spirits going back and forth. For the first time since autumn, I laid eyes on this sight that I had missed so much, and I felt an unexpected pang in my chest.

If my mother hadn't left me with Nyaa-san, I would never have been able to see this spectacle. If I had lived in the human world instead...the scene that met my eyes now would have been extremely different.

I had been a small child who couldn't do anything for myself. My fate had been entirely up to others. First my mother, then Nyaa-san, then Shinonome-san and Noname... If any of them had let go of my hand, my life would be unrecognizably distinct from the one I led now.

I had grown up, and now here I was, leading a happy life. Instead of abandoning me, the people who raised me had ensured this outcome.

Wasn't it amazing that things had turned out the way they had?

"Kaori? What's wrong?"

As I sank into a reverie, Nyaa-san peered at my face. My friend seemed worried. I hastily wiped away the tears that had welled up.

"Nothing. Winter always makes me think too much, and I need to stop that. I hope spring comes soon."

Smiling slightly, I called out to Suimei, who was waiting for me outside. At his feet, Kuro wagged his tail happily.

"Hey, there's a food stall over there!"

"What kind of food?"

"Yakisoba!"

The scent of the savory sauce irresistibly rushed toward me.

"Great, let's go and get some! I'm having a large portion. With extra pickled ginger!"

"I want mine with extra meat!"

"Good grief... You two are so greedy."

"It's because I haven't had lunch yet. Nothing wrong with that, is there?"

"Don't come crying to me if you get fat..."

As Nyaa-san and I bantered in our usual fashion, I realized that Suimei was watching me intently. Tilting my head, I smiled at him.

"You seem to be in better spirits," he said.

"Yeah. Thanks to you inviting me out, Suimei."

If I had been left to my own devices, it probably would have taken me much longer to put those feelings behind me and move on.

Probably—no, certainly, from now on, whenever I happened to think of my mother, I would feel a little down. Now that I knew her fate, I couldn't avoid it. I couldn't return to the me I'd been before I had found out, however hard I tried. I had to quickly put my feelings behind me and move forward. Anyone could see that.

But I was a coward, and I had hesitated to take that step forward. Suimei had given me the push I needed.

Yeah, I really do love him after all.

The simple act of leaving the house where I'd shut myself away—to someone else, that wouldn't seem like anything much. But the companion who had provided me with that small impetus was precious, and because that companion was someone I loved, this seemed like a priceless thing.

"Thank you."

When I smiled gratefully at Suimei, he turned his back. Clutching Kuro with one arm, he held his other hand out toward me. I hesitated, unsure of what he wanted me to do.

"Our path to the food stall is absolutely crammed with spirits," Suimei said, still facing away. "It would be a pain if we got separated."

In other words, he was telling me to hold his hand.

I startled, feeling my cheeks grow warm, but I gently took his hand. I grinned uncontrollably as I walked along behind him. Pulling the scarf around my neck up to my mouth, I watched Suimei as we walked along in silence.

Mom, I'm doing well. I'm having fun. I'm in love. There's so much for me to be happy about. I miss you, but I'm living life to the fullest.

As I thought this, I walked through the spirit realm town, where the new year was in full swing.

After that, we ate yakisoba and drank amazake. As I stood around talking to the neighbors I hadn't seen in ages, watching the spirits performing at the side of the road, I noticed that a crowd had formed in a particular place.

"What's happening?"

"Shall we go and see?"

Along with Suimei, I wove my way through the crowd of spirits. In the middle of the crowd was a familiar face. I called out to her.

"Otoyo-san!"

"Oh, Kaori-chan. Happy New Year!"

It was Otoyo-san, the onibaba who lived next door. She was wearing a gorgeous outfit: a kimono patterned with pine, bamboo, and plum—perfect for New Year's. Her belly jutted out even farther than it had the last time I saw her, and she seemed to be having some trouble moving.

"Happy New Year! Are you all right in this crowd, Otoyo-san?"

"I'm fine, thank you. And never mind that, Kaori-chan—look!"

Otoyo-san pointed excitedly to a certain place. Stretching up on tiptoe, I peered at where she was pointing.

It was at the heart of the crowd. I could see someone sitting with their back to a house.

Ta-wang. Twan twan twannng...

I heard the timbre of a biwa. The performer was a woman in an amigasa straw hat and a striped kimono.

Placing a bamboo basket next to her, she skillfully strummed the biwa strings. She was dressed in simple traveling clothes and wasn't pretty by any standard, but the sound she drew from the biwa was astonishing. Her playing was truly incredible, and I listened, spellbound, to the pleasant low tones of the instrument.

Then I saw her face. Beneath the braided hat was the face of a cow.

"Ox-Head?"

"No, she's not one of the demons from hell, she's an Ushi-onna. But never mind that, look what's next to her!"

"Huh?"

Otoyo-san thumped my shoulder several times in excitement. Puzzled as to why this might be, I realized that the spirits around us were gazing eagerly at the bamboo basket. It seemed to be the reason why so many spirits had gathered.

The basket was about the right size to be carried in both arms, and it looked very similar to a kind of straw house for cats called a neko-chigura. It was dome-shaped; the inside was hollow, and I could see a soft, fluffy cushion laid out within it.

But the creature inside the basket wasn't a cat—it was a tiny little spirit.

I gasped in surprise. "Is that a kudan?!"

Otoyo-san nodded vigorously.

A kudan is a strange-looking spirit with the body of a cow and the face of a person. These spirits come up in legends from China, Shikoku, and Kyushu, and they're said to appear at times of great social change, such as wars and natural disasters. They die soon after they're born, leaving behind prophecies. And these prophecies *always* come true.

"That's ominous," Suimei said in a low voice. At some point, he had come to stand next to me without my realizing it. Kuro also looked nervous from his place in Suimei's arms.

And to be honest, the prophecies left by kudan were often inauspicious. In the past, they had been said to have predicted plagues and world wars, as well as major defeats during those wars.

Otoyo-san laughed as she looked at the two of them. "Oh, my! Ominous? I suppose you might think so if you lived in the human world for a long time. Didn't you know the kudan was originally known as a good omen?"

Pictures of kudan became popular as amulets around the time of the Great Tenpo famine.

A kawaraban newspaper from the seventh year of the Tenpo era had said, "The kudan is a beast that tells of abundant harvest... When one wears an image of this beast, one's family will increase, and they will not be struck by evil or disease. This beast invites not disaster but summons great returns. It is truly auspicious."

This trend died out in the Showa period, and instead kudan had come to be known for troubling predictions. That was probably why Suimei and Kuro thought it ominous.

But, in the spirit realm, kudan were still good omens. Moreover, the spirit realm was characterized by stagnation, and if any change occurred, it was extremely gradual. Great disasters and calamities rarely came about. As a result, the prophecies given by the kudan could only really be good things, and the appearance of a kudan was in turn an obvious good sign.

When I'd explained this, Suimei shrugged, slightly exasperated. "What kind of reasoning is that? That just means that's how things have been *so far*, doesn't it? A disaster might still happen."

Nyaa-san laughed scornfully from her place on my shoulders. "Oh my. You're more of a coward than I was expecting, Suimei."

"I'm just pointing out that it's a naive way of looking at it. Besides, I don't understand how you can feel grateful for a creature that dies right after it's born."

"It's all right. Souls circulate. It will die, but before very long, it will come back again."

Nyaa-san and Suimei glared at each other as they argued, quietly but heatedly.

The source of their quarrel was a fundamental difference in opinion on the subject of death. However similar the positions of spirit and human on this subject might be, they inevitably differed.

For a human, life was something that happened only once, and death, well, that was the end. Ideas such as the circle of transmigration existed, but they were often thought of as fictional.

But it was different for spirits. As Nyaa-san said, they knew souls circulated and came back. To them, death wasn't an end, but a departure. Spirits could always afford to wait until a certain soul returned. One could even say that they saw being able to wait as a virtue precisely because they lived eternal lives.

Chuckling, Nyaa-san glanced sidelong at Suimei. "Wow, people brought up in the human world really are delicate, aren't they?"

"Weren't you born in the human world in the first place?"

"That was so long ago, I've forgotten all that."

As I listened to their back-and-forth, I gazed at the kudan curled up in the bamboo basket. Its face was the very picture of a newborn baby's. But just as the folktales said, its body was that of a calf. It seemed to be sleeping, its breathing comfortable and even as it lay on the soft-looking cushion.

Although I knew that kudan were good omens, they appeared only rarely in the spirit realm, and this was the first time I had seen one. *I wonder what it will predict.* My heart throbbed with anticipation.

"A kudan appearing in the year my child is to be born... How auspicious!" Otoyo-san seemed to share my feelings. She rubbed her belly dotingly.

Ta-wang!

At that moment, the biwa rang out especially loudly.

Everything around us grew silent as the gathered spirits' attention focused on the bamboo basket.

"On this auspicious day, when the new year has been safely reached... A kudan has appeared in the spirit realm, as you can see.

Now, will the words that the kudan bequeaths unto us be omens of good or of evil?"

Ta-wang!

"Even I, an ushi-onna, do not know. And now for the prediction that this newborn infant will make in exchange for its life. Please listen to the end, everyone, so that you don't miss a single word."

With this, the ushi-onna put down her biwa and bowed her head. Swept up in the atmosphere—it was like a scene from a play—I watched so attentively that I forgot even to breathe.

The kudan who had been sleeping within the bamboo basket began to speak in a small voice.

Everyone gasped as they watched. Perhaps because it was still asleep, the kudan didn't produce any words. Maybe because the woman had warned us not to miss a single syllable, everyone focused their entire attention on the kudan's every single move.

That's when it happened.

There was a loud thud. A pile of snow had fallen out of a pine tree that stood next to the eaves of a house. Under it was a spirit who had been watching the kudan.

"Whew!"

Letting out a wild cry, they jumped up and down, making a clamor—perhaps the snow had gone down their back. Because I had been bracing myself so assiduously, a sudden laugh burst from my throat.

"Oh, what a mess!"

"You're ruining the tension!"

As the jeers flew about, the spirit who had taken a direct hit from the snow smiled awkwardly, embarrassed. Everyone else broke into a grin, their attention diverted from the kudan.

Then it spoke.

"The spirit realm's winter will never end," the kudan said.

A dead silence fell. Faces drawn with shock, we all stopped moving and turned only our eyes toward the kudan. When I saw the kudan's eyes, I bit back a scream.

In the eyes of that newborn's face, I saw the entirety of the cosmos.

They had no pupils or irises, let alone white sclera. Beyond their eye sockets was the limitless sky, teeming with glittering stars. Their eyes crinkling with delight, the kudan spoke fluently with a mouth that had never even suckled at a teat.

"However much time might pass, no warm wind will blow. Though they long for the brighter seasons, the buds will stay closed up tight. The water will freeze over and will not flow. The infants will die, and the mothers will shed tears of blood. These red tears will make the spirits forget themselves, and unable to bear the cold, they will pour out into the human world."

The kudan twisted their neck around. Those bottomless eyes... I felt they were looking straight at me, and I almost screamed in fright.

"If you wish for the spring to come, you must bear a child. That child will pray for the world's well-being and will bring the warm winds into the spirit realm. This child, born into this realm, will cleanse it of the impurities of sin. The child's birth will not be easy. Pardoning your hateful mother, you must love the child, and work together for its sake. If you do not..."

The kudan stepped out of the bamboo basket. Slowly, sluggishly, it walked over the trodden snow and gazed around at the gathered crowd. "If you do not, the child will die, and its corpse will keep the spirit realm locked in winter. Spirits who would summon the spring... If you do not do this, the end of the spirit realm is near."

With this, the kudan slowly lay down where it was. The regular rise and fall of its belly became slower and slower, until it stopped altogether. Its life was over.

"Agh..."

Otoyo-san cried out in pain. Averting her eyes from the dead kudan, she clutched her swollen belly and began, silently, to weep.

After the kudan finished its prophecy, the gathered spirits scattered in all directions. During this time, I led a sobbing Otoyo-san back to the bookstore.

"Where's her husband?"

"He's at work right now. I've sent Nyaa-san to tell him."

I made Otoyo-san sit down next to the brazier in the living room as Suimei and I spoke quietly to each other.

When I told Shinonome-san about the kudan's prophecy, he instantly sobered up from his drunken haze, his face growing solemn.

"I heard! About the terrible prophecy," Noname said as she appeared. Throwing her fur coat to one side, she knelt to embrace Otoyo-san, who was hanging her head. "It's all right. It offered a solution at the same time, didn't it?"

"But... But..."

"Calm down. If a mother cries, the baby in her belly will be sad too, won't it?"

"Yes..."

As Noname gently rubbed her back, Otoyo-san closed her mouth tightly, trying to hold back her anxiety.

Noname's eyes had softened as she turned to me. "The kudan said that a child had to be born in order to bring in the spring, didn't it? I wonder how many spirits in the spirit realm are due to give birth this winter..."

"Ho ho, not all that many," said the hoarse voice of an elderly person.

Glancing toward the sound of the voice in surprise, I saw a beautiful gray-haired girl drinking tea. A half-transparent jellyfish floated lightly around her, and she was wearing a lacy dress in the gothic style. When she noticed my surprise, she smiled. "Excuse me."

"Nurarihyon?" Shinonome-san casually identified them.

When I realized who this beautiful girl really was, I let out a sigh of relief. "You always show up suddenly. So you're a beautiful girl today? Please don't startle me like that."

"Sorry, sorry. I like seeing surprised faces."

"I *told* you, that's in poor taste."

As my shoulders slumped in defeat, Nurarihyon laughed.

Nurarihyon was also depicted in Toriyama Sekien's *The Illustrated Demon Horde's Night Parade.* In the picture, the back of his head is elongated, and he's dressed in an expensive-looking kimono. He is shown alighting from a palanquin, about to enter someone's house.

He's also depicted in the *Bakemono Zukushi* "monster scroll" and *The Illustrated Volume of a Hundred Demons*, but no explanatory text accompanies the pictures. Therefore, few details are known about Nurarihyon, and as a spirit, he remains shrouded in mystery.

The Nurarihyon that I knew was the foremost leader among the spirits. His appearance was different every time I met him, and he was a regular at the bookstore. Before you knew it, he'd be mingling and chatting along with any group of people. He was a walking encyclopedia, and everyone adored him.

"To get back to the topic at hand... Most spirits are of the nesting kind; they'll already have given birth to their children. The only spirits giving birth at this point are the ones who live in town. There are two in the tenement houses and two on the main street. I think that's it."

Nurarihyon slurped his tea and let out a long breath.

"Luckily, many spirits have easy deliveries and lots of young, like cats and dogs do. Toochika is making preparations with a doctor in the human world for all of them. Giving birth certainly isn't easy...but if we're prepared, we can avoid an unhappy outcome. We have the medical advances in the human world to thank for that," Nurarihyon smiled brightly.

"But they're spirits, right?" Suimei asked, frowning slightly. "Are you suggesting we get them examined by a human doctor?"

"No need to fret, boy. The worlds of spirit and human are closer than you think. There are spirits who have become doctors, and human doctors who look favorably on spirits. Just leave it to me. Connecting people and spirits is the duty of their great leader."

Striking his slight chest with his fist, Nurarihyon picked up a winter tangerine from on top of the kotatsu.

Realizing how relaxed Nurarihyon was, I let out a sigh of relief. If the guy in charge was so nonchalant, the situation couldn't be so terrible.

But my naive assumption was instantly destroyed by the very person who had given me such confidence.

"The problem is you, Otoyo. Are you still estranged from your mother?"

Otoyo answered Nurarihyon's question with silence.

If you do not forgive your hateful mother, love this child, and work together for the child's sake...the child will die, and its corpse will keep the spirit realm locked in winter.

I shuddered at my memory of the kudan's words. Did they refer to Otoyo's child?

Clenching her fists, Otoyo glared at Nurarihyon, who was idly peeling the skin off the tangerine. "Do you really think I can forgive her? The birth mother who dragged my child out of my swollen belly?"

"Well, it won't be easy," Nurarihyon said with a philosophical expression, only chuckling at her shocking question. "But a long time has passed since then. I understand why you'd be unable to forgive her, but aren't you tired of being at a standstill?"

He tossed the tangerine into his mouth and screwed his face up tightly.

"Ugh, that's sour. Listen, Otoyo. There's still some time before your child is born. You can think it over until then. Don't grapple with this by yourself, okay? There's a chance that the child in the kudan's prophecy could be someone else's."

Pointing at the rest of us, he smiled prettily, as if he really were a beautiful girl.

"The quiet winter is the best time for talking to someone. If you're worried, that could have an impact on the birth. Luckily, there are plenty of good-natured people in the spirit realm. Pass the time peacefully with someone. That is my request."

"Thank you for looking after my wife."

"If anything happens, please tell us at once."

"Of course. Thank you, as always."

Once Otoyo-san's husband came to pick her up, we left her in his care and returned to the living room.

Nyaa-san had come back with him. Thanking her, I prepared some tea.

"I never knew that Otoyo-san was dealing with that," I murmured.

Noname and Shinonome-san looked terribly pained.

"Humans who become spirits are always dealing with something," said Shinonome-san.

"I did know," Noname admitted. "But I thought it had already been settled a long time ago. So when I heard she was going to have a baby, I thought everything was all right. I was so relieved…" She sighed.

"Noname, can I ask you…about what happened to Otoyo-san?" I asked timidly.

Noname looked torn for a moment and then turned to Nurarihyon for help.

Peeling his third tangerine, Nurarihyon nodded serenely. "All right."

"Understood. It's a fairly well-known story. You'd have heard it sooner or later anyway." With a deep sigh, Noname looked down and began to tell me the tale.

It was an unspeakably tragic account, the story of a mother who became an oni and a daughter who was killed; no one was saved.

"A long time ago, in a noble's mansion in Kyoto, there was a servant—a woman named Iwate."

Iwate was the wet nurse of a princess named Tamaki-no-miya. But the princess suffered from an illness without remedy that no doctor could treat, and this grieved Iwate terribly. One day, Iwate embarked on a journey to find a remedy for this illness that could not be cured. Leaving behind her own young child, she traveled to the east and to the west. Then she heard a rumor that the princess's illness would be resolved if only she ate a liver taken from a living fetus. In order to obtain one, Iwate settled down in a cavern in Adachigahara to wait for a pregnant traveler to pass by.

"She believed such a preposterous rumor? There's no way something like that would work." Suimei sighed.

Noname slowly shook her head. "The Heian era tanka poet Taira no Kanemori composed a poem that says: *They say that in Adachigahara of Michinoku, in Kurozuka, some oni live in hiding, but is this true?* This took place before even that. Medical treatments weren't as developed as they are today, and since the liver of a fetus was extremely hard to get a hold of, she might well have believed that it would cure an otherwise incurable illness."

She must really have felt cornered if she decided to try and get her hands on a fetus's liver.

Although she had only been trying to help her ailing princess, Iwate's heart had probably already become inhuman by the time she transformed into an oni.

"Iwate waited and waited for a pregnant woman to pass by. At last, one day, a husband and wife came to the cavern and asked for lodging for the night. The wife was pregnant. Iwate was delighted, and she gave shelter to the couple. Then, while the husband was absent for a moment, she strung the woman up and cut open her belly."

"Ugh..." That was so sickening, I thought I was going to throw up. Suimei rubbed my back.

Dropping her gaze to the floor, Noname continued her story, looking pale.

"Iwate dragged out the fetus, and when she had removed its liver, she realized something. In the luggage belonging to the woman she had killed...was an amulet she had given to her own daughter before leaving on her journey. The woman was the daughter whom Iwate had left behind in Kyoto."

She had killed both her daughter and grandchild. When Iwate realized this, she lost her mind.

"Because of this, Iwate transformed into an oni. She became an onibaba who preyed on travelers and ate their livers, tearing them from their bodies while they were still alive. Many things are said about her end—that she was defeated by a traveling monk, or that she herself became a high-ranked priestess after repenting her sins and entering the priesthood..."

Finishing her story, Noname fell silent.

The daughter Iwate had killed was probably Otoyo-san. How could Otoyo-san not hold a grudge against her birth mother for killing her and her unborn child? That must have been why she herself became an oni as well.

"Hey, Noname." Kuro, who until now had been sitting silently by Suimei's side and listening, spoke up. His eyes were wetter than usual as he stared up at Noname. "What happened to the sick princess?"

Noname shook her head slowly. "I don't know anything more than what the folktale says. But Iwate wasn't able to bring medicine back to the princess. That much is certain."

In the end, it seemed no one ended up with a happy ending.

"That's too sad... Why did that happen? Why?" Kuro sobbed, large tears falling from his eyes. His pointed ears drooped, and his tail flicked anxiously back and forth.

Suimei scooped Kuro up in his arms and stroked his back.

"Everything started out with good intentions. But because she happened to believe that stupid rumor about the liver of a fetus... she was doomed."

Iwate killed her daughter and grandchild for the sake of her dear princess. Otoyo-san lost everything because it was taken by her birth mother. Is there any chance at all for these two to reconcile?

My heart throbbed, and I frowned.

"At any rate, all we can do is support her until the baby is born," Shinonome-san murmured. "We have to resolve to do this much amongst ourselves."

"You're right." I happened to glance out of the window, and I sighed at the sight beyond it.

It had started to snow again. The snow falling ceaselessly from the sky blanketed everything in white and brought stillness back to the spirit realm, which had been so excited about the new year.

"The spirit realm's winter will never end."

This was kudan's ominous prediction. They said a kudan's prediction always came true.

I wrapped both arms around myself and longed from the bottom of my heart for the bright days of spring.

The winter will never end. As if to prove the prophecy true, large snowflakes continued to fall for several days.

There was so much snow that if we'd let it be, it would have buried the bookstore up to the windows. Even Shinonome-san, who usually lazed around all day, worked diligently to clear the snow.

Now that she was in the final stretch of her pregnancy, Otoyo-san's stomach grew larger by the day. Someone went to the house next door to visit her every day. For instance, Noppera-bo from the confectionery shop delivered various treats so she could keep up her strength. Sometimes Otoyo-san would come to share them with us, assuring us she'd been given more than she could enjoy.

Noname and I went to her house often so that we could make help Otoyo-san make diapers, swaddling clothes, and socks. Noname was the one to teach us, of course. As an apothecary, she came into contact with spirits of all kinds on a regular basis, so she was excellent at looking after babies.

"You can never have enough diapers. Let's make lots. In the spring, when you hang them out in the garden, you'll have a whole curtain of them."

"Really?! That's going to be tough..."

"It's all right. I'll help you, and all the women in the neighborhood are ready and waiting to care for your darling baby."

As she talked, Noname continued sewing a diaper, her hands not stopping for even a moment. She was amazingly skillful; in a flash, she had finished one. In contrast, the cloth I was supposed to be turning into a diaper was a complete disaster. *Ugh, I hate how clumsy I am...*

Like me, Otoyo-san was locked in a struggle with the diaper she was making. "What should I say?" she murmured. "I'm grateful, but is this really okay?"

"We're all in the same boat, aren't we? The next time a child is born, you can help their mother too, Otoyo-chan. That's what we've all always done. You don't have to worry."

Otoyo-san stroked her belly nervously with a shy smile. "That's true, isn't it? There's nothing to worry about..."

On the surface, Otoyo-san didn't seem particularly bothered about the kudan's prophecy. She had also been checked by a doctor, as arranged by Toochika-san. According to the doctor, there was a lot we wouldn't know until the baby was born, but for now, he couldn't detect any abnormalities in her unborn child. That was welcome news.

"This is none of my mother's business. I can give birth to this child by myself," Otoyo-san grumbled.

However, I couldn't help feeling uneasy. If, by some chance, Otoyo-san's child was the child from the prophecy...

But there was little we could do. I was frustrated that I could only stay by her side, but I carried on steadily preparing for the birth.

In the blink of an eye, two months had passed. Before I knew it, it was the month in which Otoyo-san was due to give birth.

I wonder what happened to her mother? I had questions, but I couldn't ask her straight out.

Thoughtlessly barging into someone else's affairs would have been rude. I felt Otoyo-san and I had become close by this point, but we were only neighbors. It would have been different if we were good friends, but I wasn't sure someone like me should butt in.

In the meantime, other pregnant spirits had given birth one after another.

Winter in the spirit realm had grown a little livelier, but by March, there was still no sign of spring, and everyone was worried.

On one March night, a strong wind battered the bookstore, making the glass doors rattle. We had covered the windows with boards so that the glass wouldn't be shattered by miniature avalanches of fallen snow, but wind blew in through the cracks and shook the doors powerfully, and my anxiety was mounting. And on that night, someone knocked at the door to our entryway.

"I've come to share this with you." Otoyo-san had appeared in the middle of the furious snowstorm.

I quickly invited her inside. It was awfully dangerous for a pregnant woman, due to give birth any day now, to be walking about on a day like this.

"What's wrong?" I asked. "Has something happened? You look a little..."

"I'm not ill. Don't worry. I was given too much again."

Otoyo-san held out a parcel of meat. I was pleased to be given a share, but I was more worried about her tormented expression.

"Is your husband at home?" I asked.

"He's on the night shift tonight. He'll be back at noon tomorrow."

At that moment, there was an especially strong gust of wind and a loud bang that made the whole bookstore shake. Otoyo-san clung to me. Trembling slightly, she hung her head and tightly closed her eyes.

The wailing of the wind sounded just like a vengeful ghost. Being alone on a day like this must have been frightening for her. I ran my hand in circles over Otoyo-san's back, massaging it gently.

"That startled you, didn't it? Otoyo-san, would you like to stay with us tonight?"

Looking up in surprise, Otoyo-san nodded repeatedly, her eyes overflowing with tears.

"Thanks for turning to us." I smiled.

Otoyo-san shivered violently—and gently sniffled.

The snowstorm outside showed no sign of abating. In the meantime, Otoyo-san and I cooked and ate dinner together, then bathed. Laying out two futon in my room, we lay down to sleep.

"Aren't you cold, Otoyo-san? Do you need another futon?"

"I'm all right. Thank you, Kaori-chan."

"If you get cold, you can borrow Nyaa-san instead of a hot water bottle."

"Thanks, but no thanks. I'd probably handle her too roughly."

We chuckled as we waited to fall asleep. Outside, the storm continued to rage. The rattling of the glass still startled me, but with three of us there, I wasn't at all afraid.

"You really helped me out, Kaori-chan. I was so, so worried. I was terrified of going into labor on a day like today. It's bad enough already with the kudan's prophecy, you know?"

"Yeah. Of course you'd be worried."

"Besides, recently I've felt like someone's watching me. It's frightening."

"Huh?"

When I lifted myself up to look at her, Otoyo-san let out a slightly troubled laugh. "I think I'm just sensitive because I'm waiting to give birth. I feel someone's gaze on me, but then it disappears straightaway. I must just be imagining it."

"Well, I guess that's okay, then..." Exhausted, I lay back down. Petting Nyaa-san, who was curled up next to my stomach, I looked intently at Otoyo-san. "If something's bothering you, tell me straightaway, okay? Otherwise, I don't know if there's something on your mind."

"Thank you. It's reassuring to hear you say that."

Suddenly, Otoyo-san looked straight at me. As our eyes met in the gloom, my heart pounded, and I averted my gaze. Otoyo-san said abruptly, "Hey, Kaori-chan. Could I ask you a...difficult question?"

"Huh? What...?"

"You don't remember your mother at all, do you?"

This perplexed me. Nyaa-san squirmed about inside the futon; stroking her back slowly, I spoke, choosing each word carefully. "Yes, that's right. I only have memories of the time I've spent in the spirit realm."

The time I had spent with my mother, the warmth I'd felt from her, should by all rights have been a part of me, but I remembered none of it. I could listen to Nyaa-san talk about her, but I couldn't feel those things for myself.

I had a mother. That person used to exist. The "mother" inside me is nothing but information. Her smiles, her tenderness, her warmth, her kindness—none of these things have stayed with me.

A pang of sorrow lanced through my chest. All the love that she had devoted to me had trickled through my fingers. Things that slip away from us like this never come back.

Well, there's nothing I can do about it. I was too young back then. And I understand that, but human emotions are beyond our control...

However much time passed, this would stay with me, like a lump in my heart.

"Why do you ask?" I said to Otoyo-san, gathering my thoughts.

She was silent for a little while. "If, hypothetically, you were reunited with your dead mother, are you confident that you'd know straightaway that she was your mother?"

"Uhh...?" I hesitated, unsure of what she meant by that question. Tipping my head to one side, I imagined the situation Otoyo-san had just described. "I'm pretty confident that I wouldn't recognize her at all."

"Pfft..."

I realized that Nyaa-san, inside the futon, had burst out laughing. Indignant, I stroked her harder on purpose.

"You're completely different from Akiho," Nyaa-san said. "That girl... When you went missing, Kaori, she was full of confidence. 'We're parent and child, so I know she's alive!'"

"I can't stand the thought of that. If by chance I got it wrong, the regret afterward would probably kill me," I protested.

"Wouldn't you know her because her face was similar to yours?"

"Huh? I don't even know whether or not she looked like me. It would be different if we were like two peas in a pod," I pouted.

Nyaa-san chuckled. "I bet Akiho would cry..."

"In which case, I'd apologize to her. Just because we're parent and child doesn't mean we'd understand everything about each other!" I said despairingly.

Just then, I met Otoyo-san's gaze by chance, and I realized that her eyes were wet. I hastily sat up.

"O-Otoyo-san?! Did I say something wrong...?!"

"S-sorry. It's not that..." Brushing away her tears with her hand, Otoyo-san gave me a troubled smile. "Ahh... I was just thinking what a fool I am." Sitting up, she stroked her swollen belly slowly. "Do you know what happened between me and my mother, Kaori-chan?"

I nodded.

Otoyo-san looked at the patch of scarlet spirit realm sky that we could see through a gap in the curtains. "My mother was a wet nurse. She was always looking after someone else's child, and she never spared me a glance. All I remember is her back. I was so lonely when I was little, I used to follow her around and annoy her all the time."

She probably doesn't have many clear memories from when she was so young.

Otoyo-san scrunched up her face, pained. Looking down, she continued her story. "In the end, my mother set off on a journey to search for medicine. She left everything behind. Her household. Me. And then *that* happened. I hated my mother so much, it was enough to turn me into an oni."

"I mean..."

"But!" Cutting me off, Otoyo-san looked up, smiling through her tears. "I really do understand. That was all just me being selfish. Being a wet nurse was my mother's job; she was simply trying her best to carry out her role. She was wet nurse to the princess's brother too. My own brother was able to get a high-ranking post because of my mother's efforts. If the princess's illness had been cured, I—as the princess's friend—would have received good offers of marriage as well."

Her tears fell in large droplets as she said hoarsely, "In the end, my mother did everything she could for me. If only I'd waited patiently for her to return, none of this would ever have happened. If only I had recognized my mother's face when I met her in the cavern..."

Oh. So that's why she asked me that question.

I finally understood the meaning of Otoyo-san's question. Her mother, separated from her when she was little... Otoyo-san had only had vague memories of her. By the time she had grown up, found a partner, and become pregnant, too much time had passed. When she arrived in Fukushima after her long journey, Iwate's appearance must have been quite different from when she was a wet nurse in Kyoto.

Her face crumpled in distress, Otoyo-san spoke as if to the baby in her belly. "But I wanted to show my mother the baby I was going to have. I wanted her to hold her grandchild. I wanted her to praise them and tell them how cute they were. I wanted my mother, who always had her back to me, to look at me."

That was a very normal wish for a child. And yet this parent and child had ended up hopelessly at odds with one another.

A mother who had gone on a journey for her child's sake and ended up forgetting that child's face. A daughter who had followed after her mother, but who, by the time she left on her journey, had forgotten her mother's face.

Neither was in the wrong. How had things come to this sad conclusion just because they had loved one another?

"It wasn't your fault, Otoyo-san. It wasn't anybody's fault..."

Otoyo-san wiped away each falling tear with her sleeve. "No... Which is why what you said just now saved me, Kaori-chan."

"Huh?"

I stared at her in puzzlement, surprised by her words.

Otoyo-san chuckled. "'Just because we're parent and child doesn't mean we'd understand everything about each other.' That feels exactly right to me. I... This whole time, I've been blaming myself. Telling myself that I didn't love my mother enough as her daughter."

We're parent and child, so of course we should have understood one another. I ought to have recognized her at once.

Perhaps those were the kinds of words with which Otoyo-san had been cursing herself.

"That's not true at all," I insisted. "It's not like you're a god; there are some things you'll never realize."

"Yeah. That's right. I think that's true. Thank you, Kaori-chan." Otoyo-san smiled peacefully, looking relieved.

"Um... Otoyo-san," I said, wavering slightly. "Do you think you'll be able to forgive your mother?"

Otoyo-san avoided my gaze for a moment, and then, slowly,

she shook her head. "She killed my child; that's a fact. If I could forgive her easily, I wouldn't be so troubled."

"Uh-huh," I murmured.

Flopping back onto the futon, Otoyo-san looked up at the ceiling. "Why does the heart have to be so troublesome? If only it were less complicated...I would have been eagerly awaiting the birth of my child by now, with my mother to help me."

She closed her eyes. A single tear rolled down her cheek, reflecting the starlight that filtered in through the window.

A few days after Otoyo-san had spent the night with us, her labor pains finally began. Noname and the women of the neighborhood ran about, preparing furiously for the birth. Suimei, Kuro, Shinonome-san, and I—and Nurarihyon—gathered in the bookstore to discuss Otoyo-san's situation.

"So it was no use, then?"

When I told the others that Otoyo-san still hadn't reconciled with her mother, Nurarihyon looked down at the floor, sipping his strong tea. Today, Nurarihyon was a bright-eyed, handsome youth. Dressed in a school cap and uniform with a stand-up collar, he had the air of a Meiji-era schoolboy.

"I didn't think it would be easy. But this has become rather complicated," he said.

"So, what now? The other pregnant spirits have delivered safely, right? In other words—the prophecy was definitely talking about Otoyo-san. If she doesn't forgive her mother, her baby will die, and spring will never come to the spirit realm," Shinonome-san said, irritated.

Gazing at the full moon hanging suspended in the sky, Nurarihyon spoke in a detached manner. "I'm not just waiting for the baby to be born. I have taken measures."

"Stop putting on airs and tell us what you're actually going to do, Nurarihyon. I trust you, but the baby's going to be born soon. This is no time for lazing around!"

"Well now, hang on a moment. They say haste makes waste, don't they?"

"But...!"

Shinonome-san was impatient, but all Nurarihyon said was, "Just wait, and you'll see."

The dent between Shinonome-san's eyebrows deepened, and an extremely unpleasant atmosphere filled the living room. Just then, I realized that there was a commotion going on outside the front of the shop.

"Wh-what's that?"

As I puzzled over it, I heard furious footsteps and realized that someone had come in. The sliding door was flung back, and several faces appeared, their expressions totally at odds with the atmosphere in the room.

"Hey! Excuse us!"

"Hello. We've caught him!"

"Ba ha ha ha ha, how run-down this place is! It's even worse than I imagined it would be! I hardly think it's worthy of Fuguruma-youbi, but she's very good at concealing her displeasure!"

"Wow, there are so many books! I wonder how many love stories you have here that I don't know? Kami-oni, take me over there."

The ones who had just barged in were Kinme, Ginme, and—being carried bridal-style by Kami-oni—Fuguruma-youbi.

With them, they had Tamaki-san, who was being held by the scruff of the neck and seemed to have been dragged here against his will.

All at once, our ranks had swelled, and now we were all packed into the bookstore's living room. In that horribly cramped space, Nurarihyon listened to the report Kinme and Ginme delivered.

"We went all the way to Fukushima, but there wasn't really anything there."

"Well, that's because it was turned into a temple. I hardly thought that the onibaba would still be there."

Nurarihyon had sent the twins off on an investigation. They had checked every place that had a connection to Iwate.

There is a temple in Adachigahara, Fukushima Prefecture, called Kanze-ji. A capstone kept there is supposedly the remains of the cavern where Iwate settled down—and a pool of blood is where she is said to have washed her knife. But even in Kurozuka, the place near to where Iwate is said to have been buried, they apparently found neither the remains of the cavern nor Iwate herself.

"You didn't find even a trace of her?"

"Not the slightest sign. I'm telling you, no spirit has lived there for a long time."

"We looked high and low for her throughout the spirit realm too. There wasn't a single spirit who said they'd seen her."

"I see... Where in the world has she wandered off to?"

At the twins' words, Nurarihyon's face took on a pensive expression, and he looked down.

Just then, a shrill voice piped up. "Wow, how wonderful you are, sir. My name is Fuguruma-youbi. Please look favorably on me."

"Huh? Why, you're a beauty, aren't you?"

At some point, Fuguruma-youbi had started to lean against Shinonome-san, and now she was trailing her fingers flirtatiously across his chest. And wasn't that my adoptive father laughing foolishly, not looking nearly as troubled as he ought to?

"Shinonome-san... Now isn't really the time for that, is it?" I asked in a low voice.

Flustered, Shinonome-san avoided my gaze. "Ack! Ah...Kaori, I was just..."

"Oh, do stop it," Fuguruma-youbi chided me. "Women's jealousy is unseemly, don't you think?"

"I'm not jealous. He's my father!" I burst out, raising my voice.

"I was joking," Fuguruma-youbi chuckled.

For some reason, Shinonome-san looked shocked.

This has gone off the rails...

The serious atmosphere from a few minutes ago had completely vanished.

Also, Shinonome-san didn't realize it, but Kami-oni was glaring at him with bloodshot eyes.

"He's seething!"

That's scary... Earnestly pretending not to notice, I turned to Nurarihyon. "And why did you summon these three?"

"I was brought here against my will! Like a condemned man being sent to the gallows!" Tamaki-san declared, seemingly mortified.

"I caught him myself! Pretty good, eh?" Ginme said proudly.

Just when I thought the chaos had finally reached its peak, Nurarihyon laughed. "He may not like it, but he's the best hope we've got to search for Iwate. You'll come in handy, Tamaki."

"Don't talk about people as if they're tools, oh great leader."

"Ho ho. You're telling me not to treat you as a tool because you're a genius who's painted countless yokai portraits? How stingy you are with your gift."

Nurarihyon took a book out of his jacket. It was old and bound in the traditional Japanese style. The cover read *The Illustrated Demon Horde's Night Parade, Volume 2: Yang.* It went without saying that this was a book of pictures by Toriyama Sekien; I had read it several times.

"Why did you bring that?" I asked.

"It's here somewhere... Ah, here we go."

Nurarihyon opened it at a particular page and showed it to me. Along with the heading "Kurozuka," it bore the explanation: *An oni from Adachigahara in Oshu, mentioned in old poems.* There was a picture of an old woman wearing a ghastly smile while she stood in front of a bamboo basket full of severed heads and chopped-up legs.

It can't be! Is this...?! I stared up at him. "A picture of Iwate?"

"That's right. And I understand that this man drew the spirit himself. Isn't that right, Tamaki...or rather, Sekien?"

Tamaki-san grimaced, silent but unabashed.

I, meanwhile, froze, open-mouthed with shock. *Tamaki-san is Toriyama Sekien?*

Toriyama Sekien was a master painter of yokai illustrations. In terms of modern-day artists who drew the same subject matter, most people would have thought of the mangaka Mizuki Shigeru. It's true that he had an enormous influence on the way yokai are depicted these days, but many of Shigeru-sensei's pictures were based on images by Toriyama Sekien. Given this, it could be said that the foremost creator of images of spirits in Japan was Toriyama Sekien.

To think that he was so close by... I stared at Tamaki-san in amazement.

"Stop it. Please, stop it. I'm not the same person now as I was then." Shaking his head vigorously, Tamaki-san dropped his gaze to the floor in annoyance. "Now, I'm just the remnants of when I was Sekien. I am Tamaki; Sekien has already left the stage. So please, leave me alone..."

If I was remembering correctly, Toriyama Sekien had lived a full life as a human. Yet Tamaki-san only looked like he was in his forties, at the very oldest.

A human who's died, being transformed into a youthful-looking spirit... Does that kind of thing happen?

"Nurarihyon. He doesn't like being referred to by his original name," I said. "We don't really need to be talking about that now, do we? Let's get back to the matter at hand."

"You're right. I did something I ought not to have."

"Oof..." Shinonome-san fell silent, looking as if he'd just swallowed a bitter-tasting bug. I didn't understand why, and it made me even more confused.

Just then, Suimei rounded on the grinning Nurarihyon. "Damn it. Why do all spirits talk so carelessly? Explain so that other people can understand you!"

Nurarihyon's silver eyes were like the full moon, full of a cold light. "Think about it calmly. There have been many stillbirths in the spirit realm before this time. But the spring has always come."

"Is that so?" Frowning slightly, Suimei looked away, perturbed. "I thought this was because...surely there would be changes in the spirit realm because dead children would trigger their mothers' negative emotions. I was sure that was something like a natural phenomenon here."

Nurarihyon laughed. "No, no, though that line of thinking is very suited to an exorcist. That didn't occur to me at all."

"No way..." Suimei seemed to have realized something. His face grew solemn again.

Nurarihyon took off his school cap and, tapping it lightly against his chest, turned toward us with an affected air. "All this strife in the spirit realm is likely an intentional attack, wrought by someone who bears ill will toward this world. It seems there is a group that wants to prevent spring from coming to us. But giving birth is already a game of life and death. Shouldn't we be off to punish those who have thoughtlessly butted in?"

Putting his cap back on his head, Nurarihyon grinned, showing his white teeth.

We tidied the living room and spread out a sheet of washi paper as large as two tatami mats. Tamaki-san sat in front of it, having taken off his splendid haori. He knelt down and perched on the soles of his feet, staring at the paper. His right arm hung loosely at his side. The hand peeping out of the cuff of his open-necked shirt was inflamed and looked as if it didn't move well. I realized then why, at the Christmas party a few days ago, he'd said, "This is my non-dominant hand." This also had to be why he usually kept his right arm tucked inside his haori. I frowned.

"Darn, I wanted to go too."

"Bring us back a souvenir!"

When the rest of us had made our preparations to head off after Iwate, the raven Tengu twins had been sent next door to help out. The birth was finally approaching, so someone needed to be on hand to assist. Smiling awkwardly at Ginme's look of displeasure, I hoisted a sleepy, yawning Nyaa-san onto my shoulder. Suimei had just returned from replenishing his paper talismans, and he and Kuro watched Tamaki-san nervously.

Taking up the brush in his left hand, Tamaki-san muttered, "I'm just the remnants...I can't guarantee the quality."

Even so, he put all his strength into his arm holding the brush, from which ink began to ooze. With a bold stroke, Tamaki-san brought it down onto the white paper.

The brush danced smoothly across the surface of the paper with no hesitation, just as if he had input instructions beforehand.

The jet-black wall of a hovel, through which pillars and a central support were visible. A bucket with the dismembered head of a woman peeping out of it. An onibaba, suppressing an eerie smile, unconcerned that her kimono had fallen open. She was eating someone.

"This brings back memories," Nurarihyon said softly. "Back then...all the spirits would gather around you, begging you to draw their portrait. You hardly took time to sleep, Tamaki, you were so busy drawing them."

It seemed as though Nurarihyon's words weren't reaching Tamaki-san's ears. His whole attention was focused on the movements of his brush. At last, he wrote, *"An oni from Adachigahara in Oshu, mentioned in old poems."*

Then, mysteriously, those characters alone sank into the paper and disappeared, as if they had never been there.

Tamaki-san let out a long breath and stayed sitting where he was. Then, gazing at the finished picture, he called out, "Kurozuka."

At that moment, the onibaba in the picture changed. The mask of a demoness appeared on her eerily smiling face. A knife, dripping with blood, manifested in her hand. Blood splattered here and there across her body. She trembled for just a moment, then looked up to the heavens and screamed.

"Aaaaaaaaaaaaaaaargh... Aaaaaaaaaaarrrggh!"

The next moment, she was gone, as if she had dissolved.

"Wh-what...?"

I was bewildered. Shinonome-san, Suimei, and Nurarihyon were likewise transfixed. Only one person among us was smiling.

"Well then, everybody. Shall we go? Not as a parade of courtesans, but as a parade of spirits?" asked Fuguruma-youbi. She looked at each of us with a charming smile.

Just then, a sweet scent tickled my nose. It was an elegant aroma, not overly sweet.

Oh... It's the scent of wisteria flowers.

I had smelled that fragrance recently. I began looking around for the flowers. But those beautiful, bluish-purple blossoms were nowhere to be found; there was only the courtesan, blooming in her full glory.

"Well, now, everyone. Please come a little closer to me. Normally, it would be uncouth to approach someone with whom you are not intimate, but this is a special occasion. I am going to show you the whereabouts of all the sad feelings etched into this paper."

Blushing, Fuguruma-youbi cast down her eyes, framed by their long eyelashes. Her gaze fell on the paper. "I am the spirit of a person's feelings which were written into a letter but never delivered," she said with a lilting sadness. "Concern for their friends, love for their parents, the feeling of missing someone, gratitude... People really do express all kinds of feelings on paper."

Kami-oni picked up where Fuguruma-youbi left off. "They commit curses to paper too. Hexes, grudges, the intent to kill—they put feelings on paper that are so sordid, it makes you want to turn your eyes away."

Fuguruma-youbi gazed fondly at Kami-oni, and a single tear fell down her cheek.

"Paper is the medium that connects everything. Dreams, feelings, stories; it catches everything on its snow-white body and conveys it to someone else... Ahh." Closing her eyes tightly, Fuguruma-youbi wiped away her tears. Then, as if she were reciting a poem, she said, "What an unhappy creature a mother is. Because she is a mother, she cannot compromise at all, and with one mistake she can lose everything. Her child's happiness or unhappiness—she bears it all on her back, but because she loves her child, she cannot give in. Ohh... Look, there she is, the demon who killed her own child. Right there."

She clapped her hands together, and a dazzling storm of wisteria petals sprang up.

"Wha...? Wait..."

My vision filled with blue and purple. Automatically, I closed my eyes. It took a little while for the howling of the wind to die down. When calm finally returned, I timidly opened my eyes again.

They went wide with shock. We seemed to be inside the ink-wash painting.

There was no color anywhere to be seen. We stood in a monochrome world, represented through the light and shade of ink. The sky alone was the vivid red of blood. But I recognized the scene. It was the street in front of my own house, which I knew all too well.

"Hey, Kaori! You all right?"

Suimei came running up to me. Kuro was at his feet.

I looked around and saw that the others had been thrown into this world along with me. Apart from Fuguruma-youbi, Kami-oni, and Tamaki-san, we were all here.

Leaping nimbly down from my shoulders, Nyaa-san looked about warily. Her eyes fixed on one particular spot, and she said sharply, "Over there!"

I followed the line of Nyaa-san's gaze. The instant I saw the scene unfolding there, my entire body broke out in goosebumps.

Birds.

Large birds with jet-black wings and bloodred tail feathers had lined themselves all along the eaves that faced the street. Their coloration alone wasn't so different from that of birds in the human world, but one part of them was definitely uncanny. They had no heads. Instead, the torsos of naked women extended out from their chests. Full breasts, plump stomachs, and slender waists. Normally, these features would have emanated sexual allure, but they were as pallid as corpses, and instead they repulsed all who looked upon them.

"Kokakuchou..."

These birds, also called Ubume-dori, were said to have originated in China.

Many had lived in what was once Jing Province, where they had transformed between this shape and that of women; when they donned their feathers, they were birds, and when they took them off again, they were women. Furthermore, according to classics such as the *Keicho Kenmonshu*, the *Honzou Kibun*, and the *Compendium of Materia Medica* and the *Dictated Compendium of Materia Medica*, they were wrathful deities and often took human lives.

These spirits were also known to harm children.

"Waaahh... Waahh..."

With unsettling cries like those of infants, the Kokakuchou stared out from the eaves at a certain spot. They were gazing at the house next to the bookstore... Otoyo-san's house.

They seemed to be lying in wait to steal the baby that was about to be born. Huddling together, they moved toward Otoyo-san's house in fits and starts, as if to peer inside and see what was going on.

But they were entirely prevented from ever reaching it. As they approached the house, someone drove them all back.

"Iwate-san?!"

"Huff...hff...hff..."

It was Otoyo-san's birth mother, Iwate. Panting heavily, she had no breath to respond when I called out to her.

Just like in Tamaki-san's picture, her face was covered by the mask of a demoness. Her tattered kimono was spattered bright red with blood, and sweat beaded her exposed skin. In her hand, she held a knife; every time the Kokakuchou approached the house, her knife mercilessly slew one of those grotesque birds, which sank into a pool of blood.

Just how long would she stay there and fight? In this monochrome world, the only bright colors came from the redness of the sky and the blood shed by the Kokakuchou.

"So this is where you were, Iwate," Nurarihyon muttered bitterly, watching her.

"Um, Nurarihyon...where are we?"

This monochrome world, the swarming Kokakuchou, Iwate fighting on, covered in blood. The whole situation baffled me. Nurarihyon stroked his beardless chin with a murmur.

"We seem to be in a dimension that someone intentionally created. You might call it the world behind the scenes."

"Why is Iwate-san in a place like this?"

"She's probably here to protect them from beings she realized were out to hurt her child and grandchild. This world is separate from the surface world, but the two are extremely close. If the child had been harmed before it was born, we wouldn't have stood a chance. We have Iwate to thank for the fact that the child has made it this far."

"Recently, I've felt like someone's watching me."

Otoyo-san's words came back to me. She had also said that their gaze disappeared straightaway. I didn't know whether that gaze belonged to Iwate or to the Kokakuchou who were trying to steal her baby, but either way, it meant that Iwate had been by Otoyo-san's side this whole time.

"Here...all alone?"

While I spoke with Nurarihyon, Iwate slaughtered several more Kokakuchou. The blade of her knife was already worn; rather than slicing through them, it was more accurate to say she was mowing them down with all her might.

Iwate's wounds were grievous and clear, but she made no

move to leave her position in front of Otoyo-san's house. Her posture said clear as anything: that which was behind her was more precious than herself.

Hers was the figure of a mother fighting, at the risk her own life, for the sake of a child. But a single, decisive error had left a deep gulf between this mother and her child, and they could not make amends. Even so, she kept on standing there, wretched to behold.

Just then, a voice spoke, one that sounded out of place.

"Argh... What a bother this has become. Ugh, now the master is going to be angry with me."

The voice was languid, as if it came from a person holding back a yawn. It definitely didn't fit this ghastly place where dead bodies were strewn all about.

The owner of the voice came slowly closer, trampling on the dead Kokakuchou without paying them any mind. "I thought this was going to be an easy job. Why did it go so wrong?"

It was a humanoid spirit with pale and bloodless skin to which her straggly, oily black hair was plastered. From the waist down, her body was covered by a blood-drenched kimono, and her deeply shadowed face held no vitality—it was corpse-like, and it seemed to produce a feeling of visceral disgust in anyone who looked upon it.

"Oh, but maybe it's a good thing I got to meet such a lovely girl. Yes, this job isn't completely without its charms." With a sweet smile, the spirit turned toward me and waved.

"Kaori, get back," said Suimei.

"Behind me," Nyaa-san directed.

"Grrrrrrrr...!"

Kuro joined them to step in front of me, and before I knew it, Shinonome-san was also there at my side. This mysterious spirit frightened me, but now I felt a little relieved.

"You're just like a princess, aren't you, with everyone looking after you? I'm jealous." Laughing low in her throat, the spirit turned and began to walk toward Iwate. "Well then, shall we finish this? It seems I was a little too careless."

She raised a hand in the air and turned it suddenly toward Iwate. Then, as if she were suggesting they go for a picnic, she said, "Everybody! Kill her, please."

At that moment, all the Kokakuchou lined up along the roofs took off at once. Wailing cries like those of newborn children, they rushed Iwate, who was still fighting alone.

"Iwate-san!"

"Damn! Hey, come on, let's go!"

"I don't need you to tell me that!"

Shinonome-san and Suimei broke into a run. Suimei's talismans flew up, and Kuro snapped at the Kokakuchou. Shinonome-san leapt resolutely at them too. But all they could do was remove the Kokakuchou on the edge of the flock; they couldn't sweep away the ones swarming Iwate. They were just wasting their time.

"Iwate-san!" I cried. *Otoyo-san's mother is going to die!*

The more time passed, the more hopeless things seemed for Iwate, who was surrounded by Kokakuchou too numerous to count. I didn't know what to do. Frantically, I tried to hold back my desire to start running. As if she'd read my mind, Nyaa-san instantly stopped me.

"You mustn't, Kaori. You have to stay here!"

"I know! But..." I shook. *Argh, why can't I do anything?!*

It was so frustrating. Nevertheless, wanting to do *something*, I yelled, "Iwate-san! The baby is going to be born very soon! This time...this time, for sure, please hold your grandchild! Please tell them how adorable they are!"

I channeled all my feelings into that shout. It didn't matter if it didn't reach her. It didn't matter if she didn't hear me. But if I could just support Iwate even a little... With that thought in mind, I shouted loudly enough to make myself hoarse.

Just then, something strange happened to the Kokakuchou.

"Eeeeek!"

Shrieking as if with the agony of death, the Kokakuchou flooding around Iwate were blown away. In the midst of those Kokakuchou, which fell like rain, a cheerful voice rang out.

"Ho ho. It's just as Kaori says. The birth of a child is an auspicious event, but when the grandmother is in this state, we'd better worry about her first. After all, she should be the happiest of all."

"Nurarihyon!"

It was the head honcho of the spirit realm himself. He had moved to stand by Iwate's side and summoned a jellyfish twice the size of his own body, which completely blocked the attacks of the Kokakuchou.

"How deplorable. Kokakuchou steal people's children, but there's no reason it has to be Otoyo's child. Hey, you, Ubume... No, something that *looks* like an Ubume."

The thing he had called an Ubume frowned, the expression on its lifeless face full of wrath. "Wh-what are you saying? I only did what's natural for a spirit to do. When there's a child about, I hunt them down. That's completely normal for a Kokakuchou."

"What kind of logic is that? That's absurd." Nurarihyon sighed deeply and wrapped himself in the blue-white lightning of the jellyfish. "I don't know what kind of misconception you're laboring under, but spirits do not indiscriminately attack children. Oni who eat people, spirits who menace people traveling at night, even Kokakuchou who hunt children—they each have a reason for doing what they do. Spirits are not senseless monsters!"

Then he released the stored-up lightning. That blue-white flash lit the sky and landed a direct attack on the Kokakuchou who had regrouped to attack Iwate. The Kokakuchou let out their final death screams and thudded to the ground. All the color drained from the face of the spirit Nurarihyon had called an Ubume.

Nurarihyon turned his cold gaze on them. "Why, I'd say your way of thinking is terribly human. Where did you put on that Ubume skin?"

"Damn!" The Ubume leapt backward. "Ha ha. Of course I'd be at a disadvantage, going up against the spirits' great general..."

Then they turned on their heel and fled, swift as a hare.

"Hey!"

"Wait, you bastard!"

But the Ubume stopped in their tracks immediately. Suimei was standing in front of them, blocking their path.

"Don't you dare run away," Suimei snarled.

"Hello. Could you let me through, if you don't mind?"

"Don't talk nonsense. There's something I want to ask you." Talisman at the ready, Suimei glared sharply at the Ubume. "Which exorcist sent you? Why the heck are you doing this?"

Scratching at their cheek, the Ubume gave a small shrug. "Well, I have no reason to tell you the truth."

"Is that so? In that case, I'll *make* you tell me. Kuro!"

"Understood! Leave it to me!"

As Suimei yelled encouragement, Kuro flew toward the Ubume like a bullet. Closing in on the Ubume's feet in an instant, he swiped his long tail. They nimbly avoided it, but were hit by a time-delayed shock wave, and fine cuts appeared all over their body.

Red blood spurted forth from their wounds, and as the Ubume closed their eyes in pain, Kuro wasted no time unleashing another attack. His tail hit the Ubume right across the face. Crouching down, they clutched at their face, unable to bear it.

Suimei approached the crouching Ubume and looked down at them coldly. "If you don't want to die, tell me the truth. Why were you after this spirit? Why are you trying to keep the spirit realm locked in winter? Bear in mind, if you do any further harm to any spirit, I'll have no mercy left for you."

The Ubume stayed silent.

"Hey..."

But just when Suimei was about to speak a second time, the Ubume suddenly burst out laughing.

"Ha... Ha ha ha... What the hell? If I harm a spirit, you'll have no mercy for me? Ha ha..."

Startled, Suimei drew back slightly. Kuro let out a wary growl.

The Ubume slowly lifted their face. "What are you saying? Weren't you a savage hunter of spirits mere months ago? You bathed in so much spirit blood that even you found it unpleasant. You killed *countless* spirits. So how can you stand there and say that as if you're so innocent?!"

As the Ubume let out a heartbroken scream, their face split horribly. Their human skin tore away, leaving their insides visible. Anticipating a sight too painful to behold, I started to avert my eyes—but what was exposed beneath the skin was so unexpected that I couldn't look away.

The skin of the Ubume had parted to reveal the face of a beast with red eyes and jet-black fur.

I froze in shock. The Ubume took advantage of our surprise to slip past Suimei and break into a run.

"Damn... Wait!" As Suimei was about to dash after them, there was a scream from behind us, and he stopped short.

"Aaaaaaagh... Ugh...gh!"

"Nurarihyon!"

Nurarihyon had screamed. He was crouching down, his face contorted with pain. Someone had cut him from behind.

But who would... When I looked behind Nurarihyon, I saw someone totally unexpected.

"Huff...hff...hff...."

Standing there, her shoulders heaving, clasping a blood-soaked knife in her hand, was Iwate.

"Iwate-san?! Wh-why...?"

"Ha ha...! Serves you right!" the Ubume snarled in a grating voice. Staying a safe distance away from us, they whined, like a dog running from a fight it had lost. "According to the plan, that onibaba was supposed to attack her daughter! The negative feelings that would have surged forth when mother killed child a second time—they would have been immeasurable! That's why I put on this mask... But she defied us with an iron will and indiscriminately attacked anything that came near the house."

A smile appeared on their half-torn face. They waved a human hand. "Well, do the best you can. It's been quite a struggle for that one to stop us from breaking through thus far."

"Wh-what are you talking about? How can you do something so cruel?" I stood stock-still, dumbfounded by their selfish, heartless plan.

If Suimei was right and this Ubume was the pawn of an exorcist, then the one plan was the work of a human.

Could a human wound someone so easily, so pitilessly? No. I don't want to believe it.

"Kaori! Don't just stand there!" Shinonome-san snapped.

I came back to my senses. As I looked hurriedly up, I saw someone running toward me. They held a bloodstained knife aloft as it gleamed a deep red in this monochrome world. Iwate.

"Kaori, run! Hey, you, protect Kaori!" Shinonome-san howled in a terrible panic. It looked like he'd been attacked by Iwate too; blood was pouring from his arm.

Nyaa-san, had immediately covered me from behind. "You let your guard down, Shinonome!"

"Shut up! What else was I supposed to do?! I didn't think she would hurt—oh, damn it!"

During this exchange, Iwate rapidly got closer.

"I told you to stop!"

Taking on her gigantic form, Nyaa-san leapt at Iwate and tried to pin her down, but Iwate nimbly avoided her. Keeping her stance low, Iwate headed for me, getting faster and faster.

"W-wait, Iwate-san!"

"Damn it! Kaori!"

Suimei turned toward Iwate and threw a talisman. But before it could reach her, that bloodied knife was already staring me in the face.

I'm going to die! I squeezed my eyes tightly shut. I could feel my regret spiking. Was this really how my life was going to end?

But the pain never came.

Wondering what had happened, I timidly opened my eyes— and there was Iwate, still poised to attack me, frozen in place. But her face was turned to look behind her.

"Wh-what...?"

Desperately fighting my urge to sink to the ground where I stood, I followed Iwate's gaze. She was staring at Otoyo-san's house.

"Ouahh... Ouahh... Ouahh..."

We heard a tiny little voice, crying. Quite unlike the cries of the Kokakuchou, it was sweet and frail, expressing the shock of encountering this world for the first time as best it could.

"They've been born?" I murmured.

At that moment, there was a dry clang as something fell—the knife Iwate had been holding. It slipped from her grasp, damp with blood and gore, and stopped where it had fallen, trembling slightly.

Ahh.

Warmth overflowed from the depths of my heart, and I gently approached Iwate. I slowly reached out for the demoness mask and removed it from her face.

"Congratulations. Your grandchild is crying very healthily."

The face that appeared from under the mask looked nothing like an oni. It was that of an old woman with completely white hair, and features very similar to Otoyo-san's. The moment Iwate stared in the direction of Otoyo-san's house, her lip began to tremble.

"Finally." Then, slowly, she looked away, her eyes downcast.

The quiet tears that flooded down her face were almost completely clear.

We brought Iwate with us as we returned to the world from which we had come. I left the injured Shinonome-san and

Nurarihyon to Suimei and Kuro, then headed for Otoyo-san's house along with Iwate.

"I...will go home."

But Iwate stubbornly refused to come with me and tried to leave, saying that she had already fulfilled her role.

"That won't do. Please take a look at your grandchild's face," I insisted.

"But..."

Keeping a merciless grip on Iwate's arm, I dragged her toward the house next door. "Hey, Granny, don't you want to see the face of your grandchild?"

"Grann..."

"I think your grandchild will want to see their grandma's face."

Iwate fell silent. It seemed to me that she really did want to see her daughter and grandchild.

When we reached Otoyo-san's house, Noname came out to meet us. "Good grief. Are you really going to go meet the baby in such a state?"

"Oh."

Come to think of it, both Iwate and I were covered in blood and dust.

Borrowing a hand towel soaked in hot water, we hid ourselves behind the partitioning screen in front of the entryway and wiped our bodies down. As we did so, I heard the healthy crying of the baby, and my face naturally softened.

When we had finished our preparations, we headed for the inner part of Otoyo-san's house, walking gingerly so that our footfalls wouldn't make a sound. It seemed that Otoyo had given birth on a futon laid out in the living room. It was awfully noisy on the other side of the sliding door.

As I imagined the adorable baby, I excitedly put my hand on the door.

Iwate caught my hand in hers.

"Wait." She was trembling, her face pale, and her eyes downcast.

Perhaps she was afraid of Otoyo-san's reaction. There was no way around that. After all, Iwate had killed her own daughter and grandchild.

Just then, we heard voices on the other side of the door.

"At any rate, Otoyo-chan, I'm glad the birth went smoothly. It's been two hundred years since you married your husband, hasn't it? I wondered if you were ever going to have a baby." It was one of the women from the neighborhood. Her tone was worried but curious.

That's a bit too blunt, isn't it?

Though I frowned at the impolite question, Otoyo-san's laugh was unexpectedly pleasant. "We always intended to have a child. But I had to wait."

"To wait? What for?"

"I decided to wait until my dead child came back." Otoyo-san explained.

Souls circulate. To a spirit, that's obvious—it's common sense. Those who die go around, then return to this world. So no one in the spirit realm really minds death; that's why they're so relaxed about it.

"My husband is one of the demons of hell, so he made a special request to Enma-sama. He asked that my dead child be returned to me."

"Then—you don't mean...?"

"Yes. This child is the same child as the one before. It took two hundred years. But they've finally come back to me."

At that moment, we heard a weak little voice. Otoyo-san instantly began to soothe it, her own voice gentle. "Good girl. There's a good girl... This time, I'm going to make you happy."

The baby stopped crying at once.

Exhaling deeply, Otoyo-san chuckled. "This moment has made me glad I was able to turn into an oni. None of this would have been possible if I'd stayed a human. With this...with this, *I can start again.*"

She sniffled slightly, but she spoke earnestly. "Now everything is as it was before. In this way, I'm alive, and my child has been born to me again. I no longer have a reason to feel bitter toward my mother. At last...I can forgive her."

"Ahh."

The moment she said that, I heard Iwate gasp. She stared at the sliding door as if she couldn't believe it. Balling her hands into tight fists, she shook her head over and over, utterly unmoored by Otoyo-san's words, which she couldn't process.

Letting out a breath, I put my hand on the sliding door, and I called out in a soft voice. "Otoyo-san? May we come in?"

"Kaori-chan? You're here? Please do."

I opened the sliding door to see Otoyo-san sitting on the futon, holding her baby.

"Congratulations. May I see the baby?"

"Of course! Here, hold her."

"Thank you! Also..." Casting a brief glance behind me, I moved to the side and sat down. "Can she come in too?"

Otoyo-san's eyes went wide with shock. Reflected in those olive-brown eyes was an old woman whose features strongly resembled Otoyo-san's. But her eyes quickly grew damp with tears, submerging the reflection.

"Of course. Of course she can. Thank you, Kaori-chan..." Though exhausted from the birth, Otoyo-san got to her feet, holding her baby in one arm. "Mother. Look, it's my child... Isn't she lovely? I did the best I could. Agh..."

Of course, she soon staggered.

Without a moment's delay, Iwate moved to support Otoyo-san as she tottered. "You mustn't push yourself! Silly. Don't underestimate what you've just gone through."

She patted Otoyo-san's back gently. Otoyo-san blushed like a little girl and gazed at Iwate with sparkling eyes.

"Okay. Okay... Sorry, Mother. I just wanted you to hold her as soon as possible."

"Good grief. You always were impatient, weren't you? That hasn't changed, even now that you're a mother yourself."

"Ha ha... I'm sorry. That's no good. I'd better become more motherly."

Giggling, Otoyo-san showed Iwate the baby in her arms. Iwate nudged the baby's plump cheek with a wrinkled fingertip— and her face slowly began to soften.

"She's lovely. Just lovely."

Awkwardly, she hugged both Otoyo-san and the baby to her chest—and, in a quivering voice, she said, "I'm sorry. I'm so sorry. I was desperate to get back to you as fast as I could, and to find medicine for the princess... I'm so, so sorry."

Iwate pressed her cheek against Otoyo-san's. Her voice was terribly hoarse. "I didn't realize... I didn't realize at all that my lovely Otoyo had become a splendid young woman. I'm sorry... I'm sorry for being such an awful mother!"

These were the same feelings of guilt that Otoyo-san had harbored.

Their faces captured the tragedy of a mother and child separated for so long that they no longer recognized one another. Until today, the two of them had been at odds, even as they held the same feelings in their hearts.

"It's all right. It's all right... I missed you, Mother. Mother, Mother... Ahh!"

Calling loudly to Iwate over and over, Otoyo-san clung to her mother—crying just like a newborn baby.

On the Day of the Thaw

"**A**H, WELCOME BACK... Huh?"

Leaving Iwate next door, I returned to the bookstore by myself. I opened the sliding door to the living room with a clatter, revealing Shinonome-san being patched up by Suimei.

As soon as my father saw me, he let out a hysterical, "Why are you crying?!"

"Shut up!"

I firmly wiping away my tears and flopped down next to the window, sniffling, where I hugged Nyaa-san, who was close by. Nyaa-san looked annoyed for just a moment before sighing and giving in.

"Good job, everyone. That must have been tough." At this point, Noname turned up, carrying a tray with several teacups on it. Sitting down next to me, she passed me one of them. "There was some sake lee left over, so I took the liberty of making this. You drink amazake, right?"

"Thanks..."

295

White steam drifted lightly upward from the cup. I took it and blew on the contents to cool it down. I sipped cautiously and found that it was extremely hot, so I hastily drew my mouth away.

"Oof."

"My, my. You're all over the place today, Kaori." Smiling cheerfully at my teary-eyed state, Noname patted my head gently. "You must be tired. I'll make dinner tonight, so you just relax."

"Okay. Sorry, Noname. You've had a hard time too."

"It's all right. I did it because I wanted to."

I watched her stand and leave, saying she was off to prepare dinner. Then I let out another sigh. Noname immediately stopped and said brightly, "Oh, that's right! This is what you need right now, Kaori. Tee hee hee, I'm sorry for being tactless, okay?"

Suimei was clearing up after treating Shinonome-san, but Noname grabbed his arm, dragged him over to me, and made him sit down.

"Hey. What're you doing?"

As Suimei pouted and glared at her, Noname gave him a playful smile.

"Now, now. You settle down and rest too."

"Hey, hold on, Noname. Why are you putting the boy next to Kaori? Agh?!"

"You should help out sometimes," said Noname. "That injury of yours is just a scratch anyway."

"Ho ho. In that case, maybe I should help too."

"Oh, Nurarihyon! I'm so glad. But you'll be joining us after as well, won't you?"

Bantering merrily, the three adults disappeared into the kitchen. At once, the living room grew quiet, and the only sound in the room was the kettle on the portable stove.

"Are you okay?" Suimei asked timidly as he glanced at Kuro, who was sleeping next to the brazier with his belly showing.

"Ha ha. I'm all right... I think? I don't know." Stroking Nyaa-san's chin, I gave him an anguished smile.

I understood the meaning of my tears. I was just...jealous.

"I wonder what my mother was like. Was she as kind as Noname?" I murmured, burying my face in the back of Nyaa-san's head.

Iwate and Otoyo-san. I couldn't help being dazzled by the sight of them embracing each other and crying, and before I knew it, I'd been crying too. Of course I was happy that they had been able to make up, but I was simultaneously overcome by a feeling like that of a child begging for something they couldn't have. There was no use fighting it.

Suimei listened to me in silence. Then he spoke softly. "My mother...was kind."

"You saw her again in the spirit realm this past autumn, didn't you?"

"Yeah. Only for a few days, but I was able to see her." As if lost to the memory, Suimei smiled, a faraway look in his eyes.

If I remember correctly, Suimei also lost his mother in early childhood. *Ahh, why were we so unlucky with our mothers?*

"I bet she'll come back," Suimei said.

Surprised, I cast him a sidelong glance as he continued.

"Souls go around and come back, right? Someday...somewhere, you'll be able to meet her."

I smiled and poked Suimei's cheek. "You've taken on quite a spirit realm way of thinking."

"Quit it!" Suimei gave me a sour look.

Shooting him an awkward smile, I went back to looking at the garden. With the snow piled up, it still had a wintry appearance; there wasn't the slightest sign of spring.

According to the kudan's prophecy, spring would come if the child was born, but...

"Spring's late. I wonder if there's still something wrong?" Without quite knowing why, I leaned against Suimei's shoulder. I felt his body stiffen. "Oh, sorry. Too heavy?"

"N-no, it's okay..." Suimei coughed as if he were trying to cover something up. Then he frowned slightly. "There's also that Ubume-like creature. It disappeared somewhere. We'd probably better not let our guard down."

That's true. While we'd been struggling with Iwate, the Ubume had disappeared.

Even with all it had said, we had no idea what it was planning. Nurarihyon had been all worked up about it, saying he would have to come up with emergency measures...

"Besides, that mask..." Suimei's gaze moved to a corner of the room. The demoness mask that Iwate had worn lay there. When he'd returned here, Suimei had said he'd investigate it.

"Did you figure something out?"

"I couldn't discern any details. But there was a talisman stuck to the back of it. It was similar to the kind an exorcist uses when they make a shikigami. Humans are definitely involved in this in some way." Frowning, Suimei looked intently at me. "I've got a really bad feeling about this. Don't go out alone. If you need anything, come get me first."

I blinked over and over at his words—and then I exploded into laughter. "Ah ha ha ha! Our positions have completely reversed. When you came here this summer, I told you not to walk about by yourself!"

"It's been almost a year. Even I've changed."

"You've turned into someone I can rely on. That makes me happy."

"Don't make fun of me, idiot."

Chuckling, I buried my face in Nyaa-san's fur.

"Kaori, that hurts..."

"Sorry. Just bear with it a little..." I pleaded. *Ahh, my face is hot. If he sees my face now, he might find out how I feel. I just want to avoid that.*

Just then, I heard a dull thud. Raising my head quickly, I looked outside. The snow that had piled up on a tree in the garden had fallen off.

I had a hunch about this. I released Nyaa-san and went over to the glass door. I slowly opened it and stared out at the tips of the tree branches.

"What is it?"

"Ugh, Kaori, all the warm air is going to escape."

Ignoring their puzzled voices, I strained my eyes to look.

Everyone who had been preparing dinner in the kitchen spilled back into the room, asking to know what was up.

"Ah!" I spotted something in the garden and turned to them all. "Look! Over there! A bud is swelling!"

"Really? Where, Kaori?"

"Oh my, that's wonderful. Come on, show me too!"

"Ho ho ho. Haven't you people ever heard of a seniority system?"

"Hey, don't push. Stop it! I might fall!"

As they made this racket, we suddenly heard the cry of a baby from the house next door. We looked at each other. If she'd been sleeping, it was possible we'd woken her up.

We all fell silent.

But, still smiling, we gazed at the bud that had begun to grow.

Ahh, the breeze feels warm, somehow.

Water droplets began to drip from the roof. At this rate, the snow would gradually melt and disappear. The long spirit realm winter, a winter that had been disturbed by the kudan's prophecy, was finally coming to an end.

After winter, the gentlest season of all would come around, the one where everything buds and is bathed in soft sunlight. It's the most beautiful season of the year.

However, the remainder of winter would have its own ups and downs, and that made me anxious.

Even so...

"When the spring comes, let's go flower viewing," I said.

"Oh my! Well, in that case, I'd better do my best making

bento," Noname declared. "Suimei, will you and Kaori stake out a good spot for us?"

"You save your place in the spirit realm too, then?" Suimei asked.

"Get Kinme and Ginme to tell you all about it," said Shinonome-san. "Going flower viewing in the spirit realm will be fun, don't you think?"

"Hrmm. Flower viewing?! I heard you were talking about flower viewing!" Kuro said excitedly.

"Oh, be quiet, you mutt!" Nyaa-san scolded.

I felt sure that, if we were all together, things would work out.

"We should have sushi wrapped in fried tofu in our bento! Lots of different flavors!" I said cheerfully to dispel my unease, as I waited for the bright season that was to come.

Afterword

HELLO, this is Shinobumaru.

What did you think of *The Haunted Bookstore—The Black Cat's Old Friend and Gemstone Tears*?

Personally, I'm very happy to have finally touched on Kaori's past. Having written three volumes, I've reaffirmed to myself how important mothers are.

Right now, I'm writing while bringing up a four-year-old, so when I think about something happening like it does in the story...my chest starts to hurt. At the same time, as I think about how I want to continue raising my child with care, I feel unending gratitude toward my mother for bringing me up until now.

When I think about my own mother, I imagine her with her face wrinkled and her mouth wide open in a great burst of laughter. Her laugh is like sunshine, so I've always had the impression that, just by being there, she makes the house bright. The fact that she likes pickled food. The fact that her fingers are surprisingly dexterous. The fact that she loves alcohol and can drink a lot of it. I could give endless examples of my favorite things about my mother, but perhaps my strongest impression of her is her lively spirit.

But I also find myself thinking of how small she's become since she became ill.

I thought that, while my father was ill, I'd already reflected to an unpleasant extent on the fact that one's parents won't necessarily stay healthy. But my strange assumption that my mother would always be healthy keeps getting in the way. A child will always be overly reliant on their mother.

At the same time, even as I'm thinking that I want to be as healthy a mom as I can be, I've definitely inherited my own mother's love of alcohol... Yeah, maybe I should stop drinking. (That seems a bit difficult.)

Although my resolve to abstain from alcohol is already wavering, I'm going to move on to the acknowledgments.

To Munashichi, who was responsible for the cover art, thank you for your work on all three volumes! Double-coated cats! Shooting stars! Rustic hot springs! Giant-sized Nyaa-san! Every time I received your illustrations, I gaze upon them, spellbound. Thank you so, so much! To my editor, Sato—it was hard bringing these three volumes into the world. Thank you for telling me it was all right to let my middle-aged male characters squeal like schoolgirls. I never thought I'd be able to. Middle-aged guys are a gift, aren't they? They really are... In addition, I would like to express my gratitude to everyone who has been involved with this book up to its completion, to my adored husband and child, to my mother back in my hometown, and to all my readers.

Finally! Comic ELMO has started turning this series into a comic! The pictures will be drawn by Medamayaki-sensei, who brought my *Isekai Omotenashi Gohan* to life as a manga. Please give it a look, everyone.

Written in the season when
the plum trees bear fruit,
Shinobumaru